Critical Praise

I read *Barrio Bushido* in short doses, braving the pain and suffering and violent life of its young characters and their/our world. Suspense pulled me onward; I had to know how crimes, wars, hopes come out, but more importantly: Will the author be able to pull off a novel with meaning, or will this be another nihilistic thriller? On the level of world politics, is there homecoming for the Iraqi war vet? Benjamin Bac Sierra has taken upon himself the labor of Dostoevsky writing *Crime and Punishment*. Is there redemption for those who've lost God's love? The reader feels the joy of murderous combat, and the heartbreak of compassion.

MAXINE HONG KINGSTON, *The Fifth Book of Peace*

Benjamin Bac Sierra moves from lyrical beauty to savage brutality with all the grace of the symbolic matador who haunts his gripping novel of criminal life in a California barrio. Bac Sierra's voice gets inside your head and stays there, binding the reader to the compelling narrative as tightly as the novel's characters are bound to the twisted code of criminal honor that leads to their tragic downfall.

KARL MARLANTES, *Matterhorn: A Novel of the Vietnam War*

Feral and poetic, *Barrio Bushido* is a cautionary tale about the dangers that lurk behind brotherhood and honor, love and loyalty. A gritty, relentless, unforgiving portrayal of the equally unforgiving world of the barrio.

NAMI MUN, *Miles from Nowhere*

With energy that explodes on the page *Barrio Bushido* is rough, raw, uncompromising, and unflinching. Ben Bac Sierra has created three modern day musketeers that define the country we will live in for the next hundred years.

ALEJANDRO MURGUIA, *This War Called Love*

As if delivered in a single, sustained breath line, Benjamin Bac Sierra's *Barrio Bushido* alternates rhythms of waiting and combat, reverence and mayhem, the sacred and profane. As in vertical time, the end is in the beginning, no spoiler alert sparing us from the weight of its final chord. Irresistibly, we are bound to Lobo, Toro, and Santo; since we cannot save them, we go down with them. Read this: dare to know.

SANDRA PARK, *If You Live in a Small House*

A truly poignant, lyrical novel. Ben Bac Sierra gives a steely eyed lesson in barrio-ology as only a true homeboy can. A must read.

PROFESSOR PEDRO RAMIREZ,
San Joaquin Delta College; Lead English Professor of California Statewide Puente Leadership Conference

Barrio Bushido tells the story of three young Latino men in the 1990s struggling to live by the homeboy code in a California neighborhood rife with poverty, drugs, and violence. Bac Sierra uses a generous narrative voice and surreal absurdities to illuminate harsh realities, creating a world that straddles the line between myth and actuality. *Barrio Bushido* brings a Latin American literary tradition to American soil, situating Bac Sierra among magical realists such as Mario Vargas Llosa and Gabriel Garcia Marquez.

SHAWNA YANG RYAN, *Water Ghosts*

A Latino Elmore Leonard.

Bac Sierra's novel about three homeboys living in a California barrio speaks of the wounds of poverty and racism and of the world of crime and heartbreak. Ultimately the novel is about what both bonds and separates us from our friends, families, and homes. Written in gritty and evocative language, *Barrio Bushido* resonates with a raw energy that sings off the page.

Ben Bac Sierra sears the pavement with his bleeding-edge account of the barrio and its three most vital inhabitants: Lobo, Toro, and Santo. As rough as asphalt, as true a vision as you can find, *Barrio Bushido* demands to be read.

Barrio Bushido

A NOVEL
by Benjamin Bac Sierra

EL LEÓN LITERARY ARTS

Berkeley

El León Literary Arts is a 501c3 nonprofit foundation established to extend the array of voices essential to a democracy's arts and education.

The generous support of Peter Yedidia is gratefully acknowledged.

El León Literary Arts books are distributed by
Small Press Distribution, Inc.
(800) 869-7553
www.spdbooks.org

El León books are also available on Amazon.com.

El León website: www.elleonliteraryarts.org

Publisher: Thomas Farber
Managing editor: Kit Duane
Cover designer: Andrea Young
Text designer: Sara Glaser
Proofreader: Sunah Cherwin

ISBN 978-0-9795285-5-2

Dedicated to

Mi Madre Querida, Margarita

and

My Soul Brother, Jeff

Contents

Losing Balance

Man's existence is absurd in the midst of a cosmos that knows him not; the only meaning he can give himself is through the free project that he launches out of his own nothingness.

WILLIAM BARRETT, *Irrational Man*

It was a soft sunny spring afternoon when God stopped loving them. Lobo, Toro, and Santo were relaxing, passing around a frozen forty ounce bottle of Olde English, and shooting the shit on the cracked cement stairs of an old woman's iron-gated house in *Montaña,* their neighborhood, their *varrio.*

"So we were sixteen, up in the summer time," Lobo said, "one of those hot ass crazy nights, and Toro had snatched Ginger's purse. The bitch was so stupid she called the cops over to my hole in the wall. There we were—me, Toro, Lil Toon, and these two broads we picked up at the bus stop. Everyone's all snapped— Toro's layin flat on his back knocked the fuck out in the middle of the kitchen with his eyes popped open and drooling out the side of his mouth—cause you know he can't never hang with that red devil dust. I just let Toro's ass lay there while the rest of em were cows staring off into green pastures—complete fuckin retards." Lobo gulped a refreshing guzzle off of the forty and passed it to Toro, who listened with humble silence and curiosity at the escapade he had taken part in but could not remember. "But you know," Lobo continued, caressing the bushy goatee around his mouth and under his chin, "I had an ace up my sleeve, cause I didn't hit the *leño* too hard cause I knew after I got this broad whacked out I was gonna really whack her out."

"How'd she look though?" Santo asked, hitting hard on his Marlboro cigarette and exhaling perfect halos into the windless air.

"Bro, this was a straight up big titty bus stop bitch. Down for the count. I swooped em up in a stolen Caprice while they were waiting for the bus. The other broad, her homegirl, was kinda nasty, but that's why I gave her to Lil Toon. It was gonna be *firme* cause everyone had his own girl, but Toro's dumb ass fucked it all up." Lobo play jabbed a left at Toro's face, and Toro freely accepted the pretend punch.

"That shit wasn't my fault," Toro responded, "cause I had told Ginger she was gonna have to put in some money for the *leño,* but after we got it, she said that since the other bitches didn't have to put in, she wasn't gonna put in. I had put in my last five bucks, and, fuck that shit, that bitch must have been out her mind if she thought she was gonna get tight on five bucks with me," Toro puffed and flexed his rocked biceps. "So I wrestled her purse from her, took her cash, and booted her out the pad for giving me an attitude." Lobo and Santo gazed at Toro's striated arms and *morillo* muscles protruding out of his white tank top. Toro stood firm, short and stocky, brutal fists balled up at his side.

They all simultaneously hooted out deep belly laughter.

2

"Yeah," Lobo started up again, scratching the fleas in his crotch and adjusting the mad-dogger shades on his face, "you know, I don't even think Ginger was pissed about the money; she was mad about not gettin high! Called the cops cause if she wasn't gonna get a PCP hit, everyone else was goin to jail. Fuckin snitch ass ho. But anyway, they'd all smoked that shit, and I was in the bathroom with this broad, and I had her tight T-shirt pulled up, suckin on these big ass bus stop titties, and she was hella horny. Before she got high, she had told me she thought I was fine, so now she's rubbing my head like a crystal ball, fuckin up my greased back hair, and all of a sudden she starts moanin—this real crazy fuckin moan—like ooooowwhhhhhh!, ooooowwhhhhh! like if it's *Halloween* or *Friday the 13th* or some shit. These titties, man, they were beautiful, and my dick was steel, but I wanted her to shut the fuck up—and I heard the bang on the door, but I didn't give a fuck about a punk knock—she gets down on her knees, still moanin, and I'm about to shut her the fuck up when someone shouts 'Open up! Police!'"

"Nah!" Santo exclaimed, crossing his arms in disbelief.

"I wish, homes," Lobo replied, his big white teeth glistening in the glare of the sunlight, "cause I was standing there about to stop her moan when this cop fucked it all up. I told him 'Hold up!' and he must've thought I was robbing someone cause the asshole busted the door down," Lobo grinned and took another chug off the forty. "Stupid ass Lil Toon was only about eleven years old at the time, and he had let the cops in cause he was trippin too much off the *leño;* it was the first time he ever smoked a raw one. He told me later that he thought the cops were spacemen visitors or some shit. We all got hauled in but got let out at nine the next morning. By ten Toro was back up in there cause first thing he did when he got released was go bust out all of Ginger's windows." Smiling,

Lobo and Santo looked at Toro.

"She must have been out her mind to call the cops on me," Toro calmly declared as he wiped sweat from his shaved head. Lobo and Santo nodded in agreement.

They spent the afternoon reliving stories of this sort, and it felt odd for them to reminisce like this because it meant they actually had something to reminisce about. Robberies, drug deals, sexual feats, and acrobatics—these were the sort of stories spit out kicking back that only experienced homeboys could pull off with a smile. The stories they told that afternoon, after not having been blessed with each other's united company for over a year and a half, represented stories that meant that they had crossed over into maniacs' maturity: they were salty old soldiers of the streets—*veteranos* at the tender age of twenty-one—*veteranos* because they were still alive after their many battles, still down for crime at any time, and they were still not completely hooked on any junk. They were true *veteranos* because they stood for something, something that runts like the ones who toddled up on that soft sunny afternoon could worship and emulate.

"Ay, we were just talking about whuppin your ass, Lil Toon," Lobo, with skinny chest sunk in, exhaled out as the runts walked up with Little Cartoon at the lead.

Baseball hat on backwards and black jeans sagging low, Lil Cartoon stopped swiftly, pushed the runts that crowded around him off of him so he could have room to maneuver, and elegantly danced his dukes in the air. "Bring it on then, bitches!" he shouted.

Lobo smiled, Toro snorted, and Santo stared.

Santo pushed himself off of the stairs, marched up to Lil Toon, and looked into him. Lil Toon stood at the ready. "That's why Lil Toon can kick it with us anytime," Santo said with a straight face.

He eased his arm around Lil Toon's neck. "Come on," Santo said, downing the last drops of the forty ounce, "let's stroll down to the park."

Taking the lead was the holy bronze Santo in the solid five-foot-ten, one-hundred-eighty-pound frame, scraggly two-day-old-stubble beard, and medium length wavy brown hair. Behind him seven brown *bandidos* bounced down the street as if on a class field trip; each one carried a forty ounce or two from a quick detour at the corner liquor store; each one mastered the mask of machismo that was embedded in them like the *sangre* in their veins.

When they reached *Bajo* Park, the park that was the entrance into their humanity, they pitched quarters against a playground wall and breathed in the sweet stench of the *varrio* air. For them the grime and graffiti was more dazzling than a Disneyland parade. They laughed and drank and didn't even mind they were going to go to sleep hungry. Then, with good buzzes in them, Toro and Lobo challenged the runts to validate their worthiness to claim the fame of their game.

"What the fuck have you runts done?" Lobo demanded, stretching out his kinky neck and shouting at the top of his lungs. "By the time I was your age, I'd already scalped a man and been up inside many a tender young lady. We owned these *calles*, member Toro?"

"I remember," Toro answered solemnly. "Fifteen years old we were the baddest boys in the world. Fifteen years old, I was already buffed as fuck, and this world was ours. You needed to pay the toll to pass by this park."

With awe and respect, the open-mouthed teenagers listened to the young men—more so than they listened to or respected anyone else in the world. For most of them, their crazy-junkie-prostitute-kick-around-don't-really-care-about-you-except-that-you-get-them-a-welfare-check parents had not made it. Their parents, the ones who hung around, no longer had a connection to them that compared to the bonds they felt for these young men of iron and wood. Crazy-junkie-alcoholic-not-knowing-what-to-do old folks had lost, surrendered to life and searched for death all day every day through a bottle, needle, or pipe, or worse yet, maybe even minimum wage slavery. Because of this, the runts had stopped listening to the establishment a long time ago.

Varrio Montaña, this hood in the middle of the Tumbletown district, was their *varrio,* and this *varrio* was all that they had.

"Damn, we were some sick ass motherfuckers!" Lobo exclaimed to the dark red sky.

From beyond, Santo listened to life and looked around slowly at his environment. He viewed the runts as innocents who talked shit but hadn't done anything to speak of. He knew they wished that one day they could talk authoritatively about bloody fights, potent sexual escapades, and violent robberies and drug deals. Santo saw that these runts wanted to laugh as he and Toro and Lobo laughed, about bullshit—worthless garbage that did not signify or show any-thing. Sitting down solitary on a splintered wooden bench with his legs crossed, Santo saw this and realized that these boys could never learn the harsh lessons of the *varrio* laughing and bullshitting.

From within, Santo listened to life and looked around slowly at his environment. Laughing, a family played basketball down at the courts. They were smiling, sweating, having a great time. The father drove down for a layup only to be swatted from behind by his teenage son. When the father pressed him back hard, the lanky boy passed the ball to his uncle, and he rode in hard and shot a hot layup. Happy, the boy and uncle high fived.

We *are* some sick ass motherfuckers, Santo thought. He beckoned Toro to his side. The short stomper suspended telling his war stories to the runts and trotted over to his friend.

"Ay, Bro, are we sick?" Santo, his dark, penetrating green eyes staring straight ahead, asked Toro.

"You know it, homes—sick as fuck," Toro answered as he sat down next to Santo.

"Then check out," Santo said. Lowering his already calm voice, he scooted closer to Toro. "We got tradition to uphold, cause homeboys before us have been sick with it. They got our name hit up in many worlds—they're down for the brown. Now it's our turn, homes, and we got to pass on the torch, *entiendes?*" Santo looked into Toro.

"You want to fuck someone up? *Orale,* let's go down to the other *varrio* then—light it up!" Toro sharpened his horns.

Santo looked through Toro, into the family playing basketball down at the courts.

A pause for hard reflection.

"You want to get ruthless, *que no?*" Toro asked, patting the short spikes of hair on his scarred up closely cropped head. "Fuck it, what's up?"

Santo glued his eyes to the family playing basketball.

Toro did not understand until the silence forced him to understand. "Bro, that's just a *familia,* homes, they ain't *nada.* They're just kickin it," Toro said.

"Are we really sick?" Santo asked.

Toro stepped up to Santo's heart. "Yeah, Bro, but, but…, come on, you're tripping. You know we could fuck them up. They ain't disrespecting. They're just playing."

"Are we just playing? Are we runts like these kids?" Santo looked over at the runts who were laughing and slap boxing amongst themselves. Lobo orchestrated the whole gang of them, inciting them all to fight each other. "If we are sick," Santo said, "we got a lot of responsibility with that title. It means we live the life, and we die. That's it. It means we don't give a fuck. It means we *know* we don't give a fuck."

Toro knew this to be true, but he still could not bring himself to accept such a ruthless role. "What the fuck is wrong with you, Bro. That shit aint right." Toro glanced at Santo's cauliflower ear. "You hearing me?" Toro asked.

Smoking a cigarette, Santo gazed into the white cloud of smoke he breathed out.

"Hey, would you fuckin hear me if I shouted?" Toro questioned on.

Santo followed his smoke until it dissipated into the heavens. "I hear what doesn't shout," Santo answered. "I hear what no one else has the guts to listen to. So you can go ahead and scream out like a little bitch if you want, but I aint hearing shit if it's above the sound of a whisper." Santo knew what he expected to hear from Toro. "So if you aint down with your homeboy, don't say shit and just walk away. But if you got it in you to do some dirt with your everlasting brother in arms, no more questions need to be asked."

Although Toro wanted to argue further for the souls of the family, for the soul of himself, he could not. His mouth was sealed. He was, however, dying to say more—was being smothered inside himself with blasphemous thoughts and words. He wanted to tell Santo that the plan was deranged, taboo, unforgivable, beyond the norms of even the most fucked up *cholos*. The family was chaste: they were civilians; but it was Toro's heart, Toro's bleeding red heart, that told him to bite his tongue. *Give your old homeboy Santo the benefit of the doubt,* Toro thought. Respect your down ass homeboy and keep shut the fuck up. And Toro did.

He stayed silent because Santo had always been there for him. There had never been a time in his twenty-one years that Santo, the lion, the angel, the devil, the man, had ever let him down. For him, Santo had willingly stuck his neck out on the guillotine dozens of times. Santo performed miracles for Toro without a word needing to be uttered, simply on the pure strength of their *varrio* homeboy *amor*.

Sitting silent looking into each other's eyes, Toro knew just how solid of a homeboy Santo was. He remembered the time that he was going to throw blows with Mister Puppet from Swamp, the other *varrio*. They were seventeen years old, and Toro had accepted the challenge as always, with no reservations. For some unexplainable reason, Toro knew he would be unable to defeat Puppet, and Santo realized what time it was that night.

"Toro," Santo had said, "you got to jab at him for awhile, until he gets tired, cause I know he gets tired hella quick. He's a heavy smoker. Then let go with hard right hands."

"Yeah," Toro stated. It was then that Santo glanced into Toro's coffee colored eyes. It was then that Santo knew Toro was about to get his ass kicked. And after Santo gazed into Toro's heart, after Santo understood his friend wanted the cup lifted off of him, Santo took a small sip off of his just opened beer, gargled, spit, and threw the rest of the full can square into Mister Puppet's face.

"Did you want a beer, homes?" Santo had asked Puppet, "or did you want this?" It was at that moment, on that night, as the crickets chirped and the field mice squealed in the sparse green wooded section of *Bajo* Park, that Santo pulled a six-inch steel blade out of his back pocket, glided up to the young man in his black tank top who was ready to fight the good fight, and repeatedly stabbed poor Puppet in the stomach and heart. Toro watched this for a moment dumbfounded, relieved. With newfound confidence and strength, Toro then drilled, kicked, and chased away Puppet's startled homeboy.

That's what true friendship is all about, Toro now thought, and Santo never even asked for or expected a thank you. Looking back at this, Toro started feeling ashamed for questioning Santo. Who the hell was Toro to be preaching to or questioning a great angel like sick Santo? Toro was no one.

"Fuckin Santo, I gots to love you, Bro. You know I gots to love you." And with these words, this unbreakable oath, terrible Toro sealed the letter that was his life.

Santo stood up peacefully, confidently, pulled out his pack of Marlboro Reds and handed a cigarette over to Toro. They both smoked, as the condemned do with their backs against the wall, facing the firing squad. Once the *frajo* was down to its butt, Toro rose, considerate of what had to happen. Laughs, shouts, and a ball bouncing were the last noises they heard while God still loved them.

Crushing the cigarette butt as if it were a bug, Toro advanced steadily forward thirty yards towards the basketball courts. Santo joined his partner's side. Lobo and the runts saw that they led, so they took the smiles off of their playful faces, and they followed.

"Foul!" The teenager cried as the father elbowed him and took the ball. The father laughed and shot from the corner of the free throw. Two points.

Toro charged directly up to the father. *"Puto,"* he said, "you got to pay the price." Toro kicked the basketball out of the father's hands. The tall man was shocked. He did not understand what was happening. The uncle and teenager also did not comprehend what was going on. They just stood there as if under a spell, a trance, as if in a nightmare that they could not wake up from. Although they desperately tried to, they could not even speak.

Toro slapped the father in the head as if he were a pesky fly.

"What are you doing?" The father asked perplexed, looking down into his empty hands. Toro answered him with a flurry of furious combinations in the face.

Consenting to the punches, the father then shouted "RUN!" out of his dazed bleeding mouth. The uncle darted off, and Santo gave chase. The teenager ran towards the runts, but the runts did nothing. The boy was about to break through them all when Lobo's long skinny legs tripped the adolescent. Lobo looked down at his scared eyes and knew he could not beat him, so he started kicking him. The youngster curled up on the ground, and Lobo kicked the boy in the legs and ass as hard and as fast as he could. The runts, like the family earlier, stood there trying to remain cool, trying to understand what was happening, but they were in complete shock.

Meanwhile, Toro leaned the father up against the hoop pole and repeatedly kneed him in the groin and elbowed him in the face. The father's shut face was a busted bloody mess. He was out cold, but Toro refused to let him fall down.

Lobo, however, finally tired of kicking, allowed the teenager to limp away. "Where's Santo?" he shouted. Toro heard this question and let the father's cold body slide out of his hands and onto the ground. He scanned around for Santo.

"We got to go," Lobo coolly stated, somewhat understanding the consequences of the actions they had just committed. Toro, nevertheless, was concerned only with Santo. Once he saw the struggle going on at the top of the stairs from the basketball courts,

Toro ran full force up the three flights while Lobo followed, panting through exhausted lungs. "We got to go!" Lobo huffed. The runts took this command as an opportunity to leave.

Toro reached the top just as Santo shot in on the uncle's knees and dipped him on the head. Quickly mounting him, Santo punched the man in his face, and Toro joined in with kicks and stomps to the legs and head. Out of breath, Lobo finally reached the top of the stairs, immediately searched the man's pockets, pulled out his wallet, and declared once again, "We got to go!" But Santo and Toro heard only the crisp sounds of their fists and feet pummeling the man on the ground.

"Please!" The uncle finally whimpered through knocked out teeth.

Santo stopped for a moment to study the man. Toro also paused in respect to this reflection. Lobo counted the money from the wallet.

"I got to do this, man," Santo, his knuckles ripped up and bloody, explained to the uncle. "It'll be over in a minute and then you can return from whence you came. You'll be all right." And Santo slammed left, right combinations into the man's understanding eyes. The uncle never pleaded again.

"Let's go." Toro lightly touched Santo's arm, as police sirens grew loud. Santo stopped punching, and the three of them ran up towards the street and in the direction of the crumbling abandoned shack they used for homeboy parties.

"I need a beer, Bro," Toro stated as they ran.

"Fuck that shit! We're gonna get busted!" Lobo protested.

Santo smiled. "We're already busted, homes. Let's get a few beers," Santo said this as he remembered the stolen money from the uncle's wallet. "You're buying, Lobo."

They ran into the store and bought a tall bottle of Christian Brothers brandy and some Cokes instead of the beer. Sirens and police cars cornered the streets outside, so they stayed inside of the store thumbing through magazines—as if they could actually outsmart the Omnipotent. When the noise finally died down, and they felt it was safe, they sauntered back outside to the streets they knew so well. At first glance it looked as if the coast were clear, but in actuality the coast would never be clear again. They were in uncharted waters and knew forevermore that they had no favors left. Knowing that they had been caught, a deep feeling of somberness overcame them, yet they strutted down the street.

They were flat busted in the worst way.

El Lobo

No; it was no accident, and he would never say that it was. There was in him a kind of terrified pride in feeling and thinking that some day he would be able to say publicly that he had done it. It was as though he had an obscure but deep debt to fulfill to himself in accepting the deed.

RICHARD WRIGHT, *Native Son*

What was I supposed to do? Serve some penance, forget all of the beautiful bloody bullshit, and trade in my khakis and All Stars for a nice, neat holy hood? Get the fuck out of here. I could never trade in my heart. I could never trade in my soul. So you ask me—no, you tell me—as if you knew what time it was, "What's wrong with you? Don't you have any remorse? Don't you know what you stand for? You're oppressing your own people and giving them all black eyes. You are merely a worthless pawn in a game of shame." So let me ask you—no, let me tell YOU—Whose pawn are you? Is your game nicer—is everyone a friendly fool? Is it safer—does nobody die? Is it better, more civilized, less animalistic—are the bathrooms prettier? Is that it? No oppression? Now, what planet have you been living on? Every nation has oppression; every state, city, neighborhood, street and household owns its own unique flavor of dictatorship and persecution. The truth is that if I was gonna lose my mind somewhere I was gonna lose it anywhere. What threads would have prevented that? What would you have had me don? Would you have suited and booted me in Brooks Brothers' finest, had me speak with a smile, and fooled yourself into believing that you put a poor down and out *vato* in paradise? Or would you have actually rather proved prejudices, delivered justice, and seen me mad dog you caged up in penitentiary blues?

None of it matters anyway cause I was on a mission to kill even if I'd spent a million years clothed in a monk's dress in a Buddhist temple. I was on an expedition to doom gloom, living the life that could only end with a violent red KABOOM! The world was twisted upside down and earthquaked every day like one a them little Christmas village decorations in globes filled with snow. You shake it around just so you can see how much of a blizzard you can create.

So I tell YOU, did you think that just because there's an invisible standard of how society is supposed to be that that is the way it must be, that I'd have to conform to norms to be happy, productive, alive? Hey, I'm a survivor of many battles, many tragedies, and my experiences make me unique—*solo*—different than any other person in the world, yet I've also laughed a loud proud universal chuckle with the best of em and shot my even louder prouder nut up into the worst of all of em, and I've tasted the happiness of sweet watermelon on a sunny day and the sadness of mama stuffing scorching peppers down my cursing throat. It's not a boast; it's the ghost of my life. Tears, smiles, and laughs got me right here to this predicament, and now I'm here, and I don't know what the hell I'm supposed to do, but live, but die, but be who I am and sing my song, but wear my *Pendle-Tone,* with all of its moth-eaten holes and rusted homeboy medals pinned right above my pumping heart, and struggle and hustle every moment I have.

So I'm an ignorant fucker, eh? Yes, I am, ignorant of quitting when all says I should. If I would have listened to bright ideas, I wouldn't have been a *cholo* chasing *loco* dreams like a dog chasing his tail. I would have done great in school, graduated *magna cum laude* and been a gangster doing civilized business in honestly filthy places—but because I couldn't make it legitimately cause of all the shit I've fucked up, then I'm a fucked up ass motherfucker—the worst piece of shit in the whole world. Cause I don't half ass my life with anything. *Nada* or *todo.* I mean, I guess that's what makes these days so fucked up; people don't know how to get their hands truly dirty. Don't know how to feel around in the toilet bowl for that lost tooth.

Yeah, a lost tooth in a shit filled toilet. You ever done that? Could you, would you ever do it? Get your grill busted by a cop on a night of riots, not protesting over civil rights or human rights, but over get your motherfuckin money rights. Jump in a store, grab a TV, and get busted on the chops by a pig having a field day on anyone out on the streets. And then one day, months later, you're so damn drunk you swallow the fake tooth you got so you can smile like a proper wolf, the tooth that cost you the change from two liquor store holdups, and when you wake up all hung over you actually appreciate you risked your life and could've got busted and got locked up for a dime, or you could have got really sick with it and blasted your way to kingdom come and been a flower loving corpse. So after you take your shit, you get down on your hands and knees, and you dig into the holy toilet bowl because you realize you don't give a fuck about too much, but you give a fuck about a little piece of ivory that gives you the illusion of humanity.

I still smile.

Sheila told me once that I had a funny smile.

"You got a funny smile," she said.

"Funny? Like how?" I said.

"You smile like if you're not really smiling at all or like if you're not smiling because you're glad to see me, but like if you got something else to smile about; like if you know something." She concentrated on my teeth.

"Maybe then I should frown. Would you like that better?"

"No, I think if you did that you wouldn't be so damn funny anymore." She rolled her light brown eyes.

"I think if it wasn't for this damn funny smile I would've never got up in your panties."

"No, you got something funnier than that smile." Her fluffy brown hair bounced as she giggled. I took off my boxers, chicken legs proud, and I made her laugh loud all night long.

When daylight broke into her dingy dungeon, I stretched out and watched her slobber on her pillow. She was beautiful, with her eyes closed and mouth open, but I had to take care of business. I caressed my spotless white T-shirt, folded creased khaki pants, and super clean white Converse All Stars, put them on with silent pride, and started for the door.

"What happened?" she blurted out quickly, still half asleep.

"Nothing. Stepping out on the sly. Go back to sleep."

"OK. Bye." She put her soft face onto the lucky pillow, and I sucked in the stale aroma of pussy that dangled around in her unventilated room.

I walked out to the scenes and shouts of the cold morning streets. Middle-aged pudgy Latino men were unlocking their fruit and vegetable stands, buses full of rowdy high school kids hooted and howled, and the bums from around the way added shots of cheap whiskey to their morning cups of coffee. I walked into Taco Loco, the best *taqueria* in the Swamp, an ally *varrio,* and bought two super tacos *de carne asada* and a Corona. I sat down at the multi-colored tiled table and wolfed down grease and hot peppers. Eight thirty on Thursday, September 12, 1991, I pondered about how I was gonna handle Kwai Chung's *problema.*

Kwai Chung was my homeboy from old days gone by. His mom and pop owned a little fish and poultry market in *Montaña,* and he'd gone to the same high school as the rest of the homeboys. He was an average Joe kind of kid that no one even noticed, a teenager who stuck to himself and his few Chinese immigrant friends. But in February of 89, we both woke up to each other's reality. While I was on the bus going to see some broad, and he was headed to the community college with his fat backpack, we got to talking. Sitting behind him that morning, I saw him reading the sports page. While I was no expert on any one sport, I prided myself in keeping on top of the boxing game. He had folded his newspaper into a neat, precise half square and was reading up on the upcoming Duran-Barkley fight that was gonna be happening on that next Saturday night. I had to put in my two cents as to what I thought about the fight.

"Hey," I said, tapping his shoulder, "Duran is the man."

He nodded his flat-top haircutted head but said nothing, didn't even look back at who was talking to him.

"What do ya think?" I asked.

"Duran very good fighter, Lobo, but..."

"But what?" I snapped back, "He's gonna whup Barkley's ass."

"Duran very good fighter," he said calmly, "maybe win, but he not knock Barkley out."

"What the hell you know about boxing? This ain't Kung Fu. This is *mano a mano,* beat the bum to the ground, and hug and kiss afterwards. This is Hands of Stone against a two bit tomato that couldn't beat his way out of a paper bag. You better stick with Bruce Lee, and let the big boys worry about brutality." I said it pumped up and without hesitation.

He reflected.

"Are you certain? Would like to wager on it?"

"Wager? You mean bet, don't you? You want to bet me that Duran won't knock his ass out?" I laughed. "How much?"

"Not exactly fo money. I give you fifty dolla you win, you do fava if lose."

"Favor?" I asked. "What favor?"

"It is small fava that will not bother you."

"Fuck it. I aint losing. It's a beh—I mean a wager." I put my hand out to him and gave his dry hand a homeboy handshake.

He nodded his square head, but did not even look back.

That Saturday night they fought a damn fight. Duran backed Barkley up, and Barkley bombed back. Duran, though, charged forward slipping and sliding with snapping left hooks and devastating crooked right hands. Barkley stood his ground and let loose with stiff elbows and upset uppercuts. Ten rounds of close, hard fighting that could have been held in a telephone booth. Then, in the eleventh, Duran threw a flurry of punches at Barkley against the ropes and did combos up and down his head and body. Like a tree in the forest, Barkley hit the dirt. I slammed my beer thinking about the fifty bucks I was gonna buy a half gram of angel dust with. I'd roll six fat *leños,* smoke a pregnant one, and sell the rest of em for thirty bucks a stick.

But Barkley rose. And he blasted back with his eyes swollen

shut. And he hurt Duran. And the fight started. The crowd cheered *"Piedras!"* and Duran hammered stones onto Barkley's open mouth, and Barkley, I swear, smiled. For four more rounds the fighters fiercely warred. They took turns pounding each other in the face and body, but Barkley, though he was gettin tattooed all over the place, never let up. There was no technique or science in Barkley's punches, but the motherfucker put up a hell of a fight. It turned out to be a split decision. Barkley, Mr. Tomato Can, was not knocked out. I owed Kwai Chung a favor that would change my life.

I wasn't tripping too much off the bet cause I was always into something: looking for new victims, fresh blood, and fluorescent green dollars. So, two weeks later, when I saw Kwai's bony little four-eyed ass walking through *Bajo* Park while I was shooting dice with the homeboys, I didn't even say nothing, but neither did he. Kwai Chung walked right by me without even glancing in my direction. I saw him clear as day, but he didn't even seem to care that he'd won. I was just gonna stiff him anyway, but he didn't even give me the pleasure of coming up to me and telling me I owed him; he didn't even let me stiff him to his face, and for this reason I was interested in him. Was he scared of coming up to me? Had he forgotten? Or had he known that I was just talking out of my ass, and did he view me as a low down rotten scoundrel that wasn't good on his word? I had to look at his face.

"Hey," I shouted to him as he walked further away, "you won."

He stopped, but did not look back. "Yes," he said.

"You got a favor coming to you," I said.

He turned around and looked me in the face; his thick, Coke bottle glasses reflected off the sun and blinded me. "You do not owe me fava unless you want to owe me fava."

Motherfucker. "What the fuck? I want to owe you a favor!" I said a little aggravated. The homeboys stopped bullshitting and turned their attention to us.

"Let's go talk this over there." Kwai Chung pointed to a wooden picnic table we used for playing cards and dominoes. Walking over with him, I noticed he was calm in the midst of walking straight into the entrance of our *varrio*. I am sure he knew that at any moment we could have become annoyed at his presence in our blessed sanctuary and robbed him or beat the shit out of him, but he seemed relaxed, as if he knew he was untouchable.

"I do not fight," he said looking me in the eyes. "I do not drugs or drink. I not interested in be gang memba. I respect you and yo friends because you cwazy. You truly not care about life or death, and for this you take my respect; you must give cwazy man respect if you value life."

I grinned a proud, closed mouth grin at his statements. No one had ever confronted me in this way, so he had my complete devoted attention. I remember every word because he spoke to me as no one had ever spoken to me before: with meek authority.

"I am not, however, pure," KC kept on. "I man like you, and man is corrupt. I know boxing. I know football, baseball, basketball, and hockey. I even know golf. I know for long time. Right now I run bets to markets and homes here and in Chinatown. I doing this since I arrived in this country and have learned much. I run many miles for others; now I want to sit."

"You can have this seat, homes. Anytime you're tired you can come sit down." I brushed off the wooden bench with our graffiti carved all over it.

He did not want my seat.

"I want my own chair," he continued, the yellow skin around

his lips cracking. "I know outcomes and want to begin my own side bets with many of customers I know. There is, howeva, noooo respect. They know I value life. They will not cheat my connected bets, but they will cheat me if they know they can." He looked around to make sure no one was listening. "This is fava I ask: collect my hod payments. Just mere presence of yo face will let people know you are man to respect. You be rewarded well." He bowed his head and fooled a fool.

"Yeah," I said, "I'll hook it up."

"Good. We meet here tomorrow at twee o'clock and you can come with me to make my rounds and yo presence, I sure, will be all that is required."

That next afternoon I took a little stroll with Kwai Chung. I carried a .38 and a forty ounce, and we went to neighborhood liquor stores and little alley homes. I just stood there while Kwai Chung collected money, wrote down figures on a notepad, and smiled. Rarely did he even break anyone off any green. I realized then that gambling is for straight losers. Still, it surprised me just how many people actually bet on bullshit. His customers were old men and women who went to church on Sundays, blue collar Joes with big beer bellies, local store and business owners who made it day by day on the pocket change and food stamps of the community—he even had homeless bums from the shantytown under the freeway calling odds and placing bets with bags full of change. Everyone put their seasonings in KC's stew, and everyone was satisfied with putting a buck on their own personal long shot or sure thing.

There was no problem. For two and a half years, I walked with Kwai Chung every couple of weeks, and there was never any problem. I would put on my face of stone, KC would take care of his business, and I'd get a C-note for my troubles. Wonderful. In that time Kwai Chung prospered. He had become an underground superstar with my help, and everyone was happy with him because they felt he was honest and fair. His side bet customers dealt with him instead of the other connected knuckleheads because they knew with Kwai there would never be any overblown garbage like there would have been dealing with *cholos* like me. With Kwai Chung you got paid, and you didn't get no bullshit. You paid cause to not pay ruined your bets with the fairest man in the business. His customers cared about being on the up and up, and when they saw me, the good kind of *gente* they were, they would figure they should also pay cause it was in their and their properties' best interest to pay.

For two and a half years it was beautiful like that. On Wednesday, September 11, 1991, Kwai Chung beeped me at Sheila's house and told me some Chinese dude wasn't paying his dues. Kwai had always dealt with this guy on a personal one-on-one type level. When KC first started the racket, we'd go over to this dude's house, on the outskirts of *Varrio Montaña,* and Kwai wouldn't even want me to meet homeboy, so I never even seen dude. Smoking a *frajo* or two, I'd just wait outside, about a block away. Then, for some reason, we didn't have to go over there no more. Now Kwai told me that this guy needed some talking to or whatever. He didn't tell me, but I knew I had to take his ticket.

There was a bomb hovering above me since we fucked that family up. That shit had been all on the news, and, yeah, some people were scared, but I also knew some people were brave. Already in the six months since we fucked that family up, we, our *varrio,* gained some really fucked up notoriety, but I knew some shit was gonna get fucked up somehow. This was the beginning. Someone didn't want to pay. Someone figured homeboys were soft. Maybe I was being paranoid, but I felt this dude must have heard we were the lowlife punks who did that shit to the family back in March and figured he wasn't no punk like that. He must have figured I, being Kwai's muscle, was some kind of sissy beating up on a teenager and old uncle. I was a damn cream puff. I accepted those beliefs and knew what I had to do to set them straight.

The night before, over the phone, while Sheila was licking my neck and tickling me under my armpits, KC had given me the address. I laughed and knew I had to make my mark.

That next morning, Thursday morning at 9:00, I sat at Taco Loco, after finishing my beer, and realized the scope of what I had to do to get back some respect. I smiled.

And it sounds fucked up that I could smile about such depraved shit, but you gotta understand I've done a lot worse than smile. I used to keep the smiles locked up inside me and just grin or chuckle every now and then—that is, until we did that shit. Before that family, I would bullshit, tell meaningless funny jokes, and glide my way into the good times, even though I knew there was no such thing. But after the incident, I knew who I was, and I knew who I had to be. So I put my head up and started the journey that we all go on—that long hard journey to hell—cause I knew I wasn't right, but neither was anyone else. No one got the answers, so I made up my own answers. Cause when God stops loving you there aint nothing you can do but go on. Like I said, I used to figure I could slide my way into the good grace of the Almighty if I bullshitted enough, but after what I did, and don't get me wrong, I've done some pretty fucked up shit, but the incident was different; different cause I knew I was really fucked up. I did worse than kill bodies; I killed souls; I knew there were no more favors; I knew I had purposely challenged God, yet I couldn't shed a tear cause it wouldn't do me no good. So I went on. *El Señor Lobo* was on his own, and that meant I had to be down and dirty; sly, slick, and wicked; and, most importantly, I had to smile.

After my breakfast, I ordered a cup of coffee from a chunky little *señorita* in a *huipil*. I slouched forward on my Taco Loco table and blew into the strong odor of the *café*. I thought about how the past six months had actually been the happiest time of my whole life, and I knew it was because of Sheila. Back in March of 91, the night after the family incident, I met Sheila, and I smiled. It was my honey, my little baby doll, my stranger who did not smile back. Of course, I had just returned from an all night mission to set a world record for the most snapped out on PCP you can get, the most stupid drunk, the most senseless, idiotic, armed robbing, car jacking, stick my knife to your throat; the most stabbing, stealing, stampeding young *cholo* in the universe, and the darkness vanished, it turned to sunshine in the middle of blackness, and I confronted her. Young homegirl challenged by young *cholo*.

Cholo,
Latino,
Hispanic,
Chapin,
Mexican,
Salvatrucho,
Central American,
Indian,
Spick,
Wetback,
Warrior,
Hombre.
Thee Lobo.

But my name really didn't matter cause I could be a nigga or a white boy too. I listened to the screaming soul oldies and loved those all American Chevy Impalas. I could, if I had to, say good morning with a smirk on my face or break dance like a little crab on the ground. I was a true rainbow *loco,* and I didn't give a fuck. Call me, label me, tag me or stamp me whatever you want; just give me your money, and keep your damn mouth shut.

Universal as a hungry man.

And, oh yeah, there she was, and I smiled, and she mattered, which is more than I can say for myself because I was *El Lobo:* a fighter, a robber, and a mack to the fullest. I would let my false tooth shine in the brilliance of broad day and be a mean mugging monster in the majesty of the moonlight. I didn't matter cause I didn't give a fuck if I mattered or not.

But she did. She mattered because I saw that she didn't give a fuck either.

On that sultry night, I was kickin it, choppin it up with the homeboys at our corner liquor store. With just one look, I knew I had to have her. I examined her walking down my street with her face painted up like a beautiful Bozo the Clown, her hair a tall brick wall of hairspray, and she was shaking her sexy thick ass like the Playboy Playmate of the year. She was a diamond in the mud. And even though she was baby doll fine, I didn't think of just going up in her at the time, didn't think of only tearing off them panties. For her to address the world with such style, I appreciated she had more than a body. What I really wanted was her soul. I wanted her to give me more than just her cooch; I wanted that woman to devote to me her eternal faith.

It was my once in a lifetime chance—my dream girl was in my presence, and I had to impress her, shock her, and love her right at that moment or never again. One shot, one kill. So I prowl up, smile, and says, "What's up, gorgeous! You are a wildflower blooming in front of my eyes. I've been waitin to pick you all my life, and now you're here, and it's not a dream. I'm in your face as a man that aint got too much on the materialistic side, only got a good time when you're with me. I want to fall in love with you tonight and forever."

"Huh?" she snarled, as if I could give her some nasty disease, "Are you serious or just retarded?" I sucked in the cotton candy scent off of the angel's mouth.

"Yeah, I'm serious as a heart attack." I took the stupid smirk off of my face and stared her down as if I was the incarnation of *El Diablo* himself. "Check out, let's go get us a coupla forties, sit down at *Bajo* Park, and talk about life. Let's go kick back, listen to some live ass homeboy soul oldies, and let's laugh about the act I'm gonna play for you and the Academy Award movie star you're gonna be just for me." She unfolded her arms. "We'll do this much for each other, and we'll give each other illusions of how we wish we were, we'll laugh at our insecurities, and we'll love each other for less than a second yet pretend it's forever." I released a genuine smile from somewhere mysterious in the depth of my soul, and I yanked her into my heart. She gave me her unyielding faith by flashing me her precious sunbeam. I captured her around her little waist and confidently led her into the world of my truth.

It was paradise. We'd wake at three in the morning and start out our day after having gotten drunk off our asses the whole day before. We'd walk five miles, catch the bus, or steal a car and cruise to the beach to watch rats and raccoons duke it out for scraps of trash. We'd stroll down the shoreline listening to the splitting waves crash on the beach front, and I'd make love to her right there on the freezing sand as fantastic fog rolled in over us. Afterwards she would embrace me with all of her strength and tell me, "Don't ever leave me, Lobo." I'd answer her by prying her off me, jumping my naked ass into the forty degree ocean, and shouting, "Never!"

It was three weeks later when she doubted me. She had her homegirl's Regal, and it was her, her chubby cousin Tracy, and me. We had just bought some forties and a bottle of Wild Turkey and were on our way to have a good time somewhere by the beach or at the pier, but she gave me a fucked up attitude cause I busted open my forty in her homegirl's fucked up car, like if I was gonna contaminate the interior with a few spilled drops of malt liquor foam. And so she pulled the car over, all high and mighty, and commanded, "Lobo, put the cap back on until we get to a cool spot." As if she was the leader of something. And so I said, nice and sincere, like only a charming *cholo* can—

"Bitch, fuck you."

Her mouth dropped. Who in the hell did I think I was? I can't talk to her like that, oh no, she's a lady, a princess, a goddess. But Goddess didn't have a chance to say none of that nonsense cause I just took my forty, adjusted my pistol under my shirt, stepped out of the car as if the past twenty-one days of falling madly in love with her didn't mean anything to me, and left her listening to James Brown with her mouth open and no words coming out. I walked away without looking back.

I always look forward.

So I'm a wolf on the prowl and dead straight in front of me there's a flock of business guys in suits strolling down the street that beautiful Friday morning in the downtown, busy ass traffic city of Inten, and I pulled out my .38 from my pants belt, ripped out some stomach hairs in the process, and said...

28

"Your fuckin money." Sober and serene as a priest at mass. They all jumped like little bunny bitches and strangely started throwing their chump change on the sidewalk as if they expected I was actually gonna bend the fuck down and pick up their leftovers like some stereotypical garbage man. I smashed a heavy redneck in the head with my forty. My forty, for some reason, didn't break, but he buckled to the floor anyway.

"You," I pointed my gun directly at the glossy forehead of the guy who was standing behind buckler, "grab the fuckin money and give it here." He bent over and scooped up the money that was shining and sparkling on silver and gold money clips. I stayed looking at his four eyes as I put my forty down on the hard ground and accepted the money from the scared man that I could tell had never met a true garbage wolf up close and personal. He had never known that garbage wolves have honor too. He'd never known how it is to live in the garbage can, without hopes and dreams—except for distorted fantasies of going to *La Pinta,* selling drugs, or getting killed. I stuffed his dirty honest money in my pocket and dropped the weight of my gun and the full force of my arm on top of his bald eagle head. I grabbed my Old E and walked back to Sheila in her piece of shit, fat homegirl's Buick.

She hadn't left. Nope, not my Goddess, the car door was still open, just like her honey filled mouth, inviting me inside. She had thought I was actually gonna leave her. Silly rabbit.

"Drive," I said as I scooted in and shut the door. I didn't look at her as she drove away, and she didn't look at me either. She simply drove, and her love was telepathically proved. She had the passionate love of a true believer, a partner who would never leave my side.

Mi amor. My love.

Vida Loca. Crazy life. The homeboy philosophy. My philosophy—cause it didn't make any sense to do the shit I did, but it did. It made me normal in a world where I had to fuck a motherfucker up to feel good inside, to be accepted by the *locos*, to keep my respect as a man. I had to get over on someone and make them feel like shit so that I could say I was a true street soldier. I couldn't justify or explain it. It went beyond justification. It went beyond the simplicity of an explanation. There was no explanation or theory that could satisfy the lust of *La Vida Loca*. All I knew is that I was there, and I had to do what I had to do to keep the little piece of planet that was the *varrio* mine. Reality is what counted, and it is what was strong. The crazy life was reality—as real and genuine as the crazy death.

After Goddess demonstrated how genuine she was, I trusted her to suck my dick and not bite. That's a beautiful kind of love when you can just lay back and not worry—the kind of love that don't need words, the love I searched for all my life, and all my life it was never there. So I let go. After we'd be wore out and sweaty from fucking for over an hour, lying on her twin size mattress on the floor of her cold gray basement spot in the Swamp, I would tell her who I was.

"I am so, so bad cause I always get my prey. I go high, and I go low, and sometimes I even pretend I aint shit so I can sucker a fucker in, and then I pounce, love. I go in for the kill. I am a man of many different masks, crooked as my smile." But Sheila would blow O's of smoke from her Marlboro Reds and wouldn't be impressed, didn't care about those things, looked at me and kept silent, cool, so I told her stories, adventures, misdeeds, and craziness that I was proud of. "One time when I was fifteen, solo *cholo*, getting off the bus late night after boning this broad from *Pueblo*, the enemy hood,

I had to transfer over to the next bus. I see this mob, this gang of nuts, but I gotta get past them and fuck that shit if I'm gonna walk around them, fuck that shit if I'm gonna punk out—cause even though there's no one there to see me, I know what's right and what's wrong. I walk right up to all of them, bold like a full ass pimp, lean and mean, a hundred fifty pounds soaking wet, just a little lighter than what I am now, and I recognize this dude, motherfucker, I whipped his ass before, tapped that ass real good, and he recognizes me, but I don't give a fuck. 'What's up,' I say and look right into his eyes, and he must have thought I was cuckoo comin into his *varrio* and not giving a fuck, yet I stayed there looking into his eyes when I should have got on, gangster-strutted the fuck away, but I stood there like I'm invincible, cause I got a bulletproof heart, and in that second I could hear the beat of my *corazon* booming in my ears—'You go wherever you want cause you aint scared of shit.' That second was victory, and then *puto* says, 'You still wanna fight?' Two seconds later, I heard the pride of knuckles and the laughs of feet up my ass. All them punks jumped on me like if I asked for it. All them *putos* blazed on me, and I ran away. Yeah, I ran away, and they were shouting out *Pueblo, Puto!* and throwing bottles, and I blasted off like a rocket even when I knew there was no one behind me anymore. I ran to *Varrio Montaña* as fast as I could, ran to the base of the hill which is *Bajo* Park, then up to Tip Top's, our bar, searching for the homies. No one was there, so I dashed up to the top of *Varrio Montaña,* Tweak Peak, and homeboys were all *snapped*—Toro's a cow grazing in green pastures and whispering sweet nothings to a tree, Santo's sitting cross legged on a big rock, eyes closed, nodding up and down, drooling, and singing songs. I see my good ass homies are drugged out fucking retards, and I know I got to have this one down on the exact number.

"I'm calling the shots.

"I reach into Santo's pocket and pull out his .22, and I'm off, running back to the scene of the crime, but those *putos* aint there no more. But I know where dude lives, right in the middle of *Pueblo*. I knock on the door at two in the morning, and when the door creaks open with the flimsy little chain still trying to show some force, I bust through like a rabid wolf, and this little old lady in her flower print muumuu starts screaming and yelling, and I rush into the room, about to unload, pointing the *cuete* up and down, but homeboy aint there. The lady's Chinese. It aint even the right fuckin house! So I took her little black and white TV and got on. I saw the dude two years later, and I jumped his ass right in front of his mom." I'd tell Sheila this shit, and she wouldn't even change her expression, wouldn't seem as if it mattered to her, had no prejudice or emotions, but just stared right back at me in my face, listening, but not judging—knowing the life. As time passed, and I told her so much, after I let her know my weaknesses and strengths, I had to look away.

That's why I loved her, cause I wasn't worthy to even look at her. She was that damn beautiful, so damn gorgeous, nice light titties, smooth soft skin, full lips that never refused my kiss, and I hated to drink beer around her cause then I'd have to go take a piss, and that was a minute I didn't have her in my arms. I hated to have her scream and moan with her slender legs wrapped around me and her fine fingers scratching my back cause that meant it was the beginning of her end—but I'd deny my own pleasure—stop, hold my breath, bite my tongue, and go on and on; deny myself cause I never wanted to pull out of her endless black hole—never tired of planting my tree. And when I had to leave her to go handle mines, and leave her for a day or a week, my life was not worth living. I'd smell her on my arms, in my fingers, on my goatee, and she smelled like pears, but that's not what I'd tell her, 'Did you take a shower? You stink.' And she was no damn good cause she'd laugh at my jokes, and I'd play jab at her face, trip up her legs, and chuck her onto the bed, and damn if she wasn't the best bitch I ever smelled!

One day in May, we went to the zoo. You know, ate popcorn and peanuts, and we heard the lions roar and saw the gorillas swing. I hugged and kissed her, and I won't bullshit you—I even held her hand in public. I was proud. It didn't matter that I was hung over. It didn't matter I was half broke and that I had made her jump over the gate of the zoo so we could get in for free. And I didn't care that my stomach grumbled and turned from the burrito I'd eaten the night before. Machine-gun fire rattled out of my pants, and I knew I positively loved her when I didn't want her to see me sweat. I held it in—held my shit in with a straight face and acted as if everything was fine. The peanuts got to me, the buttered pop-corn kicked in, and the burrito tried to break me down. I smiled, walking sluggish but proud until I seen the head. I excused myself like a gentleman for her. Sometimes, though, I couldn't help but be who I had to be.

One night in June, I went to her place all bloody, shanked in my side by a hater at a birthday party. Should have gone to a mother-fuckin hospital, should have called a damn ambulance or cried for help, but I went over to her basement, and she was waiting. She opened the door and didn't say shit, just took off my blood soaked shirt and kissed my wound. And I threw up from all the brandy I'd drunk, kept throwing up, and I felt I made a mighty great mistake coming over cause I really didn't want her to see me like that. She lifted my head up out of the toilet bowl and kissed my closed eyes, stuck her tongue deep in my mouth, put a patch on my flesh, and made me feel like no one ever has, like a human fuckin being. She gave me what I needed, and what I needed was her tender mouth and silent comfort. She made it seem as if there was nothing I couldn't do, no world I couldn't conquer, no happiness that was impossible.

At some point she stopped asking me what I did. She knew what time it was. So, after awhile, I told her not about what I did, but who I really was. I opened up my pie hole about no mama or papa, about all my time locked up in the Hall and reading poetry and drawing hearts, let go most of what was inside of me, showed her what I could never show anyone else. Cause for everyone else I had to keep my teeth sharp. For everyone else I knew there were boundaries, but for her there were no lines, for her there was only infinity, and all I could do was jump into her tenderness and never land. I flew in space with nowhere to go, lived like if there was no tomorrow, loved like if I invented the shit. And it wasn't the meat anymore—it wasn't the chase or the kill—it was the life I wanted! I didn't tear her body apart without respect. I was a good Indjun. I bowed my head for her, said a prayer for her, gave her all my love cause she sustained me and kept me alive even though there was death and despair all around. She kept me going even in my hardest times. I depended on her more than I depended on myself. Some people might think she was weak for being my angel, but I only wish I had her strength.

My mistake was that I gave her garbage, and she gave me roses, yet she never complained about it, never preached or nagged or ever looked away. She saw beyond my player face, right into the tootsie roll pop center, but still she couldn't see the real animal I am. I was always an ideal to her. She didn't know, even though she seen it with her big *café con leche* eyes, that there was a *man* inside of this fur: a man who didn't just bleed, but howled in the middle of the night about all those things that could never be let go to anyone. But I forgave her naiveté, forgave her because she was right in her own way. She had me right on the dotted line. Those damn lines, lines that never break or falter, lines that are straight forever. She had me plotted and mapped, and she knew one day I would jump over and cut that line. One day I was gonna hog and smash that line, and she was right to fear me or pity me or love me because I do go all the way; I do go up and pop, pop, pop, and I do leap over that basic human condition of survival and those abstract norms of the world. I do drink blood and stick my tongue way out there for a little piece of wafer. She was right to keep some silent distance because she was smart enough to know what she was getting into.

She must've thought I'd eventually crack like an egg, break like glass. She thought I'd give her weakness instead of strength because of all I let go, but she didn't know that my wall was bigger than she could imagine, bigger than the one in China, stronger than steel bars in prison cells, higher than the Empire State. See, I make magic, am a wonderful trickster of deception.

Allow me to amuse you with my sadness.

Back at Taco Loco, eleven o'clock in the morning, smoking a cheap GPC cigarette, sipping on my third cup of coffee, bullshitting with bums who begged for scraps. The Chinaman was priority. I knew I could have been the sly, slick, and wicked wolf stalking his prey, catch him by surprise and put a bullet through his head, but I figured I had to make my mark. I had to be known. I had to do it sick so everyone would know my true wrath: I was capable of more than just slaughtering lambs. This territory was mine, and if you fucked with my shit, then you had to pay. For this, I had to be the vicious wolf, the *lobo* that takes more than what he needs. I left a five spot as a tip and strolled to a *cantina* downtown and drank a few beers and Bloody Marys. After a solid buzz, I caught a movie show and then waited around looking at legs till late night.

No money for bus fare left, I hiked the three miles to the dude's house and rang the doorbell, as if I was gonna ask him for some sugar. I thought, this poor little guy, I'm a do combinations on his mug and put him in the sleeper, choke his ass out to the next world, kill him with my bare hands. Gonna get this shit over with nice and personal, and leave him lying right on his front door so that when the mailman trips over him, they're gonna know something completely psycho went on. I rang the doorbell again cause there wasn't no answer.

A slightly tan slant-eyed giant with a Michael Jackson Jheri Curl, a fat tat on his neck, and a dull black pistol in his left paw finally answered the door.

I was bewildered, in a maze daze, going round and round, feeling my body up above me and looking down at me. I was Krazy Glued to the ground. "The TV," I blurted out. "I came to buy the TV."

"Come in," he said, and for no logical reason whatsoever I walked in as if I wanted a TV and as if he was really gonna give me one. "Right down this way." He guided me down some steps, and I didn't know what the fuck I was doing. In a trance like a zombie—stiff, straight legs plodding and arms stretched out in front of me—I walked down the stairs, into the abyss.

Her eyes purple black, Sheila was sitting on a couch with her duct-taped hands clasped. Her mouth was bloody, her makeup was streaked all over her face, and her hair was pulled out in bald patches all over her head. "I've been expecting you," the Sasquatch said. "I knew you'd come."

OK, I snapped out. *OK, gotta see what time it is*, I thought, *she's fucked up, he knows who I am, he's got this thing figured out.* With only a few front teeth, Sheila smiled at me.

"Muthafucka! Thought you'd give me a ticket, but your ass aint even got a badge!" He pocketed his gat and pulled out a giant butcher knife from a cabinet drawer. "Sorry ass bitch didn't want to say your name, but I already knew who you were!" I stood statue still. "You didn't know who you was fuckin wit. I'm a nigga that don't give a fuck!" He started stabbing the couch and lampshades. "And now," he said catching his breath, "I'm gonna show you how a real nigga handles his!" He put the knife up to her throat.

OK. "All right, homes, all right! You win! Come on, please, homes. It's just me, just a dumb fuck. What you want to do this for? This between me and you, Bro. This some stupid ass shit that aint got nothin to do with her."

"Nigga," he said, "you tell me you come all this way cause this tween me and you? You don't even know me. You listenin to some punk ass Chinaman Kwai Chung and you gonna snuff me cause of what he says?! This tween me and all yall motherfuckers!"

"I got fare," I lied.

"Bitch, you aint got shit."

And then I knew. He needed something or else he wouldn't be playing me this tune. "OK, what you want?" I said. His eyes became slits.

"Now, well, well," he said with the knife to Sheila's neck as she sat silent. "I been hoggin, takin shit cause I want it all. I know Kwai Chung, and he's connected more than your ass will ever know. I can't fuck with him—that shit would be instant death, but don't think I give a fuck!" He launched his fist through the wall. "But I figured when I heard about your punk ass, you could get this shit handled, and I wouldn't even be touched. See, the Chinos don't know that Kwai's skimming off the top with your ass. They don't know bout that shit, and to be honest, I don't think they really give a fuck as long as they get their pockets fat as usual." He shaved the baby hair on Sheila's stem. "But I can't just go in and take over on Kwai's ass; them Chinamen don't particularly like me since I got out the jailhouse, but your ass aint got no strings." The tat on his neck read *Trust No Man*. "The Chinos know that your people got it sewed up inside the walls; homeboys is running that damn show. They don't want no static with yall cause they got people goin in and out too. Cause they don't want niggas comin out like me, a real nigga, they got some kinda agreement with homies for strong arms protection inside the pen. They know that yall give em good business, too, so if some spick caps Kwai's ass, aint no one really gonna say shit about me, except clip your ass. They just gonna look for another nigga to handle they shit."

"You want me to hook Kwai Chung?" I asked.

"You just aint gonna move on him in the middle of the night, nigga. You gonna walk into broad daylight Chinatown, with all the big boys watching, and get nice and bloody in front of all kinds of eyewitnesses. Aint gonna be no doubt you was fixed up with Kwai behind the warlords' backs and that a wetback did this shit. All's gonna work out fine cause after this shit goes down them Chinese aint gon trust no quiet man like Kwai to be doin business out in this fucked up ass ghetto. They gonna be looking for a sick nigga who got Chinaman blood. A nigga like me."

I was disoriented, not sure of exactly what was going on. This was real, slap myself true. He wanted me to do away with a straight ass dude. "For what? What am I gonna get out of this shit, but knocked the fuck out or have to leave forever?" I asked.

The Sasquatch smiled, revealing a gold mouth grill. "Bitch can live. Been staking you out, *lo-co;* I know you, blood, know you got feelings for this ho," he chuckled. "Thought you had it squared away, but you didn't figga on a nigga behind the trigga, did ya? After the shit I done here today, I'd never be safe with your ass alive, wasn't never safe from a fuckin psycho like you anyway. I mean, what the fuck you think you was gonna do comin up here like that? You aint even strapped! Nah, sick ass wetback like you aint worth dealing with. I know your kind, and I know you don't give a fuck just like me, but you fucked up and tore up this pussy here one too many times, fucked up and got whipped." He grabbed her by the hair. "You know I aint playin with you cause she's already fucked up as can be."

I looked into Sheila's light brown eyes and couldn't feel sorry for her. "Bitch," I said to Sheila, "what you have to fuck around with me for?!" I was mad. "Kill that ho, see if I give a fuck!" Sheila's expression remained hard as nails.

"You aint that slick, Mr. Lobo." He stepped back away from her, left her open and gave us space. I stood in the middle of the room; she sat on the shredded up couch. Circus makeup streaked all over her, fuzzy head like a baby bird, nose twisted flat, in her short red nightie, tan legs crossed. This time she did not want to look at me, and all I could do was stare and stand tall. Forget how I had just watched her this morning sleeping like Beauty. Forget the time back in July when we drove down to TJ, Mexico, and we're leaving that club at four a.m. and three fuckheads try to stick us up, and I start drilling one of em down, and they all jump on me, and damn! She banged away with me, side by side, and together we chased them fools off cause they didn't expect no shit like that. Forget how she smells, how she feels, how she was always there before I even arrived. I leaned up and stepped forward with baby's steps, giant's steps, shrinking, shrinking, going low and then down. I was looking in her face, squatting on my ankles, opening her legs and touching her jeweled thighs, then down on my knees, my head in her lap. I was a colored egg cracked open on Easter Sunday, a shattered window from a mighty home run ball.

She was my Great Wall.

"You have too much affection to be the wolf," she kissed my head softly, "too much love to be cool." She was more right than she would ever know, but I got up anyway.

"All right," I said facing Sasquatch, "how do I know you're on the up and up about her?"

"Cause I'm just like you, nigga, just like you. Even though I might be fucked up, I got soul inside this skin, just like you, homeboy, and that's better than my word."

"When," I stated.

"Tomorrow morning, you tell Kwai Chung I'm history. Tell him you did it sly, dumped me in a pond with cement shoes. I'm gonna go undercover with her. You know Kwai Chung makes a public tribute on Sundays at dusk right in that big park up in Chinatown. Them Big Timers take payments from all over the city, play *mah jong,* and chain smoke cigarettes. That's when you do it, nice and bloody, but don't hit no one else cause then they's got to do something to get all yall back, and I don't want no fuckin big war. Just Kwai, real red. You stay blasting into that body, and I'm gonna come save the day and tell em all that's been goin on behind their backs, let them know that this is what happens when you got a motherfucker skimming with wetbacks. If you manage to get out alive, you can hook back up with her and get the fuck out of here. After it's done, that's when she's let go."

A death sentence or a banishment. I understood completely. "A moment, homes," I said.

"It's all good, handle yours."

"Stand up," I said to Sheila. Rising, she kept her poise. I wanted to kiss her, hug her, take away the pain inside and tell her everything was gonna be fine. Instead, I looked her dead straight in the eyes, gave her a holy homeboy handshake, and told her, "Be cool, homes."

I made an about face and walked away. I nodded my head to Sasquatch, walked up the stairs, and out the front door. The cold wind slapped my face, and I stuffed my hands in my pockets. *Damn, I fucked up,* I thought. I was scared. I was angry. *Fuck this puto, I told myself, I'm comin back right the fuck now with someone's gat and kill this fool. Motherfucker scaring the shit out of me, nah, fuck that, this punk is goin downtown, to the fuckin morgue. Sheila, she's waitin, she's depending on me. Fuck that bitch, too. She shoulda known not to fuck around with a* cholo *like me. Man, that's my* vida, *homes, and I knew it was gonna come to this one day, especially after that* familia *business, but damn, what the fuck, I got to think. It's Thursday, no, it's motherfuckin Friday morning, Friday the fuckin thirteenth! Twelve thirty! Two days, two nights to prepare. I need a fat hit, some thick legs, need to relax, clear my head and think. Think. If I go back there, he'll take her out. If I don't show up to kill Kwai on Sunday, she's gone. Bitch! Bitch! Man, that's all she is anyway, what the fuck she ever do for me? I dicked her down and gave her some fantastic freedom. I showed her the world through a roller coaster ride. All she did was lay there. No—she took me in, took me in and looked in my big black eyes, loved me even with my big ass snout and sharp fuckin teeth. No, I got to do this one thing. But maybe I could find a way. Maybe with the help of sick Santo and terrible Toro. Maybe we could hook some shit up and get this handled, but I gotta figure this shit out. Too many ants in my pants.*

There were countless thoughts in my head, not enough words that could do justice to what I felt, the torture and despair. And I still can't believe that I'm relaying crimes and transgressions. I'm no damn good. Cause where I come from this means death; a homeboy just don't talk about these things. These are silent wonders that everyone acknowledges, but never speaks of except in whispers. It aint no fun that I'm forced to let it out, aint no happiness showing the secret road to my heart. But I can't hold it in no more, and if that means death then so be it. I've been eye to eye with that hooded goon, and he don't impress me anymore.

I jogged five miles to the beach and thought of alternatives to the inevitable. *Santo's been super weird lately, digging holes all over the place. Toro's a dumb fuck, got no brains. What the fuck I'm a get done with these idiots—what I'm doin with these fools? I'm smart, got talent. I could hustle and talk proper. I know how to smile and tip my hat. I could've done somethin special. Instead, I fucked up my life, but can't go back now. Gotta go forward. But I'm gonna advance hugging the ground, creep up to the suckers, camouflage my truth.*

Out of breath, I reached the beach about an hour later. I sat down on a log and watched the beasts battle it out. A raccoon was digging in the garbage can, daring someone to fuck with him. The rats shrieked, bunched up, moved around him, and formed a circle of no escape. They struck quick and then ran back to their circle formation. The raccoon roared and clawed a few rats and felled them, but the rats didn't lose their uniformity. The live ones kept their positions, and the circle got tighter around the raccoon and his precious garbage can. The rats that were left were the hard asses. They tore little pieces of flesh off the raccoon, and after awhile there were screams, screeches, and the gang of rats was on top, eating the raccoon's fresh flesh, all the guts hanging out. The garbage can was theirs.

It made me hungry, but I didn't have nothin, so I just walked, needed to tire my body out, needed to get some sleep, but I obsessed that I had too much shit to do. Sheila. I wished she had left me something to remember her by. I looked at her lipstick traces on my shirt. I saw the sun rise and counted the waves. After one thousand nine hundred and seventy waves, I rose and ran.

By the time I got back to *Varrio Montaña,* the sun was out in full force. Three in the afternoon, the rcc center was giving away cheese. Famished, I got in line. This young mom in back of me was hitting her kid for getting outta line and making her lose their spot at the front. "How are we going to eat if you don't stay in your place!" she shouted in Spanish. "How are we supposed to live with you always playing around?!" She smacked his ass hard.

"Mama," the little boy answered, "I don't want any more cheese." He looked up at her with honest, innocent eyes. "Mama, I want cupcakes and Happy Meals." He did not cry.

They will be taught through the mouths of babes.

Fuck this shit, I made up my mind, *I'm gonna rob all them fools. They're gonna break themselves for me. Fuck it! I want Happy Meals too! I'm a gangster. If I'm going out, then it's gonna be all out war. We're gonna break them Big Timers and Kwai's ass too. I'm gonna blast Kwai, Santo's gonna cover Sasquatch, and Toro's ass is gonna peel all the big boys. Fuck that bitch! Shouldn't have never fucked with me. She knew what time it was. She don't wanna live without me anyway! Nah, this shit aint goin down like this. Motherfucker gots me pegged all wrong.*

Santo will get down. Toro will go along, no questions fuckin asked.

But Sheila's gonna be gone.

Nah, got to get this guilt behind me, block it out with some dust and bitches. Sunday, that's all that matters. Sunday and my world is new. What do I want? Happy Meals, gold chains, convertible Impala, a finer bitch than Sheila, two bitches, a harem, fine clothes, silk shirts and leather cowboy boots, a palace with a statue. A memorial to her. Yeah, that's what I'll do, and that'll make it all better—a memorial to her in big bold gold letters and her face in bronze, and I'll leave a sacrifice of fresh lamb blood every day. She'll be in heaven, right? I mean, she's an angel, be back where she belongs. Honor, keep my honor. Man, that's just a word, got nothin to do with survival, all it's good for is to get me deeper into the hole I'm already in. Fuck honor. I'll be honorable when I handle this lick. I'll give ten G's to the old folks' home or some shit. I'll buy the runts some basketballs and baseballs, get them some box-ing gloves, and set up a ring. Shit, that'll make up for everything. The Swallowing Sheila Memorial Coliseum. That's honor, more than I could ever give her if I stayed the way things are going now. I go through with this shit on the up and up, and I'm dead, aint no good to no one. She'll meet another fool, have ten kids, and get all fuckin obese, her man'll end up in the pen, aint no doubt about that shit, and she'll be up in this line every fuckin week. Nah, honor, I'm gonna save her from all that shit, aint gonna have my best girl go through that shit, live like a fuckin pig. Mercy killing. She's through, and I'm new. This is takeoff.

:: :: ::

So I'm flying—higher, higher—but I got no place to land. I'm above everyone, and it's all about me and what I need done, and fuck everyone and everything cause this is my starship. I'm an astronaut headed for the moon. And I appreciate that I've had my good old homeboys to keep me going with a cause when I needed one, when I had nothin but time, but now I got independence. It's Independence Day in September. And I'm the only one celebrating cause now I'm in control, and aint no fool gonna overthrow my evolution.

Three in the afternoon and Santo and Toro walking straight towards me, and they can't see that I got them in my sight—right in the cross hairs—that I see em coming, that I see it all. They're so blind they don't know they're about to get got. Even though my body is down there, my head's up in the air, my brain's thinking in the clouds—perceiving all the possible options, and I just got to get back down there for one minute and do my dirt.

"What you doin, Lobo?" Santo asked as if he didn't know what was going on. He had a scruffy beard and his hair was all messy in crazy waves. It'd been more than a coupla weeks since I'd seen him.

As if I didn't see them, as if I had no sense of what was happenin, "Hey, what's up," I said. "It's free cheese time, homes. Gettin ready for the feast."

"We're about to get some burgers," Toro said, charging full force for the red cape.

"Keep that money in your pocket, Bro," I said. "Let's cut up to the front and get some free cheese. Aint no meal better than a free meal. With the saved money, we'll buy some drink."

Boldly, we cut to the front of the line, and no scarf headed little old lady complained about shit. We grabbed our blocks of cheese, went to the store and hustled some cheese to a grandma, then bought some Wonder bread and forties. We walked down to *Bajo* Park to feast.

Get em happy, make em smile, persuade em to think that there's no better place in the world than right in this filthy ass, pissed on, broken down graffiti park. Filet mignon, lobster with steak, pudding pie, and a super burrito are all wrapped into these blocks of pasty yellow cheese.

"Damn, this is some good ass cheese, aint it?" I stated it as if there were no insincerity in my words, as if there was nothing else in the world I would rather stuff in my mouth.

"Yeah, but why they got to give us cheese for? Why can't they give us steaks or some shit?" Toro asked.

That question had me stumped. Rubbing my goatee, I hesitated during the time when something needed to be spoken, a time when silence was uncertainty.

"They know what mice like," Santo answered. "They think we're fuckin mice, homes. They want to kill us mice with poison cheese." He swallowed.

That's when Santo started turnin blue, like if he was chokin or some shit. Nope, it wasn't a happy sight, but I had to prosper on the tragedy, make the most out of this great opportunity.

"Yeah, you're fuckin right, Santo. You're talking real, Bro." I slithered over to him and patted him on the back. He smelled like funky sweat socks. "You got it all figured out. You know we aint gettin shit here. You've always been the smartest, Bro. Always had that keen sense doin doughnuts inside your head. Cheese. We shouldn't be eatin cheese; we should be cuttin it, cuttin the cheese from bein full and mighty, from making our names heard round the world. Up in the highest mountain and down in the lowest valley, our names should be known. Our pockets should be fat; our smiles should be broad cause life—life don't last past the blast, Santo. We both know that reality. We got to make it count now—now that we're here, now that we got a chance we gotta take it."

He was listening closely, his face twisted, blue as the sea, knowing I was making sense. "Aint no one gonna give us shit but cheese. But we're better than that. The only thing that makes sense is prosperity. No one gives a fuck about what's goin on around here. That's the only truth I'm familiar with, Bro. I watched the news the other day, and they're telling me it's gonna be blue skies and sunny shine days, but they can't see that these times is stormin—they can't see that it's raining wolves and bulls every fuckin day. Now, Santo, you got what it takes to make shit happen; you're high class, baby—top of the tier royalty is what you are—don't let that shit go to waste, Bro. Don't tell me that what I think of you is a lie."

And Santo looked at me, but not at me, but in me—inside—and I met his eyes. But his green grenades were too solid for my spoiled plums, so I looked away cause I couldn't stare and pretend; I couldn't pretend I was pure and honest cause then he would have known, then I would have known, that I was totally false. So I spoke, "I've been thinkin about it; it's been in me a long time growing strong. A master plan of action to make some killer *ferria,* but I need some *gente* made of steel, cause this aint no little joke, homes. You and Toro and the century is ours."

I could only swallow my beer. A faint scent of her pear perfume haunted the air.

Santo pounded his heart hard, his face returning to normal. "All I got is right here," he said calmly, confidently.

Enough. Confirmation to join me; Toro, of course, would follow. Jump on in for the fly down, but there's only one parachute here, and it's already on my back, Bros.

Time to relax.

"*Orale!* It's all set to jet. Let's get a deck and a *leño* and turn this into a real party." I put my arms around Santo's shoulder. *Keep these homeboys on the positive trip,* I thought. We walked; I'm peeping into rides, and the first car I saw with a decent deck—bam—I busted the window with my elbow, jumped on in and took that Alpine CD system and them six by nine speakers, and handed it to Toro, but I knew it wasn't enough merchandise for us to be really cool for the night. And so we crept up on side streets where it was serene and quiet. A brand new Toyota pickup was in a driveway, and I tippy toed up. Right in the living room, directly above the truck, I heard voices and a TV, so I knew the stupid box would keep the victims glued while I pushed the Toyota's cracked open window all the way down, opened the door, and slipped in. I was workin with a little screwdriver on a pocketknife, with the tools of the trade. Just as quick as I'm in, I'm out. A Clarion tape deck, the speakers too shitty to even take. *Adios.*

Tip Top's bar is the place to be with burning merchandise. Tip Top's, where all the hard working blue collar suckers drink their sweat and look for deals of the century men like me to come by. Four hundred bucks worth of the highest quality merchandise you're gonna find in the stores for fifty bucks cause I'm kind, fellas. I've gotta get this party started and get my homeboys so shit faced and wired out on PCP they won't give a fuck what we do on Sunday. It don't matter that this deck is from your next door neighbor cause you're the smart one. The one with it now. Thank you very much, been a pleasure doin business with you. President Grant won the war.

Strollin in the Swamp, our *varrio* next door, one of our allies, hunting for a double lined raw one. A place where elephant tranquilizer is inhaled by wolves, bulls, and saints. But I puff lightly, let the other fools get slow and simple. I take in enough to make my head spin but still know where I'm at. But these junkies out here aint got nothin to lose cause you get busted with that shit you might as well be saving money for stamps cause you're gonna be goin away for a long, long time. That's why I never fucked with standin out on street corners. Aint nothin but a sure bust. Too much funk. Yeah, sure, every now and then I'd go out and hustle a few rocks or *leños,* but I always knew long term strategy wasn't in that game. That's why I stuck with Kwai, cause Kwai was a pajama wearing, undercover gangster who knew what time it was.

Our luck we had to run into a bunch of washed up motherfucking OG's. No, that wasn't in my plan. It wasn't in my plan, but to them, Santo had to ask, "What's up?"

"Some Bananas just took this *vato*'s jacket." A fat, sloppy *vato* named Bug pointed to some Samoans gathered around their corner liquor store across the street.

I saw Santo's look. It was that look he had at the playground that day, like if this was our cause, as if we should get involved with this bullshit and save the day or some stupid shit. Never understood that man.

I tapped Santo from behind, "Fuck these wash ups," I whispered into his ear. "This aint our *varrio,* so this aint our problem; let them handle this shit."

Santo didn't even turn around, "Let's just see if they need some backup. If they don't make the first move, then we'll get on," he said.

My dreams were falling apart. Any other day, yeah, great, I'd be all in to get down for some rounds, but I needed these homeboys healthy for Sunday, and these fuckin Sams were no joke. No, no, no, not a good idea to get killed the day before you win the lottery. But I had a happy face on cause it looked like nothin was gonna happen. We walked across the street toward the Sams, and the old *veteranos* didn't do shit but put on mean faces. When we walked back across the street away from the Sams, my heart soared like an eagle cause I thought we were leaving. I told Santo, pulling his arm, "All right, Santo, enough is enough. Let's get a *leño*." But before we could step out of the scene, Toro stepped onto the stage, horns at the objective, chest puffed straight out. Crazy, dumb ass, solid muscle Toro, solo, walked across the street toward the Sams and started the domino effect. Santo followed, and damn, I had to make sure these fools didn't get killed or else I'd be dead my damn self.

That was it. The big time washed up junkie vets got the hell out of the situation once the healthy Samoans busted out bats and pipes. Toro, Santo, and me were the only ones throwing with about ten Sams. It was mayhem all over the damn place, and when it was all over Toro was unconscious on the deck, and me and Santo lugged his ass into Taco Loco. Same fuckin booth I ate at yesterday, we laid Toro on top of it.

It was like waking up from a dream where Sheila was about to suck my nuts. No, no, no, low, Low-bo. No more fuckin plans cause I needed this fucker sucker. Crazy ass bull, don't know when to retreat, don't know how. Only knows how to get fucked up when there aint no reason. And now he's all fuckin bloody, shin bone popped out of his leg, probably aint walking for a few years, knocked the fuck out, but he's breathing—the monster lives, the beast speaks and raises his head, his chocolate eyes rolling around: "Ay, homes, I fucked them *putos* up," Toro said.

As if that matters, as if any of this bullshit means what it sounds like. Yes, Toro, you are a fuckin macho man. You got medals of honor for all them charges. You got scars all over that fat gourd, and your brain is no more. Yes, you have humongous, overgrown balls that clank when you walk. "Yeah, Toro, you fucked them dudes' hands up with your face and head," I said. I was about to touch Sheila's smooth, soft thighs once again, and then I woke up to a bloody raw steak laid out on the table. Aint no good no more, shit aint gonna happen right.

That's when my old homeboy, the cop, walked in and told his partner to call in an ambulance for Toro. Yeah, I knew the cop from days gone by. Ricky was his kid name. No fuckin worries back then. Me and that boy in blue used to kick it, and now he's sweatin me for a damn name and address, and I got to assume the position for his punk ass, and enough is enough—it's a fool moon tonight!

"Fuck it, I guess it's your fucking job, *que no?*" I said to the cop. "But I remember we used to box it up roughneck at the Boy's Club; remember that shit?" I paused and gave him a second to respond, but he didn't say shit, just kept patting me down hard. "But what about Johnny, homes. Man, that was a cool ass old man; you still keep in touch with him?"

The copper finished patting me down, turned me around, and said, "It's Officer Morales to you." Faggot seemed like he spent a lot of time patting my ass. "And Johnny, he's dead. I went to see him in the hospital last month, and you know what, I can't believe it, but he asked about you. He asked about *El Lobo* and said how you were one of the best fighters he ever saw. What a shame! He wanted you to be there, but I'm the only one who held his hand." My head dropped, and the copper continued. "So, if I remember right, seems as if you had a kid on the way the last time we hung around. You ever take care of him?"

I can't take care of myself. How the fuck I'm gonna take care of a kid. Cop asking me stupid ass questions. I know what he's gettin at. The man in blue thinks he's better than the true. He aint better than shit. I stayed. I made my name in the *varrio*, and if that name hurt his ears, he should have got out of my face and out my *varrio*—just comes to visit with his badge. Put your ear plugs in out there in that beautiful garden you live in. But you're here now, and now I'll tell you to your face who I am and what you are.

Cops don't like it when you turn em on to truth, don't like it when they can't be saviors of the world. They get copinitis: the fuckin disease that makes you think you got all the right answers. The only medicine for cops suffering from it is for them to beat down a bum. So, my hands in cuffs, me and Santo are driven to a nice, secluded spot where blood makes no noise—a mountain of pain, another one of our main kick back spots, Tweak Peak, the icing on top of the *Varrio Montaña* cake. Beat me for the truth. Scorn me for my unusual utterance. Kick me when I'm down, and keep your foot on my neck. Do me dirty as if I don't like water and soap. I won't recant, and I won't empty out my pockets for you. You can take some blood, you can leave your welts and bruises, but I keep my pocket change. My pocket change gots more worth than a million dollars of yours, and that you can't take.

"You keep your pocket change?! You keep nothing!" little officer Ricky said.

He ripped out my pockets from my pants and took my pennies and presidents from the deck and speakers, and he tried to leave me down and out, laughing as he left, as the two partners jumped in their patrol car and went to protect more citizens. As I lay out on that turf, Santo floated up to me and offered me his hand, but couldn't nobody help me off the ground I was on.

On my own, I pulled myself up and went to the top. Bright moon shining. Bad blood boiling. Beautiful bitter tears trickling down the terrace of my soul. I shout without shouting. I cry without wails. I speak without words. On top of that mountain, on top of the world, in charge of who I am and what I am to be. And there is hope for the next day, because yesterday and today has been fucked, and what more monstrosity can tomorrow bring that I haven't already seen? My head hurts, my bones ache, my body dies, but I've been dying since the day I was born, and I can handle one more day, one more night. I won't live forever; sure, one day there will be no more tomorrow, and then I'll have nothing, then no one will even remember my name. Now is the time for rhyme, the test for the best.

The lust for life is stronger than the despair of death.

I spit on my hands and slicked my straight black hair back. I took off my T-shirt and wiped my face and head; one strand of Sheila's brown hair dropped like a feather down to the ground. Gotta make some fare for the night.

Santo and I walked down to the Chevron gas station. He went towards the store, and I stood around the pumps waiting for victims to volunteer. After about fifteen minutes, they pulled straight into my pump, pulled in and before they got out, I got in. I pump gas for pussy.

"Huh?" the driver in the black convertible Mustang asked.

"I pump gas for pretty girls," I said. She looked at my bruised up face. "Yeah, so how you ladies doin tonight?" I continued. "Me, myself, I just knocked this dude out in the sixth round, and I'm ready to kick it."

"You're a boxer?" she asked parting her dark red lips.

"You can't tell? Thanks for the compliment," I said standing there lean and mean. I knew I was even more handsome with bruises on my mug. She smiled and sniffed around my bait. "I fight all around the country. You girls don't recognize me?"

"I'm not really into boxing, you know?" my girl with the cat eyes, the driver, said.

"Yeah, that's cool. Boxing aint really what I had in mind right now anyway, know what I'm sayin," I smiled.

Santo came back from the store with a forty ounce and went over to the passenger girl and said "What's up," like if he was gonna knock the bitch out or something. I couldn't let him fuck this shit up, so I said, "Yeah, that's my good Bro, Santo. He's a bodybuilder and boxer too." I looked at Santo, and he immediately understood to chill. I turned back to the driver.

She would suffice. "You look like my cat. I got a beautiful pussy at home, and you look just like her," I said.

She laughed, laughed because she did not know how else to respond to a person who would slur such things. "You're tripping," she giggled.

You gotta remain silent in order to see. If you shut up long enough, you can hear the fleas jumping and the fish swimming. Hear the melody playing, the lightning hit the trees, the waves crashing. I don't pretend to make you believe I can see with my eyes when I know it's pitch dark every damn day; every damn morning I look for the sun, but all I see is the moon every once in a great while. I've heard of light in the daytime, know of the concept, but there's only one *luna,* and the sun never shines. It was extinguished a long time ago. A long time ago.

The fire in my life is dead; it's gotta be cause if I look for smoke, I'm afraid I'll see it. Are my eyes really open? I don't believe it; I don't really know. If I knew for sure, I could come in from the cold. But if there's fire, I might get burned; I might not survive. Sheila, Sheila—I know her voice, heard it many times—THE HOWLS— she howled with me; we mated. The fire is still burning. The bulb is still hot.

This girl seems cool, crashing like the waves. Water takes out fire. Maybe she howls too.

"Just enough, enough trips to know where I'm headed right now, and that's with you—tonight—trip to the moon." I pointed at the sky. "Right there, love, right now. We'll go up and never come down." I changed her face. She had Sheila's smile, Sheila's stare. She looked exactly like Sheila; this was her twin. She spoke. I gave her Sheila's soft voice. The words didn't matter.

"Let's go," I interrupted her. "I know a cool spot for blast off, just came back from there as a matter of fact, but it's kinda crazy to get there, you know? Let me pilot the cruise, cool? Have your fine ass homegirl slide in with Santo in the back seat."

She smiled and talked to her homegirl and whispered something about "he's hella fine" and then agreed. And so now there's fine wine and good times, and we're on Tweak Peak where I got my ass kicked a few blinks earlier. And now I'm so, so live, so happy, Sheila in my arms.

"My tree house is right over there," I pointed at the biggest, bushiest tree on Tweak Peak and took her hand. Santo and the other girl stayed talkin, lookin out at the view of the city lights.

We got close to the tree, and I know what I wanted, but I know what she thought. So I said, "I'm tame, love. I seem wild, out of control, but I know what I'm doin." Then I took a chance on truth and looked in her eyes. "I'm doin dirt, baby, but aint we all?" She looked at me strange because the truth isn't very romantic.

"I'm not dirty, Lobo. I get checked out all the time. I take showers, honey."

"You're the only thing that's clean then." I rubbed two fingers under her powdered chin. "Cause I aint gonna try to jive you, jewel. You are water, and I am filthy as hell. What you think about that? About cleansing me, love, about giving me some of your perfume?" I looked at her big breasts. "I'm civilized under all this grime. I'm tender under all this toughness." I slid my hand on the back of her thick thigh.

"Do you have protection?" she asked.

"You don't need protection with me. My germs are timid. My bacteria is gentle." Softly, I caressed her made up face. I put my right hand behind her fluffy head and pulled her into my hook. I pulled her down—let her get on top. Let her pin me. My hook in her mouth, I grabbed her hand, and I forced her to touch my thin, round shoulders, my slender peaked arms, and I commanded her hand to squeeze. The muscles tightened. I led her hand down to my legs, and she squeezed the tight knots that were my thighs, and she squeezed hard all by herself, squeezed harder than I squeezed her. My hook in her mouth, she began to pull, pull at the pole between my legs, my hook in her mouth. And now my germs were brave, now my dirt was daring, now my hook was deep, and there was no way that she could ever, ever let go, even if she wanted to.

I reeled her in, reversed her over. I was on top. My muscles strong, my body tight. Her panties down, hanging off one leg. And I'm not so tame, and it's not so safe. I'm pounding one, two, three—combinations of fours and fives—and then non-stop blows—bam, bam—"Damn," she screams. Cause she wanted it gentle, wanted it soft, but she got it hard, and she got what she wanted because she didn't really know what she wanted until she smelled the must, and the must was wild. The barbarous beast is bravest. The primitive pussy is prettiest. And she is so damn pretty right now, right at this moment, snarling and grunting and umphing without shame.

But then there was a screech, and the screech was trying to be brave, trying to be wild, but it hung on to a thread of civility. "Bastard!" it yelled out, and bastard is a word in English, a word that only tame people say. And so I pulled up my pants to see what civility tried to interrupt my delightful disorder. I ran over to the noise, pulling up my pants and buckling my belt.

It was Santo's lady. She stood with her little ringed fists balled up, and she puffed in quick and hard, hyperventilating.

"What's up?" I said rushing over to Santo and his lady, a skinny doll in tight red pants and a hoochie pink top.

"This asshole is a fucking bastard." She pointed at Santo and lunged at him. I grabbed her. I had her in a bear hug and looked over at Santo, who just stood there calmly. She ranted and raved, and I looked into the silence of Santo's dark green eyes. For whatever that man was, from whatever planet he landed from or heaven he dropped from or hell he crawled up out of, he truly was a bastard, a son of a bitch, just like me. The silence proved it.

"Bitch, that's my homeboy. You better calm the fuck down before I let you go," I told her. Organizing her mashed up hair, my lady came out of the cuts. I looked at her closely, and even in the darkness, I could tell it wasn't Sheila, would never be Sheila. "Let's walk this off back to the car," I said.

We started walking down, and I got side by side with Santo, the girls about ten feet behind us. I was about to ask him what was up, about to grill him for some grease, but before I had the chance to open my mouth, his words pierced my ears.

"She doesn't know how to get on her knees," he said looking straight ahead.

It was his answer to all of my questions, and it was two plus two equals four, an unrestricted reality, a forever fact, complete sense.

I laughed because I didn't know how else to respond to someone who would slur such things. With a stale face, he looked straight ahead, gliding like a ghost on that rocky mountain. It was him and I, together, Brother to Brother, no words to be said. I heard that he listened too, so we didn't need the bullshit of babble. We just walked, and I thought of Sunday, and what my life meant. And if Sunday came and things stayed as they were, I'd sure as fuck be dead. Sheila'd be dead, and I would have nothing to show for it but anguish. The Sasquatch was no joke. He was no one to play with in his schoolyard. I would have to use all my resources, all my strength, all my slyness and wisdom to even challenge him. Then I'd need even more luck to triumph. Would these girls get me to where I needed to go; could they help me in my time of need? Only Santo was by my side. Only Toro was lying in a hospital, shinbone popped through the skin, ready to stand up at my request. The obstacles would be easy with my two Bros—even if it was the hardest thing I ever did.

We reached the car, and I opened the driver's door and looked over at my girl. "It was very nice meeting you," I said.

She stood there with a cute smile on her face, as if this was funny or entertaining. She spoke, and it hurt my ears: "I had a good time," she grinned. It was definitely not Sheila's voice.

"I want you to know I appreciate what you are going to do for me," I said as I rattled her keys in my hand.

"No, I hope it's not like this," this girl said. Yes, it was like this. I was in a desperate situation where this girl could not help me, only hinder me, only spaz the fuck out in the time of need, only not understand in a completely logical homeboy scenario. I needed to go to a park, show my face, and cap out a *firme* ass businessman, Kwai Chung. I needed to show up for sacrifice, and I knew that by doing so, I would most likely be killed by a giant sized Sasquatch or other Chinos. I needed *soldados*, arms, food, water, maps, a reconnaissance, plans, meetings, practice; and more than that, I needed to start now. Right now. I needed time.

"Yes, it's like this: there's a phone booth a few blocks down. Give me your shit," I said.

"Huh? You're not serious," she said this as I gently took the purse out of her hand.

"Get in, Santo," I said jumping into the convertible Mustang. I took the money inside her wallet and threw her purse out the window. I started the car and peeled out hard and fast.

"Fucking bastard!" she yelled.

The hospital. Jet over there and get Toro; that was my goal. In the meantime, listen to some tunes, and it was a bad ass system, must have had a box in the trunk with an amp. Clear, constant, undisturbed noise called music booming in my ears, in this sound machine, traveling at the speed of sound, down the mountain, headed for the big bloody cross at the end of the road.

No slowing down, just rolling, rolling got to keep on going. Toro is down, but he aint out. Can't and won't let me down. The faithful bull. But what can he do? Can't walk, I'm sure. Has no foundation for a charge anymore. I seen it—white bone popped through his brown skin—Samoans fucked him up. But I'll lift that bull up—I got that power—I got that game—cradle him in my arms—rock him back and forth and sing him lullabies of glory and bravery for the homeboy cause—get him ready to rage. With the rage he has down in his soul, he can win a war.

"Make a left, Lobo," Santo said.

"Yeah, yeah, I got you, Bro." The red cross was lit up and above it were magical words: Emergency Entrance. The entrance where homeboys came to know the meaning of the Lord. I parked my car, and we walked inside.

"I'm lookin for my homeboy. He had a broken leg and was busted up pretty bad."

"You mean the guy with the horns?" the white nurse said.

"Yeah, that's him."

"Well, the doctor bandaged his leg for now, but it was an open fracture. Tomorrow morning, he's headed to surgery. It will be a long time before he can sustain himself. He also had a concussion, so the doctor sent him up to the fourth floor for observation."

"Cool, thanks a lot, lady," I said and headed for the elevator.

"Wait a minute," she commanded, "you can't go up there; visiting hours are over."

I was about to tell her I was his Brother, which really wouldn't have been a lie, but then I looked at her makeupless face, tight hair in a bun, white little hat, and realized that she didn't care if I was his mother; she wasn't gonna let me in. It wouldn't do no good arguing with her cause she wanted to be boss, plus I looked over at the corner of the room, and the cop on duty had his hand ready on his holster, "What time are visiting hours, ma'am?" I asked.

"Eight a.m. to eight p.m. daily."

It was one in the morning. "Thank you very much, and you have a good evening, ma'am." I walked over to Santo, and we walked out the door. I walked to the side of the hospital and tried to open the steel doors, but they were all locked.

"Hospitals want blood," Santo said. "There's some hot blood right over there." He pointed at the janitor who was emptying cans of trash into the dumpster. We walked up to him and—bing, bam, boom—there was blood all over the place. He was knocked out, so we rushed him inside the emergency room in a panic.

"Hey, lady, this guy's been mugged! He's bleeding bad, and I don't hear him breathing!"

There was enough *sangre* for her to feel some compassion for her fellow man, cause that's what turned her on.

"Step aside," she stated seriously, almost comically, and strode over to the little Filipino man laid out on the floor. While she felt for a pulse and applied some pressure on his wounds, Santo and I slipped inside the hospital and ran up the stairs to the fourth floor. We peeked inside every room and saw stitched up faces, bandaged heads, tubes stuck in the mouths of sleeping men and women; but there were no broken legs, no fat heads with horns.

"Psst," Santo hissed as I studied the breathing motions of a man that slept and looked perfectly normal; I thought he was probably worse off than all the rest, or he wouldn't even be there—cause the scars outside don't mean a thing.

"Psst," Santo whispered, "over here." I walked to his voice. His bandaged leg suspended in the air, startling snores snorting out of his nose, *El Toro* slept like a bambino. I shook his shoulder.

"Toro," I said softly, "ay, Bro, come on."

"Wha, huh?" Toro blurted out.

"Come on, soldier, it's reveille."

"It's Marine," Toro said clearly.

"All right, Jarhead, get your ass up and snap to."

"Get the fuck out of here. I'm fucked up. Doc said I'd be lucky if I ever even walk again," he swallowed. "Damn, quit spinning the room."

"Aint no carnival ride, Toro. You just feeling a lil aftershock from your insanity. Man," I said, "you were fucking bad tonight, homeboy! You went off on all them fools and you woulda whupped all their asses if them Swamp bitches wouldn't have run out on us, but it's cool cause we took care of you, Bro."

"What you mean? I woke up, and I was in the damn hospital," Toro said.

"Oh, shit! That's right, you didn't see what your best homeboy Lobo did for your ass, did ya? Nigga, I picked you up, got them Bananas off your ass, and took you into Taco Loco, me and Santo, that is. After, some cops gave me a hard time." I smiled and Toro looked at my face. "Then we hooked up with some hos that let me borrow their car. Man, I'm ready to go kick it!"

"Lobo, I aint hearing that shit, homes. I'm out right here."

"Toro needs to be right here," Santo agreed.

"Toro needs to be with us, homes." I took the smile off my face because there was no time to waste; the clock was ticking. Sheila's heart was beating. "What you gonna do, lay down and get better?" My fingers lightly brushed the top of Toro's scar covered head. "Aint no better between us—aint no better since that day in the park, and we've been zombies walking the Earth since then—pretending this day would never come. You know that. All I've ever had is the chase; all you've ever had is the charge. I'm askin you for what you do best. This one time. *Para los* homeboys."

"What can I do for anyone?" Toro asked, breathing with difficulty. "I'm out, no good."

"So, you ask what you could do," I said with a grin turning up on my face. "You're brown down. I'll be back in a second." I walked out into the hallway, found a wheelchair, and rolled it into Toro's room. Santo and I lowered Toro's leg and put him in the chair.

"Your arms cool?" I asked.

"Yeah," Toro grunted in pain, adjusting himself in the seat.

"Well, aint no free rides around here. All I need to know is if you could roll your ass from A to B and bend your little trigger finger; be some use to the world."

"I can hack it," Toro said in his blue hospital gown, sitting on his bare ass, "but don't you take my love as a sign of weakness." And I actually saw some glitter of intelligence in Toro's eyes. "Grab my clothes in the closet," Toro told Santo. I knew that Toro would not be scared in the times to come cause what he did wasn't that scary anyway; I mean, what was really scary was thinking, what was really hard was planning, what was truly evil was me sitting on a rock with my fist on my chin and my eyes wide, wide open counting the waves.

"Come on then," I walked out the door, and Toro rolled out behind me. Santo followed.

I had the man—a crippled fool. I didn't know what he could do. I had no idea why I even bothered, but with him beside me, I felt good and strong. And if that was silly or dumb, it was cause you didn't know the power of the Bull. Didn't matter he had no leg, didn't matter he had no brain—he had a heart that could never die, and with that heart I could move mountains.

We took the service elevator down and escaped from one of the side doors. The parking lot was empty except for my car and ambulances. "How you like my new ride?" I asked Toro.

He grinned and sped up ahead of me. "Nice. Race you to it," he said peeling out before me. I hopped forward and took off, but he beat me to the Mustang.

It took a while to pack Toro and the wheelchair in, but we managed it. We then went down to the Swamp and bought a fat *leño* from Bug, one of the dudes who had run out while we were fighting the Sams. *Fuck him,* I thought and smiled broadly. *Aint got time for him.*

We drove up the road to Tweak Peak, and Santo and Toro puffed giant drags from the joint and snapped out into never, never land. I took a small hit and relaxed.

Damn, I knew I had it good. Bullshit if all this couldn't be worked out in some civilized way. I could do it if I really wanted things to be good. But I wanted it bad.

I look for problems. I search for drama. How else could I speak of this, how else could I be such a fool? But being a fool is hard—it's a hard hangover, an endless insomnia. Three thirty in the morning and stones in my head, and I'm alive, and I can't deny it. I suck in the cold wind, and it's warm to me: the only warmth I've ever known. Cept Sheila. I want the comfort of her irresponsibility, the fire of her touch. I don't want things to get better. I want things to get worse, but I want things to get worse with her by my side. Together.

"Cause I know I've used up all my aces, and now all I got is nothing. You hear me, space men?" I spoke directly to Toro and Santo—shouted in their faces as they floated around in other galaxies. "All I got is *nada*, Bros, but that's what I offer you, and it's a damn good deal. I don't know what I'm doin, don't know what I'm saying. I know I'll change my mind later, and then I'll despise you all and treat you like shit—make you go out and rush that next world for me cause I don't want to be the one, or shit, maybe your asses will get bright and beat me to the punch—figure shit out and fuck me all up, or maybe everything will be cool, and we'll leave in peace, shaking each other's hands in *firme* friendship," I shouted loud but calm.

"What friendship is there but the friendship of enemies?" Santo responded. "Your best friends are always your worst enemies, Lobo. Whatever you got to do, do it cause you know that. Give your enemies praise—thank them for helping you out." Santo slobbered on his black windbreaker jacket, and his glazed eyes almost popped out of his head. He was a bummy looking, bearded, khaki skinned OG *cholo;* he almost looked like he could have been a model for one of those Jesus pictures. "All I could ever give you is my love, and if my love couldn't do it, then it was really your enemies who inspired you. You have not submitted to their desires," he said. "You could never do that. They were the ones that gave you motivation when your best homeboys right here could not. They gave you the passion to do what you have in your mind now, what you ask us to join in on. Your enemies have made you confront your dreams, Lobo!"

"Thank you all you enemies!" I shouted to the night. "Thank you for my stuck out ears with diamond earrings and my big eyes that drive the bitches crazy and the hairs underneath my chinny chin chin that prove that I'm wise. So I built this wall, bigger than the one in China, and I put guards at the entrance, and I got a bull, and I trained him hard, and I got me the holiest man in the *varrio*, and I let him pray for me. I protected myself from my foes cause I feared them, cause I respected their strength in hate. And I thought it would be better not to make any more enemies, because I knew I already had enough to handle. But I opened up my gates, and I let her in—my worst enemy of all—and I let Sheila in cause it gets lonely inside a king's palace. It gets lonely when you all you do is talk to the bull and pray to the saint. It gets sad when you push the ground and smell the roses and you start to think that it's beautiful, but you got no one to sniff with you. Ah! Sheila was like apples, like pears and peaches just picked at the farmer's market, ones that I didn't inspect, but that were delicious anyway. A poison apple, and I never would regret that juicy bite." Will never regret breaking down to her, and the only justice I can give her, the only respect I can pay her is to use her for something big even though that is a lie, an illusion to cover up my own humiliation. Cause every day is gonna be the same old thing, just wishing and hoping for you. Aint no way to justify that I found you and threw you away, but life can't stop for no one.

This aint no sad story, this is a glad story, a bad story—what people with words would call uplifting—cause it's make it or break it, can't go wrong with whatever should come—cause come Sunday I either die and my misery is gone, or I live and my happiness just started. And I feel like this is what life should be all about—the day of reckoning, the day of dreams. My grand dreams, my soul beams. Forget about hitting home runs, I don't know about winnin an Oscar or being president. I got no clue about scoo and all the small smiles and firm handshakes that come with that. I got now, and this is what I call high—what I think of when I hear of success, accomplishment, happiness. I'm free.

Cause no matter what you tell me, I know it aint my fault that Christ hung from that cross; to try to pin that rap on me aint gonna work. I got no guilt for my glory, no second thoughts about my sins. I've done what I've done for number one.

Letter M, number sixteen. Letters A and K and number forty-seven. They also get things done for number one.

"Toro," I said realizing that the countdown was on, "who's the dude with the heavy artillery? You should know more than any-one."

"Comin down aint no joke, feelin hot all over," Toro said wiping the sweat off his clean shaven face. I'm surprised he wasn't shivering cause he was half naked. "But you're asking for that other kinda heat—that heat that puts you down and don't never let you up. I know homeboy good—a straight up old Khe Sahn Devil Dog—was in the Corps with him—call him Animo. He's got the sweet juice. Was in the war with the *vato*, solid *viejo*. He should hook us up."

"So where's Animal live, homes?"

"That fool's in the mountains, waitin for Bible times to come, and I aint talkin bout our little hill, I'm talking about the bushy ass forest. About three hours from here."

"Motherfucker! I shoulda thought about this earlier. We got to get goin, homies," I said.

We loaded up in the ride and shot off, and while we drove, four in the morning, I saw Lil Toon wearing his beanie and a black puffy Starter jacket. He was peepin up in vehicles, lookin for decks and free rides, so I kidnapped his ass. He sat shotgun and kept me in stitches, while Santo and Toro knocked out in the back seat. Top down, the cold air caressing my face. I was smoking and blowing out circles that couldn't form. One hundred miles an hour and centimeters forward on the map. Four horsemen riding out of the clouds.

THREE

Limbo

How dreadful knowledge of the truth can be when there is no help in truth!

SOPHOCLES, *Oedipus Rex*

For Sheila, the calming moment came when she finally accepted that she had never hoped for anything more. Imprisoned, gagged, she now reaped the reward of lost desire.

Initially, she had panicked. Immediately after Lobo had left that morning, there were a quick couple of jerks on the door. Bitching a little, she scurry-stomped to answer it. Still half asleep, she opened the door only to be thumped on the mouth. Knocked down, she instantly scrambled up and fought back, kicking and punching wildly, wailing furious insults. With heavy hands, the Sasquatch simply drilled her down into submission.

When she regained consciousness, she was confined in a dark moving space—what she quickly figured to be the trunk of a car. Duct tape over her mouth and around her wrists and ankles, she kicked to free herself. She shouted-mumbled to be heard. Hearing her kicking through the bass of his stereo, the Sasquatch laughed. With a smirk on his face, he cruised by cops. When he reached his rented home in the outskirts of the Swamp, he used his remote control to open the garage door. Slowly, he drove in.

Once he opened the Roadmaster's trunk, Sheila tried to spit on him but almost ended up choking on her own saliva. As if she were a sack of rice, Sasquatch hoisted her onto his shoulders. He fumbled with the keys, then opened the door into the basement living room. With indifference, he tossed her onto the downy couch. The Sasquatch ripped the tape off of her mouth. Sheila screamed. He allowed it.

"That's the last fuckin time you gonna scream." He strangled her throat until she blacked out. When Sheila woke, he was slapping her.

"Good, good." He backed away and plopped down in a fluffy beige armchair. Eye to eye with her, he began. "I know who you are. You got mixed up with the worst piece a shit in the world. Them niggas hurt innocent people and prey on the weak. He aint gonna give a fuck about you, so you might as well let me know who he is and give me what he got. Guns? Plans?"

Sheila remained silent.

"OK." Sasquatch seemed composed.

Blam, bam, boom.

Sheila gave him nothing.

Blam, bam, boom.

In order to stay strong, Sheila transferred her pain and anger to others. She tried to blame her mother, her abusive father, her teachers who had flunked her. Then Lobo came to mind, but by then she was delirious. Still, she kept silent. She did not think she was especially tough or that she shouldn't sell Lobo out, even though he was her true love. She stayed silent because she had no idea what she *should* say. Lobo, she thought, would know what needed to happen. Lobo, she had faith, would figure this all out and save her. He felt the same love as she, perhaps even more. If necessary, he would give his life for her. Once this sunk in, instead of feeling grateful for him, she pitied him for it. She did not deserve to be saved. This is when she calmed.

After approximately an hour of torture, the Sasquatch knew he could not break her. Although he had been enjoying it, instead of hurting her anymore, he resolved to admire her. Smoking a Newport cigarette, he went about his business, talking on the phone: "Nah, I don't know how it's supposed to happen, but I know this nigga got a contract out on me, but he don't know I done flipped the script on his punk ass...yeah, yeah, I gots his bitch, and he gon do exactly what the fuck I want, and I want it all." Sasquatch's laughing roar shook the room.

Throughout the day, Sheila cried on and off. Sometimes she would sob silently, other times she would become hysterical, picking her long nails at her cheeks. She found that humming to herself comforted her. Once dusk set, Shelia, exhausted, thought of her face and wanted a mirror. She laughed. Then some hours later, Lobo presented himself, and she was pleased. She saw both the wolf and the man who played the wolf role. He impressed her, as always. And he admitted loving her even though it would cost him his life. For her, Lobo had bound himself to the Sasquatch. When Lobo left, she was relieved and at peace.

Sasquatch wrapped fresh duct tape around her wrists, her ankles, and on her mouth. That first night Sheila sat and occasionally lay on the couch. Instead of finding any more weakness in blaming, she found strength in Lobo's love. She knew he was a fuckup, but his arms were like steel wires. His wit was quick. His eyes, darting around, could see clearly. She had a good man who figured things out and was exciting. He would fuck this Chinaman up good, she thought. Because she had given Lobo her best, he would be inspired. Whatever he were to do, she realized he would do it to the fullest. He was not a cliché. Yet she also believed that he could be her knight in shining armor, her *cholo* knight. That he was a fuckup haunted her. *Damn it*, she considered, *does he really have enough patience and discipline to do this for me?*

Besides making love to her, Lobo had never even romanced. She always thought he was kidding when he would tell her he was beyond romance, but now she wondered what exactly he meant by that. She thought about what Lobo would be doing at that moment to prepare. Of course, he would hijack his homeboys. Sure, they would cause chaos on the Chinatown streets. But would he do it for her? He would want to, but would he act on his desire or would he act for himself? Yes, he loved her, but he was a strange wolf. Always hunting, always changing, always so alone inside. Sheila figured he wanted to save her, but he did not believe in romance. So then why would he do it? He would do it because he would want her to live more than he himself wanted to live.

A cold snapping breeze whipped throughout her body. The independent wolf would not allow her to live without him. If he were to follow the Sasquatch's game plan, they would never be together. Not only would he get nothing out of it but also he would be forsaking her to the same bullshit as before, perhaps even worse without Lobo's love. No matter what he promised, Lobo would choose to live. An epiphany slowly enrapturing her, Sheila knew she was lost.

Never a victim, she accepted that she could make her own independent decisions. She could die feeling she was betrayed, or she could live knowing she was in command of her spirit. She, too, was independent; that is why they loved and understood each other so well. Lobo would sacrifice her; she should have expected it, regardless of whatever he had ever sworn to her or the Sasquatch. *How slick he is,* she thought and respected him for his play. Lobo was a man of greatness and a man destined for independence. She chastised herself for being selfish and wanting a savior. She had always loved the crazy life. Now Lobo was carving out something new and expanding into new areas with Chinese people. She was proud of him. He was evolving, and she knew she should not wish to hold him back. If he designed to save her, she would welcome it; if he betrayed her to live, she would accept that, too. She would not wish further damnation to the already damned. By granting Lobo her loving spirit, she would bless him.

Knowing what needed to be done, she could not help but giggle when Sasquatch entered the room with a barber's blade. Using wide slashes, he razored her face. The face she had always covered with clown makeup, the face she had so proudly peacocked, was not surviving, yet she knew these scars would create something new. They would be makeup scars to decorate her death face.

El Toro

"Que toro más bravo," *the matador said as he handed his sword to his sword handler. He handed it with the hilt up and the blade dripping with the blood from the heart of the brave bull who no longer had any problems of any kind and was being dragged out of the ring by four horses.*

"Yes. He was the one the Marqués of Villamayor had to get rid of because he was faithful," the sword handler, who knew everything, said.

"Perhaps we should all be faithful," the matador said.

ERNEST HEMINGWAY, "The Faithful Bull"

His head was a planet full of pockmarks. All over his world were big bald scars that revealed how he charged at the red cape of life. He had been stabbed countless times by many matadors and had died a thousand ugly and fierce deaths, but each death for him was a new life because each time they rammed their final sword into him, each time they left him dying and gasping for one more faint breath, each time they began to celebrate their victory, he would somehow rise, beaten and bloody, down and out, brown and proud, and charge, only to be stabbed again and again and once more again, because, you must understand, they could never kill his *corazon*. He measured his worth by scars, and although he felt he was not worth a million dollars or even a hundred pennies, Toro felt his existence was validated beyond the realm of materialism every morning when he rubbed the muck out of his brown eyes and massaged the permanent welts on top of his uneven hard head.

His body was a mountain of solid rock. His chest heaved high with every breath and his arms tightened even when he patted a delicate daisy. Like a sculptor, Toro chiseled his rock, refining and perfecting every day, in spite of knowing perfection could never be attained; for some days his rock needed to be strong and powerful to carry the heavy loads of the universe on his shoulders; other days his rock needed to be light, loose, and agile to maneuver the many obstacles of his concrete jungle. Toro's body would conform to the situation, but it could never adapt to a new way to charge. Once the battle cry "Charge!" sounded, his legs were pillars of stone that knew only fast forward. There was no alternative but to rush up with his rock of a body, horns pointing straight for the objective, and hit or be hit, because, you must understand, he could not fight backwards; he had never been taught that sweet science of moving side to side and sticking and jabbing. Charging forward as a bull meant life; moving backwards as a pretty boxer meant certain annihilation.

This was Toro's tough hide, the illusion that the rest of the world saw at first glance. It had taken many moons to shape his outside shell. It was not simply bequeathed to him as if he were royalty; he earned the planet full of pockmarks and the rock that sustained the weight of the world. He earned his characteristics just as most earn what they want to wear, whether that is to wear the spectacles of a scholar or the rags of a bum. His was a premeditative act. Without a sour face, he swallowed the fate of his costume; he swallowed with the serenity of a man who has accepted the bitter medicine of circumstance, history, and hard hearted destiny.

:: :: ::

Hard hearted destiny pounded bright and early every morning. Always waking to the sounds of housing projects' hype, Toro
opened his eyes to this world, *Varrio Montaña*—a place where
immigrants' children did without the spoils of technology and civilization in the most technological and civilized space on Earth.

Toro's mother had to earn for all of them, and with nothing
but sweat as an asset, she put her talents to use scrubbing and
sweeping old people's homes for under-the-table dollars and pennies, non-taxable money that could not be held against her by
any welfare worker; because, of course, they were also on welfare,
but the welfare joke was no longer funny to three hungry mouths.
Laughter alone could never fill bellies.

So the mama rose before dawn every morning, stomping the
cockroaches around the kitchen table and cabinets while boiling
up water for *café con leche*. The children's cue to wake, their only
alarm clock, was the slaps they heard from their mama pounding
out tortillas. Toro's year younger sister, Letty, would get ready to
go to work with mama. Toro would not get ready for anything. He
was five, not big and bad enough for third grade philosophy, still
too much of a runt to learn his ABC's. He was also not like his
sister who was nice and calm enough for his mother to sneak into
her elderly employer's house. Letty would spend the day sitting
down in the old Italian's mice infested basement without much
care required at all. A peanut butter and jelly cracker and a glass
of milk every few hours were sufficient to keep her entertained and
happy. Toro, on the other hand, could not go anywhere without a
fuss. The mama had tried bringing them both before, but Toro had
gotten into old paint cans. The mama saw no logic in paying for a

baby-sitter for Toro because that would negate her buck twenty an hour wage with her owing a baby sitter approximately five dollars at the end of the day. Toro's mother knew it was an impossible situation, but she also knew that her babies needed food.

Tiny Toro stayed home solo. He could handle sitting in front of the beat up little black and white TV watching reruns of *Chico and the Man* and *Sanford and Son* and eating bologna and mustard sandwiches. He felt that he was big and bad enough to take care of himself in the safety of four small walls, but it wasn't until one dreary overcast April day in 1975 that Toro found out that little boys are really no more than little boys.

On that early morning Toro waved goodbye to his mother and little sister as they hopped on the bus down the block from their project apartment. He stuck his neck out of the window, yelled and waved "Bye, bye!" just to be silly, but, at the same time, the lady from upstairs, who had the everyday plumbing problems common to everyone living in the projects and not knowing that Toro's humongous head was hanging around out there, threw a bucket of foul piss-shit-water out of her window. Toro felt the first few drops of liquid tickle the back of his bull neck, and then the other three gallons of slop splashed hard. His little underwear clad body charged out of the high first story window. Tumbling and tossing, flipping and fumbling, he landed flat on his back on the cold, hard concrete. Toro saw shining stars in the fogged up morning clouds.

He rose to empty sadness. *This is the world,* he thought. Toro looked up at the window, which was approximately twelve feet from the ground, and jumped at it but could not even begin to reach it. Toro looked around for help and saw his black teenage neighbor about to go to school. Embarrassed, cold and shivering, Toro asked him, "Hey, can you help me?"

The teenager looked at him bewildered. "What's wrong?"

"I fell out the window. Can't get back in. Please help me." Toro started puffing quickly. "I'll try," the young teenager said, jumping at the window. He could not reach, so he climbed the stairs, went inside the complex, and Toro followed. He shook and rattled the door, but it was locked. He pulled out his own apartment key and tried to fit it in the door's keyhole.

Hearing commotion outside her door, the teenager's bent over, nightgowned grandmother stepped out to investigate.

"What in God's name!?" the teenager's large grandma shouted. "You better get your hands off that door, boy! Don't you ever put your hands on someone else's property! Get your behind to school before I call the police my damn self."

"No, Ma, it aint like that. This boy…" The teenager tried to speak, but the grandmother interrupted.

"Boy, you better quit lying. I know what you're up to, and you better get out of here before I tell your father when he gets home."

The teenager left his mouth open and thought about explaining the situation then thought of his father's thick leather belt and knew better. He turned and faced Toro.

"Sorry, there's nothin I can do. Just wait here until your mama gets home," the teenager said patting Toro on his sharp spiked hair, the *Indio*'s Afro.

The grandma looked at tiny Toro, grunted, "Hmmph!" and slammed the door in his face.

Toro sat Indian style by his door and sucked in the stench of stale urine in the hallways. He screamed "Eehh!" when a family of gray mice scurried across the hallway. Toro jumped up and decided he would ask someone else for help outside. *Maybe the policemans or firemans will help,* he thought.

Confronting the chilly morning fog, he went outside and looked around for help. People were running for the bus and traffic lights, old ladies were washing the piss off their stoops, and a fat hairy bum was cursing the Almighty. A young man and his girlfriend, who had been taking care of business and partying all night long, tramped down the street and headed for their apartment. Clad in tight yellow leather pants and high heels, the girlfriend looked at tiny Toro standing in the center of the large project courtyard. Seeing no adults around him, she became curious. Toro tried to speak to her as she approached him, but no words came out. Instead, he just reached his arms out to the girlfriend and puffed quickly.

"Hey," the girlfriend said, "you OK, sweetheart?"

Toro reached for soft skin, but the boyfriend, who sported a bright purple brim, platform shoes, and dark sunglasses, interrupted.

"Yeah, he's OK. He's just taking a little stroll. Let him be," he said.

"He doesn't look like he's taking a stroll. He looks lost."

"Nah, he's cool. His mom probably let him out so he could play."

"In his underwear? No, something aint right." She squatted down and wiped Toro's tears from his face. "Are you OK?" she asked, "*Estas bien?*"

Toro puffed quickly and looked at the ground.

"See, he's fine," the boyfriend said.

"He's not fine. He can't even talk."

"Look, I'm tired as fuck. This runt got somebody around here watching out for him. I aint gonna get into no shit cause his momma got a unique system for raising kids. Let the boy be."

"You fucking asshole," she said rising from her squatting position and placing her right hand on her hip and pointing all around with her left. "This boy aint right. There's something wrong and you want to just leave?"

"Bitch." The boyfriend scratched his cheek, "I just want to get some shut eye. I been bustin my ass all night selling your fat ass and getting fucked up, and all I want to do is cook me up a cool spoon and get the fuck to sleep. He pulled the sunglasses down off of his eyes, grabbed Toro's head, and looked Toro in the face. Toro puffed back in stutters. "This fucking kid is retarded," the boyfriend concluded. "He's all right."

"No. He aint OK, and I aint leaving him, you piece of shit motherfucker."

The boyfriend raised his hands up to backhand her. The girlfriend raised her arms to protect her face. Toro puffed hard. The man clumped his girlfriend's hair instead of hitting her.

"Bitch, you aint shit," he said pulling her face close to his. "Stay with retard. I don't really give a fuck. But this is mines." He grabbed on to her purse, which contained their balloons of *chiva*, and he started pulling on it. She, however, held on tight as he swung her around in circles and threw her face first to the dirty cement. He stomped on her hand that did not want to let go of the purse, took it, and sidestepped away.

The girlfriend lay on the ground defeated. Toro walked over and gave her a hug. The girlfriend looked at Toro's dark brown baby face and said:

"Fucking retard! Now I aint got shit. I shouldn't even have tripped off a damn retard boy like you. Get the fuck away from me." She pushed Toro away and yelled out, "Honey! Sugar Daddy! Wait up, I'm coming!" She sprinted to her man as he walked on with his back to her.

Without hope, Toro wandered aimlessly. The little five-year-old boy inside of him pushed his way out, and hiccup bawling and cold tears showered out of his soul. Walking throughout the projects with salty water pouring down his baby face, he cried, "Mommy! Mommy pleeeease pleeeeasee pleeeease mommeeeee mommmeee!" He shouted at the top of his lungs for a mommy who at that moment was down on her knees scrubbing her employer's floor for chump change.

At the ripe old age of five, Toro gave up on life. Many people, busy with their own lives, walked by him and felt sorry for the half naked boy, but they believed someone else with more time, more energy, more wisdom would help him out soon. Someone would have sympathy, compassion, and love for the little brown boy who cried in the middle of the street as cars beeped and dodged past him. And someone there was.

Duster, a young up and coming prospect for *Cholo* of the Year, had just copped an ounce of lame brain insane dust of angels. He drove down the street with splendid thoughts of going to his apartment, cutting up his prize, and taking a taste for himself. He put a crooked smile on his face and bobbed his head up and down to the beat of Lou Rawls singing, "You're gonna miss my loving." Duster thought, *Life can't get much better than this*. And then he saw a little boy about to become ten points. He swerved toward oncoming traffic to miss hitting him. A red pickup screeched out of his way, as Duster's Stacy Adams stomped on the brakes. His Cutlass began doing uncontrollable doughnuts in the middle of the intersection. "AHH!" he yelled as he slammed into a light post and his forehead cracked the front of the windshield.

Tiny Toro stopped crying and ran down to the smoking Cutlass. The car's grill was bashed in and the engine was smoking. Toro gave Duster a hug and tried to slap him awake. Duster woke with his head scrambled and said—

"Fuck, my car's totaled!"

Toro laughed and hugged him again. Police sirens and fire engines squealing from a few blocks away, Duster knew he had to get out of there as quickly and coolly as possible. He reached under the driver's seat and grabbed the ounce of PCP that was in a brown paper bag. He pushed Toro off of him and stumbled out of his car. Toro jumped on Duster's black pleated slacks leg and clamped down as hard as he could. Dragging Toro with him, Duster staggered along the sidewalk. When he heard the police tires screech toward the accident, he pulled Toro off of him and started running with him in his arms as if he were a football. He dashed down to the playground and rested on one of the benches in *Bajo* Park. Duster put the ounce underneath some newspaper in the garbage can next to them.

"What's your name, Little Bro?" he asked.

"Toro."

"Toro, *soy tu papi,* and we've been enjoying the beautiful morning."

"OK," Toro said, patting the hairs on his head, "What's a papi?"

Perplexed, Duster rubbed his thinly manicured moustache. "He's the man, the shot caller," he reflected in seriousness, "the one you wish for every day."

"Then you really are my *papi.*"

Duster smiled. "For now, little homeboy, for now."

A police car racing down the street slowed suddenly and pulled to a stop near the playground. Duster told Toro to play, and he mad dogged the approaching officers with a silly smirk on his brown face.

"Hey, buddy, how ya doin?" The senior policeman asked as his rookie partner stood back with his hand on his holster.

"Ah? *No entiendo*. Speak no In-gless."

"ID, you got ID?"

"Noo," Duster shook his head, "noo ID."

The partner with his hand on his holster said, "These fuckers never have any ID on them. He's a damn *mojado*."

Duster nodded his head and smiled proudly as if they had just complimented him.

The pot bellied senior policeman pointed at Duster's grated forehead. "What happened?"

"*Jugando con Toro,*" Duster said and pointed at the playground structure. The rookie policeman noticed a tattooed cross on Duster's left hand.

"What's this?" The rookie asked as he grasped Duster's wrist.

Duster looked up at the sky and crossed himself, *"El Padre, Hijo, y Espiritu Santo."*

"Looks like a damn knife to me. All the wetbacks got it."

Duster shook his head from side to side as if he did not understand.

"Check the kid out," the rookie said, "he's almost naked. What the fuck? Can't he afford to clothe him?"

"Nah, these fuckin spicks don't got the sense to buy their kids shoes. They think they're back in the jungles or some shit." The senior officer looked at Toro's face. "Kid," he bent down, the spare tire on his waist bulging out of his uniform, "how's things going. You OK?"

Toro remembered the girl asking him the same question, then looked at Duster. *"Estoy bien."* Toro answered. He walked up to Duster and sat on his lap.

"These *mojados* don't know nothing about no accident," the thin rookie said. "Come on, let's go get some coffee and donuts."

The senior officer sensed something out of the ordinary going on and stared hard at Duster and Toro. Hair cropped short, mean mustached, pimply, semi-handsome face, Duster smiled and bounced Toro up and down on his knee.

"Yeah, fuck it, just some spicks in a park. Let them get used to home."

"Adios!" Duster said as they walked away. *"Adios!"* Toro laughed out as they left.

"Yeah, we're some pretty stupid spicks, aint we, Torito?"

"Real *pendejos,* Papi."

Duster reached in the garbage can and stuck the ounce in his underwear. "I got to get you home." He grabbed Toro's hand, went to the projects, and after some hard searching (all the apartments looked the same), he found Toro's place. Like the teenager, he also could not reach the window, but he did not submit. Duster stopped a mumbling bum and asked him for help. He hopped on the bum's shoulders, hoisted himself inside the open window, and unlocked the door from the inside. He let Toro in and told him, "I'm gonna call the car in stolen."

Toro turned on the TV and grabbed some apple juice from the refrigerator.

The mama and little sister walked in. The mama had called the house, and when there was no answer, she became worried. Duster stood up slowly. *"Buenos dias, Señora."*

"Hi, Mommy." Toro said happily.

"Que es esto?"

"Don't worry, *Señora,* I found him outside. He was locked out, so I got him back in. *No hay problema.* I'm just making a phone call."

Toro's mother looked at Duster and then slowly, deliberately walked up to Toro and spanked him on the leg as hard as she could, "No talk to strangers!" She turned to Duster, "*Desgraciado! Get out of here! Get out!*"

Duster hung up the phone and looked into the mother's young but wrinkled face. "He's not that dumb, *Señora*. He's just a *puro pendejo;* a down ass little homeboy. He's gonna be strong." Duster tilted his head up to Toro, "Later, homes." He walked out the open door.

That day Toro got the worst ass whipping of his young life. His mother did not want to hear his crazy story and never found out what had really happened. She worried that Toro was already showing the marks of a moron. How could he let a lowlife into their house? She belted him hard and prayed for her son, that he would not befriend the no good *cholos* from around the neighborhood. But it was too late. Hard hearted destiny had pounded, and Toro had answered.

:: :: ::

The years and tears passed. I had spent my whole life trying to fit in, struggling between mama's world and the *varrio* around me. In February of 82, I made up my mind and joined the gang. By July I started serving my first stretch at juvie hall. In December I was released. My hands were still clean, but as I had had time to stare at my short choppy fingers and thick green veins, I knew my purpose. I sucked in the sweet air of the city streets, jumped on the bus, and went to my homeboy Santo's house. I told him what was up. He grabbed some India ink, thread, and a needle. Between my index finger and thumb, Santo poked into my left hand the wicked cross, the dual mark of certain death and eternal life. *El Padre, Hijo, y Espiritu Santo.*

I remember. "Toro," the older homeboys would say, "Go get em." With enthusiasm, I'd oblige their requests and either charge with blazing combinations or grab a stick or bottle and hit home runs on anyone that trespassed into *Varrio Montaña*. Everyone would laugh and drink. I'd shotgun my bitter Budweiser and throw up all over the place. I was a good kid.

In high school I went to school but never went to class. Instead, homeboys and homegirls would meet up in the mornings, and we'd start off bright and early and get wasted out of our minds or just bullshit all day long. We'd kick it at our abandoned shack, a little house me and Lobo took over from a bum after we drank up with him. He had it all rigged for water and electricity to the warehouse next door. Said he'd lived there for years without a problem. We'd play cards, smoke PCP, drink beer, fight, and take turns macking on honeys. We never worried about the answers to algebra problems cause we didn't really give a fuck about those kinds of questions—straight F's. I got kicked out after awhile.

The hard times and space days were worth it. I never would trade them in for anything in the world. I know I did a lot of fucking up. There ain't too much more to say than that. That was my job. That's what I was there for. I had to fuck shit up and make things complicated cause that's how I liked it. Nice and fucked up. I remember once, when I was sixteen, I'd recently stabbed someone cause he looked at me funny. I was sober, too damn sober. I stood inside my mom's house with all the lights turned off, dark as hell, and I had pride and remorse both at the same time. Damn, I fucked up. Damn, I'm a crazy ass bull. Damn, the cops are coming—got to keep the lights off so they won't think anyone is home. I thought about being down. With the lights off, alone, with no expression on my face, sweat streaming down my forehead, listening to cars pass by and people walk up and down my courtyard, I clutched a dumbbell bar and believed cops were coming to get me or someone was sneaking up wanting to kill me.

And I couldn't stand thoughts, so I left my house in boxer shorts and sneakers, barrel chest bare. Gripped my dumbbell bar so tight, I hurt my hand. The wind whistled a mighty war song through the rattling leaves. It was a magical melody, and I found myself no longer walking, but charging; charging to the elements of life, Earth, and of going to confront my worst fears. And there were four dudes sitting down on some stairs near the Swamp drinking some beers and hitting on weed. They saw me, saw a beast of a man charging down towards them with a blunt object in his hand. They admired my ferocity. They wished they were me. They too wished they could charge. They were four young matadors, and I was the bull in their arena.

"Hey, what's uppphhh," the man leaning on the stairs said, but he couldn't speak right cause I chopped him in his mouth with my bar. My victim tried to feint and dodge me, but I rammed him and clubbed him on the head. Steam rose out of my nostrils. They booked.

"Yeah, motherfuckers, run your asses off. Ya little bitches." I was talking, shooting my mouth off, being a big shot as they escaped my fury. "Yeah, *putos,* beware of the *loco* Toro!" Now I was fuckin shouting, yelling, telling the world how live I was.

"No one can fuck with the *todo bodo* down homeboy! No one can lay a finger on me without going down!" Ha! Ha! I was number one, king of the Earth, the ruler of my destiny! "Next time bring Kryptonite!" With that joke, I was also the corrupter of my magic.

I heard their voices yelling back, but I couldn't exactly understand their language. It was English, I know it was, but it was now

Chinese to me. "Get the knife!" they were shouting, "Get the fucking shank!" I couldn't understand English because I was lost in another world: a dimension where people didn't speak English—only Toro talk. I was in a land where I perpetually proclaimed perfection, where the matadors had no swords and the bull always won.

I was in the middle of the street, half naked, grunting garbage.

"I got the shank! I got the shank!" the brave matador shouted.

I kicked and skidded my feet along the cement, then charged for his jacket. He shuffled out of the way. I charged again, and he stabbed down, directly on top of my head. Like a volcano, bright red blood spurted out of my head and onto the matador's face. Cause he was inexperienced he didn't know what to do from there. He just stood there without moving, and I landed hard combinations on his horrible red face. His partners grabbed me from behind and threw me to the ground. I was face down in the gutter, and they kicked my mouth. They whacked me on the legs and arms as I tried to save my head. They did elegant acrobatics and sweet somersaults on my battered body. It seemed as if they tried to kill me all night long. But finally, they became tired and content. They strutted away to the cheers of a crowd.

But I wanted an encore. On the ground I spit out profanity and blood. Laying on the red cement, I told them I was still Toro, even though my ass was thoroughly kicked. I mocked them that they weren't shit, so they returned. I don't know how many times I got kicked in the nose. The number didn't matter. Those fuckers wanted to make sure I was humbled and wretched. With my last ounce of strength, with nothing more than a faint cough, I puckered my lips and whispered, "You'll never kill my heart." *Their* hands and feet would break before they could ever split my spirit. Ultimately, it was *they* who retreated when they realized my heart was true.

:: :: ::

Six months after I finally got kicked out of my third high school, I knew my fate, but I wanted something more, something different. I was supposed to accept my death with a straight face, and I was ready. I could not choose to not be a homeboy; that would be blasphemy. No one was forcing me to stay in the *varrio;* there wouldn't be any payback if I decided to become a straight shooter. But I couldn't even imagine what the straight life meant. I was too stupid to do anything in school. Even if I tried, I was so far behind I knew I would have failed. If I had stayed in the hood, I would have chosen to be with Lobo and Santo and the rest of the homeboys who were out there banging, selling drugs, getting locked up, and dying on our bloody streets. It was *I* who would have chosen to be with them. Imagined or not, the obligation I felt to be by their side was real to me. If I were there, I could not choose to ignore them. I loved yet hated them. As a bull, I had to go forward.

How to leave while remaining true? How to escape yet be able to come back with respect and power? I had to be macho, super macho, not exactly like all the *veterano* penitentiary OG's, but at least like some of them who had been on the front line. Some of the neighborhood dads had fought in Vietnam. Our movie superstars were Rambo and Commando, action men who killed and received medals for it. Same thing we were doing in the *varrio,* but in the military, they were called heroes.

In August of 87, still only seventeen, I joined the Marines. Bullshitting with a major hangover, I told the Major, who I had to go see for a waiver cause I had a major criminal record, "No, Sir, I have never used drugs. I've been in juvie a few times. Burglary, assault, robbery. I want to be a Marine. I saw *Full Metal Jacket,* and that's what I want to do. I'm in good shape." He liked I bullshitted with a straight face. He said, "All right, son. Infantry. You leave tomorrow."

Mom had to sign the papers because I was under age. She laughed when I told her that morning I was gonna join cause she didn't think it was possible for a *cholo* like me to get in. But she signed for me cause she knew that's what I needed to do. Anyway, she didn't really know what the hell the Marines was all about and neither did I. Neither did I.

I woke up that last morning and gave my little tubby mom a hug. I told her, "You're gonna love me." And I didn't want to go no more cause I was only lying to myself. She already loved me no matter what. She loved me when she would have to come pick me up at three o'clock in the morning in jail. She'd see me handcuffed to the jail bench and walk up to me calmly, as if it didn't bother her that she had to get up out of her warm comfortable bed and catch the bus in the pouring rain or cold night and then go to work at seven a.m. Real slick she'd assault me with her purse in front of all the policemen. *"Desgraciado!"* She loved me through all the weeks or months I wouldn't come home, and she wouldn't even know where I was. She loved me enough to visit me all those times in juvenile hall. I remember on Sundays she would bring me tacos of *carne asada* with beans and rice. I would hog like a champ. We'd pretend that everything was just fine, and wasn't it? She loved me with my black eyes and bloody stitches, and I wore a baseball cap for three months when I got stabbed in the head cause I didn't want her to know, but she knew, yet she loved me even more. I'd see her on the street going to work and run up behind her on the busy sidewalk, snatch her purse, and she would sigh and shudder in fear, and I'd turn around and laugh. I'd ask her for two dollars for a burrito, and she'd sometimes give it to me. I would say "*Adios*," and go buy a beer.

No, she had to stop loving me, that's what I really meant to say. I meant I was gonna have to go out into the world without any place to come back to. I was gonna have to be Toro without the help of my *varrio*, without the strength of reputation, without the security of everything I had ever learned about life since I was born. I was gonna have to love myself or hate myself and that's what was gonna help me or destroy me in my moments of despair. This was my first moment. I hugged her, stepped out the door, and walked to the bus station. To this day, even with all of the difficult and crazy shit I've done, through months of sweating and stinking, through tough times without a drop of water for my crusted white lips living in holes in the ground in forgotten foreign lands, through headaches and heartbreaks and getting that needle stuck into my dick by the pecker checker, through pain of legs, arms, back, and shoulders from walking, humping, running, and swimming, through blisters of boiling days and freezing nights not knowing where I was, who I was, through standing up when I've wanted to sit down, through the suffering of the world that marks this reality; that morning as I walked, each step was a mountain, each swing of my arms was a thousand silent screams and tears. That will always be the single hardest thing I ever did. I joined the fucking Marine Corps.

They hated me the most.

"What the fuck are those, shithead?" Senior Drill Instructor Sergeant Smokehouse barked and pointed at the bumps and scars all over my head.

"They're battle wounds, Sir."

He laughed a good hearty laugh I didn't think could come out of such a skinny, mean faced man. He invited the two other Drill Instructors to the show. Frozen, I stood in my skivvies. "Tough guy has battle wounds," Senior Drill Instructor Sergeant Smokehouse said.

"Yeah, I saw this piece of shit at Receiving," Drill Instructor Sergeant Rectum said. "He's decorated too, gots tattoos, a big one across his back. Turn the fuck around, scumbag."

I turned around, and for a moment they stared without speaking.

"What kinda shit is that?" Senior Drill Instructor Sergeant Smokehouse asked.

"My name, Sir."

"MY! MY! MY!" Senior Drill Instructor Sergeant Smokehouse shouted as he jabbed me in the back of the head with his finger. "You are not worthy of 'MY.' You ain't nothing but a gutter trash recruit."

"Yes, SIR!" I corrected myself, "This recruit's last name, Sir."

"He likes it up the ass," Sergeant Rectum said, "That's why the fuckhead got his name tattooed there—so that his faggot boyfriend can shout out his name when he's fucking him. Fucking queer."

"He's one of them wannabe tough fags," Sergeant Widmark said.

All three of them ganged up close behind me.

"I ain't never seen more of a fruit than this piece of shit motherfuckin slimeball."

"I'm gonna make sure this lowlife cocksucker doesn't infect my Marine Corps. He aint gonna make it."

"Nah," Sergeant Rectum said, "the fruit will probably make it with all these young men as motivation. This is his fucking paradise."

Senior Drill Instructor Sergeant Smokehouse punched his fist inside his hand. "EYEBALLS!" he shouted. In a flash, sixty-eight new recruits simultaneously snapped their eyeballs towards the Drill Instructors and me.

"CLICK, SIR!" they shouted in unison.

"Listen up, maggots, it has come to my attention that we have a homo in our presence, a one hundred percent faggot. This is not the Navy! Watch your asses!"

"YES, SIR!"

I was a pretty damn stupid recruit. Couldn't do nothing right. Left face, right face, shoulder arms, inspection arms, I didn't get it. I tried my best, but I was constantly fucking up, and so constantly getting thrashed in the dirt by the DI's. But that's what I did do well. That was my talent. I pushed the ground hardest, ran the farthest, humped the hills, and fought my ass off better than the biggest maggot around. Yeah, I was pretty damn stupid—couldn't do land navigation or remember my General Orders, but going up those mountains with a full fucking pack I was a genius. Charging the obstacle course or Confidence Course or running my ass off, I was Albert fucking Einstein. And even though I was a "rock"— cause that's what they call a stupid ass recruit—I was a solid fuckin diamond of a rock.

So one fine night, a month into Boot Camp, they fired my recruit squad leader cause he used to complain like a bitch. Senior Drill Instructor Sergeant Smokehouse inspected me during our routine nightly hygiene inspection. He was supposed to walk off and inspect the next recruit standing by me—that was supposed to be my signal to carry on with my other duties. But he stayed there and then dropped the metal squad leader chevrons on the deck behind me—walked away without saying a word. With this ceremony, I was the new squad leader. I had absolutely no idea what I was supposed to do.

So I did what I felt was right. I humped the hills, and if someone in my squad was slacking, I would kick them hard in the ass. If they couldn't hack their weight, but were trying, I'd put their pack on my shoulders and tell them, "Grab onto my pack and just keep on humping." And I'd pull em up the hills looking like a little crab, a stocky little 5'6" *Indio* with a cleanly shaved head and face. When it was time to clean, I got down on my hands and knees with the rest of my squad. I remember the other three squad leaders, two white guys and a black dude, would tell me, "Calm down, kick back, and just supervise." With my knuckleheads around me, in my skivvies, I'd be down on the deck with a soaped up scrub brush. "Fuck you," I'd say.

Nighttime blackness at the recruit depot, a lullaby to put his babies to sleep:

"I do not crumble like sand or rot like wood." Senior Drill Instructor Sergeant Smokehouse would pray self-affirmations to us, infect us with the belief we were Marines.

"Haven't you observed my arms and shoulders?" he continued. At attention lying down in our racks, we snapped our fingers twice in confirmation. Marines can't speak with the lights out.

"You I can stuff into my pack, pour into my canteen, wear on my ammunition belt.

"I hump big hills, and Earth falls apart at my feet as I sing songs and travel to distant lands.

"Are you so far that I can't get there on foot?

"Is my endurance worthless?

"I challenge stars to shine as long.

"So, I understand that my manners are mean, my voice LOUD,

the silence of my stare unbearable to ears.

"But you've listened to be strong.

"Therefore, I confront you.

"Both of my arms tied behind my back, legs shackled in chains, muzzle on mouth.

"I will make our fight fair.

"I will grant you this, and you will still fight for your life, and we shall see who falls out of the sky first.

"It doesn't matter to me.

"I fly even when I fall."

I'd fall asleep dreaming Marine dreams but then wake up in the middle of the nights so I could practice marching in the squad bay. Left, right, left foot, right. And I was still a stupid son of a gun, but I tried, damn it, I sharpened my horns and charged at the red cape.

The doctors pulled out my four wisdom teeth two weeks before graduation. The Doc gave me a three-day sick rest chit, but I threw it in the garbage can cause I knew I couldn't lead a Marine Recruit squad lying down in my rack. I slipped back into the barracks, put on my PT gear, and joined in on the five mile squad run. I pushed my squad to the limit cause I pushed myself to the limit. When they bitched and moaned that I was going too fast, I shouted through my bright red bleeding mouth, "Shut the fuck up!" And we were first place squad that sunny day.

The next morning we were cleaning our M16's and the Drill Instructors called me into their private office. They never called anyone into their hooch unless he was fucked. Some recruits who had gone in there had been escorted out by the Marine Police. Fuck! They must have found out about some crimes I committed before I got in. I'm gonna get kicked out. Three months for nothing! I pounded on the door three times and requested permission to enter.

"Center!" Senior Drill Instructor Smokehouse shouted.

I walked in and centered myself six inches in front of Senior Drill Instructor Sergeant Smokehouse's desk.

"Recruit Toro reporting as ordered, Sir."

"Toro," Senior Drill Instructor Sergeant Smokehouse slurred, "What the fuck are you trying to do to me, boy? I just got a call from sick bay askin me how you're doing. You went and got some teeth pulled, didn't ya? You're supposed to be jerkin off in your rack." He got up from his desk and put his face in front of mine. The ribbons on his chest were a giant fruit salad. He continued, "Are you out of your mind disobeying an order from a Navy Doctor? (The Marines ain't got no doctors; all Marines know how to do is fuck shit up.) Are you trying to be an individual, someone with your own mind? You fucking rock—PUSH UPS!"

I flung myself to the deck and commenced pushing.

"SIT UPS!" I turned myself over as quickly as I could and repeatedly sat the fuck up. Whatever he commanded, I'd do as quickly as the words escaped his mouth.

"Look at the pussy! He can't hang," Sergeant Rectum said.

"He wants to fuckin quit! He ain't a Marine!" Sergeant Widmark added.

"BENDS AND THRUSTS!"

Sweat rained down on the deck, and my mouth throbbed violently with every movement.

"UP! SIDE STRADDLE HOPS!"

"DOWN!"

"PUSH UPS! Faster, you worthless waste." Sergeant Rectum put his foot on my back. They laughed and saw I did it even harder.

"Aint no one here now. We're the fucking gang, shithead. We control, and I say faster," Sergeant Widmark shouted.

"The asshole ran fast," Sergeant Rectum laughed. "His squad won first place yesterday."

"He thinks he's bad," Sergeant Widmark confirmed.

"Sacrifice hurts, motherfucker," Senior Drill Instructor Sergeant Smokehouse said as I pushed with every fiber of my strength. Then softly, in a murmur, revealing the secrets of the world, the key to heaven, he continued, "Sacrifice kills. Aint no glory in it, but you do it anyway. You wanna be a real Marine? Then you should know that glory is punishment. Glory gots no friends. The love aint mutual, slimeball. There's no reciprocation, and you never get loved back. Glory? Only you know the value of it, alone."

They stood in silence. I pushed with spaghetti arms.

"STOP!" Senior Drill Instructor Sergeant Smokehouse shouted after another five minutes. I rose. "You are a stupid fucking rock, Toro. You got no sense at all. I don't appreciate some pussy ass recruit trying to take my hard earned stripes from me by disobeying a Doc's orders. Next time it's the fuckin brig for your ass." Without panting, I stood locked at Marine attention as the inside of my mouth filled up with globs of blood. The left side of Senior Drill Instructor Sergeant Smokehouse's lip turned up. "Get out of my sight!"

"Aye, aye, Sir!" Blood dribbled out the side of my mouth. I about faced and marched out the door. I got a meritorious promotion to Private First Class during Boot Camp graduation.

They hated me the most.

Boot Camp was a bitch and the Drill Instructors are tough. They're tough cause they gotta make basic Marines. The DI's take care of their business, but, for the most part, they don't go too overboard. With all the mommas that call their Senators worried about their kids, all the heavy brass walking around the recruit depot, and possible snitches, DI's know they can only go so far. Recruits got to get fed, get some kind of sleep, and wash their asses every once in a while. They make basic "Boot" Marines. The School of Infantry doesn't give a fuck about going overboard. They make the pride of the Corps, what the whole nation feels secure with when they know the shit has hit the fan—the first to fight, front line, ground pounding grunts.

January 88: the candidate grunts of the School of Infantry were humping up the Transmogrifier at Camp Pendleton, California. The Transmogrifier, we were told, transformed you from a rock solid Marine Corps superhero to a soft, wet, Friday-night piece of sweet stinking poon-tang. I had a fifty caliber receiver, full field pack, and the sun's hot rays strapped to my back and digging eternal scars deep into my young, strong, dark brown shoulders. My fellow Marines were falling out all around me, and I too was close to my last breath. I was being transmogrified. I couldn't think clearly from the intense chaos of laboring upwards, but I was trying to fool myself into believing I could make it up that torturous tit with several of my usual cons that usually worked. I was BAD. I was a Marine. Do it for the homies. Do it cause I've got *CORAZON!* But I wasn't buying my bullshit on this particularly difficult day. I wasn't going to make it up the fucking hill, the mountain, the Transmogrifier. I started believing that it was OK to fall behind this one time. I felt, man, this shit is crazy. I've given it my best, done what I could, I'll crawl up there, but I just can't keep up with this troop leader—shit, he aint got this monster on his back! Even some of the best Marines I ever knew, future blood and guts Bronze Star Jarheads, were falling behind me. This will be the only time I ever fall back. Fuck it.

Not even a flicker of fire was burning in my soul when one of the hardest core professional Marines I ever knew walked next to me and read my mind. He was walking up and down the line, checking up on us dogs. He looked at me and knew what I was about to do. He knew I was about to shame my name and give up in disgrace, but he wasn't going to help me with my titanic weight. Fuck no! He was going to let me die right there in the middle of that cruel dirt road if that's what I chose to do. Sergeant Norris walked next to me and opened his mouth without a touch of compassion for my agony, without a smile on his sweaty face, without human feelings for a fellow Brother who was about to die from the weight of the universe on his shoulders—squashed like a little bug by eighty pounds of steel and gear. He almost whispered it to me—almost whispered the most profound words I ever heard.

"Either you're hard or the hill is hard." And Sergeant Norris, the motherfucker, the wise man, the sage without sympathy, turned his head away and marched on.

And those magic words gave me an angel's push when I'd been down at the count of nine, and they were going to officially pen me down in the record books as knocked the fuck out. After those words, I began to dance like a flea up that hill, and I told everyone to dance up there with me. This was a pain party, and I was dying miserably. I was in the absolute worst absolute distress of my life. I was close to being transmogrified, and how I fuckin loved it! I thanked Jesus Christ for giving me this opportunity to suffer with a smile on my face. I thanked him for my crazy life that hurt so much, but also gave me such wonderful joy and happiness. Struggling up that winding uphill road while ninety percent of the Marines fell like flies behind me, I thanked God for my precious existence, and I asked God Almighty, with the sacrifice of every strong muscle and white bone in my body, if he would please make me hard—harder than the hill.

And I actually started believing that I could make it up the damn mountain. I started believing that I was harder than that hill that had survived tragic turmoil, stormy weather, and Marines humping up it; that place that had stood since before the beginning of civilization. And I believed I could be harder, tougher, more durable, more invincible than a giant hunk of rock. Because of Sergeant Norris's magical words, the grace of God, and me conning myself with fantastic new bullshit, I conquered a little mound of dirt on a bright sunny day.

FIVE

The American Dream

"Keep, ancient lands, your storied pomp!" cries she
With silent lips. "Give me your tired, your poor,
Your huddled masses yearning to breathe free,
The wretched refuse of your teeming shore.
Send these, the homeless, tempest-tost to me,
I lift my lamp beside the golden door!"

EMMA LAZARUS, *"The New Colossus"*

Moving up, Kwai Chung felt as if he was becoming a real American. Moving down, Sasquatch also felt like he was becoming a real American.

Both had planned out their vision of the American dream. Kwai felt he could do it by working hard and paying his dues. Never had he aspired to be some crude gangster. Instead, he was using his earnings to climb into the ideal American "old boy" network. During his senior year in high school, with his outstanding 4.2 grade point average, he had been accepted to Harvard University. Proud, he had accomplished the goal he set out in sixth grade, but he had known even then he could never afford to attend an Ivy League school. His parents without money, he also knew he could not apply for financial aid or loans because of his immigration status.

When Kwai was nine, his parents had brought him from China for a trip to Disneyland. It was there he fell in love with America. His parents, seeing his excitement, never bothered leaving. They wanted the best for their only child and knew that in China his options were extremely limited. In America, however, anything was possible. Although he studied hard to be the best and believed he would somehow accomplish his dreams, by the time he was in the tenth grade he completely understood the reality of his situation. Therefore, when the opportunity arose to run bets for the Triads, he quickly capitalized on his luck. His parents, believing in his intelligence, turned a blind eye to his business, and that is exactly what they called it. An American businessman, they knew, had to be a risk taker. The Triads also liked Kwai Chung's style. They were immediately impressed by his native manners, silent ways, and cunning. He ran very fast. Kwai Chung seemed to be exactly what they wanted, someone who could run bets and collect and not be threatening, especially in the barrio. The *gente* saw four eyed, one hundred thirty pound Kwai as a mere runner, as a nothing, almost invisible. He was no threat.

Although Kwai was proud of his intelligence and maneuverability, it meant nothing unless he could live in the US as a real American. When he graduated from high school at eighteen, he decided he would make Harvard a reality. It would require difficulty and danger, but he knew that this would position him for his best chance. For two years after high school, he organized and sacrificed his formal education so that he could have a solid street base. A miser, he saved everything. Once his system was in place, he bought a fake social security number and became "Tommy Lee." At twenty years old, he began attending the local community college. In every class he received an A and was involved with many campus wide student activities. Hiring Lobo as his barrio enforcer, he began running his own gambling operation. He figured out odds and schemes and ways to shave, while the *gente* simply placed their bets on rumors and stereotypes. Now, two years later, he had gained enough money to buy himself a Harvard education. His application ready for submission, he would become an Ivy Leaguer.

Although he wanted everything, he knew he was gambling with his life. More than just to obtain credentials or to have material things, Kwai wanted to experiment with the power of the individual. Could a man, out of sheer cunning and relentless drive, truly invent whatever he wanted out of himself? Was Mickey Mouse a cartoon character or a genius? Worst case scenario, whether he stayed in the US or not, with a Harvard education, he knew he would command international respect. In capitalism, Kwai thought, it is one's duty to become a capitalist, to constantly re-invent oneself for the betterment of one's own ego and selfishness. Soon, he would receive what he felt was a guaranteed Harvard acceptance letter, and then he could stop the stupidity of dealing with barrio people and with his own people's shame, the Triads.

United States greed had embittered the Sasquatch. He had tried to believe in the country's puritanical work ethic, but either he or it had failed. His strict Chinese parents from Vietnam had told him to always follow the rules. He had accepted their commands only to be bullied in school. When he was ten, they moved out of his happy Chinatown. His parents' cheapness and greed had enticed them to buy a house in the worst ghetto of Inten city. By buying there, his parents hoped to eventually turn big profits. They did not care about what their son had to go through growing up in the hood; they had grown up through Mao! Most days Sasquatch was chased or beat up. Young blacks would purposely pick on him most because he was the biggest boy of the new Asian migration. Sasquatch's little Chinese friends would run away when he was attacked. Ultimately he decided to join with some Vietnamese kids; yet they, too, could not walk with their heads held up. They feared the blacks' savagery.

By 1984 Sasquatch was listening to Run-DMC and break dancing for money; this was at a time when only blacks and Latinos took to the streets to dance. Being enthusiastic and wanting to embrace some identity other than his Chinese one, he became a pretty good dancer. The black homeboys from his hood noticed that Sasquatch had rhythm. Hesitantly at first, they befriended him. As he grew, the Sasquatch put in work and was thoroughly accepted.

Sasquatch's parents were suffering even more from an American identity crisis. Many Chinese had borrowed money to buy houses in the hood at inflated prices, not understanding the danger that lurked there. If they lost money and needed to sell their houses, getting out could be close to impossible, because no one who knew the hood and had any money would buy there. With a big mortgage and bad credit, they borrowed from the only ones who would lend, the Triads. Like a fog, the Triads seeped their way into the hood. In 1985 Kwai Chung and a Blue Lantern member went to collect payments from Sasquatch's father. A giant, Jheri Curled Chinese youth answered the door. Shocked, they thought him a traitor, but they also thought he could be valuable.

Sasquatch and Kwai began working together, Kwai as the boss. In the hood, Kwai would have had all his money stolen. In the black hood, Sasquatch acted as his Lobo. But Sasquatch was also doing other things, such as selling crack and gang banging with the blacks. Sasquatch would give Kwai sly looks and laugh at him to his face. Although he felt safe with Sasquatch, Kwai sensed that one day this man who was like him but so unlike him would injure and possibly destroy him. One summer day after Kwai dropped a dime, the police raided Sasquatch's house. They found fifty rocks of crack cocaine. Sentenced to three years in state prison, Sasquatch got off easy.

In prison Sasquatch was initially alone and tortured. His own people abandoned him because he talked and walked like a black man, and the blacks who knew him from the streets could not convince the black prison gangs to allow him to enter. Sasquatch was in living hell and fodder for anyone who wanted him. Finally, he had to stab and steal and create his own unique gangster identity. Using women's pink rollers and Crisco cooking oil, he kept his Jheri Curl. He power lifted weights on the yard, and his sheer size gave him some status. Ultimately he banded with a crew of Samoans and a couple of blacks.

Once released, Sasquatch demanded restitution. He confronted Kwai Chung, told him that he realized he had snitched on him, and he knew that Kwai was running side bets without the Triads' permission. He shook him down in classic American fashion. Kwai Chung was cool on the outside, but inside he was jolted. Although he knew Sasquatch deserved something, he was unwilling to establish a negative precedent. Also, the amount that Sasquatch wanted would be Kwai's Harvard tuition. Kwai Chung simply could not do it. That was when he called Lobo.

Sasquatch had had time to figure out that Kwai would not go for it, and he also figured that he would get his *cholo* to hit him, as Kwai could not tell anyone else of his fraud. Sasquatch had heard of a young up and coming homeboy hustler named Lobo. He also knew firsthand of *cholos'* ruthlessness inside the walls. These people were very precise and organized when they had to be, but Lobo had never been in. Sasquatch felt that Lobo was a simple street thug who had never had real time to think. Sasquatch knew he could either kill him or weaken him even further. He tailed Lobo and waited for him outside Sheila's apartment. When Lobo exited that morning, Sasquatch had his black .45 in his sweaty hand, but he just couldn't do it. For ten seconds, he felt ashamed of himself, but he did not allow his shame to overwhelm him. Impromptu, he knocked on Sheila's door. For reasons he still didn't understand, he abducted her. As he was torturing Sheila, he realized she wouldn't betray Lobo. The word "love" didn't pop into Sasquatch's mind. He'd never felt it. But later, when he saw Lobo look at Shelia, the word occurred to him.

Before Lobo came, he made his plan. He would reverse everything. Instead of he himself being assassinated, he would have Lobo hit Kwai in front of all of the senior Triad members, on their most holy day, during their most revered ritual. Witnessing this, the Triads would have no choice but to evolve. They would choose Sasquatch because only he would know how to deal with these Americans.

If this did not turn out right, Sasquatch would be facing life for kidnapping and torture, most likely murder. Sitting there, Sheila did not even seem to comprehend her fate. He pitied her stupidity. She no longer even tried to fight back. *How weak bitches are,* he thought.

Sasquatch knew true combat and hell and figured Lobo was soft, especially because of Sheila. The street *cholos* were all a bunch of fuckups.

SIX

El Toro

In February of 91, the bombs burst and the enemy fell. It was the real shit—combat action. We, the grunts of Bravo Company, had just hard charged through miles of deadly mine fields and dangerous but feeble enemy resistance. Iraqi soldiers around us, forever slept in their trenches, while others preferred the camaraderie of being permanently bonded and melted to their tanks.

We were close to the end of our fifteen minute break as the third squad leader of Third Platoon, Sergeant Accosted, looked around at us as we lay sprawled out on the tan sand stretching out our locked up limbs and joints and trying to get some rest. He chomped on his Red Man chew, savoring the sweet juice of tobacco leaves that made his lower lip look as if it were nine months pregnant. It was time to move.

"Saddle up!" he spit out a brown geyser of saliva and nicotine syrup. We snapped out of our daydreams and dragged our tired bodies along the sinking sand. Under the pressure of M60 and M249 machine guns, M16 rifles, AT-4 tank and bunker destroyers, grenades, ammunition, and sour adrenaline, we loaded ourselves into our Amphibious Assault Vehicle, better known as our track. We were mooing like cattle when a mere man complained.

"Damn! Always fucking moving. Yo, what the fuck is up here? I'm in the middle of heating up my chow!" Corporal Ramsey got up from his squatting position by a tiny heat tab flame and violently threw down his halfway heated, ten-year-old beef stew like a baby throwing down Gerber's during a tantrum.

"Hey, spazoid," Sergeant Accosted replied, "if you're really hungry, I'll leave you here—cause ya got some ready to eat, well done crispy critters right on over there." Sergeant Accosted pointed to the charcoal Iraqi corpses sitting in annihilated vehicles. "So quit your bitchin and get the fuck on the track like everyone else."

Corporal Ramsey grumbled.

In the track, we rushed forward in the vast Saudi Arabian desert to the ultimate objective: Kuwait City. Rolling over and conquering the evil Iraqi empire, we were true poster United States Marine Corps superheroes. A rainbow of browns, blacks, and whites spanning from one coast of the big chicken to the other. We were short and stocky, black and brawny, white and scrawny. Young at heart, quick to stink, and first to fight. We were men that had never been completely fooled by old men's lies. We knew about the horrors of close combat through the flashbacks and stories of many of our senior sergeants who were Vietnam vets. Still, we were all volunteers who had subjected ourselves to mind games and torture to gain a prestigious title we were almost too embarrassed to hold. We were proud, but it was with a silent pride that we didn't flaunt in front of each other. Contrary to movie madness, we didn't shout it out constantly in each other's faces. Real Marines had shown their dignity lying silently on the black sands of Iwo Jima and in the dense green jungles of Vietnam.

On the first day of the offensive push into the ancient city of Kuwait, real Jarheads were breaching the minefields in the desert of Saudi Arabia, watching C4 line charges explode a path of attack to the Iraqi trenches. After seven infinite months of living from hole in the ground to hole in the ground like homeless bums with guns in the middle of a godforsaken scorching desert, we thought that first day of the war was beautiful. It was the undisputed best day of our lives. We had gone into the war having trained for trench warfare. Without anything we could use for cover, we had practiced charging in the middle of an open desert and jumping into potentially booby trapped trenches. World War One was supposed to repeat itself in 1991. We had crazy dreams of making it back home alive, winning some medals of valor, and killing some filthy non-human beings we referred to as "Ragheads." And our wildest fantasies were coming true better than any wet delusions we ever had about "Mary Jane Rottencrotch." We were taking thousands of friendly and grateful enemy prisoners of war who waved their white underwear as surrendering flags, told us, "Fuck Saddam!" and then spit on the ground. We attacked mercilessly without too much retaliation, blew up mine fields like crazy kids playing with firecrackers in our backyards, and stampeded out of our AAV track as if we were extras in the biggest war film ever made. We were winning the "Mother of all wars" and none of us had even sprained an ankle. We were alive and alertly awake in this magnificent fantasy that was new to most of us.

On the first day of Desert Storm's ground war, I truly believed in the almighty powerful force of *Happy Days*. For some reason, that show was imprinted in my memory bank. I kept thinking of cool ass Arthur Fonzarelli. In my mom's room, I used to mimic him while I stood in front of the full length mirror with the collar of my Salvation Army pleather jacket turned up, my hair slicked back, and my thumbs sticking up and out at the side of my hips.

"Ayy! Move aside world cause here I come!" I would say cool things to the mirror and wish with little boy bullshit that if I said enough magical "Ayy!"s I'd somehow get transformed into the coolest motorcycle gangster in the world.

On that first day of the ground war, while killing time confined inside of the track waiting for our next move, I knew I no longer needed the hocus pocus of a writer's invented word. I could whip the Fonz, and *Happy Days* was here. I'd beat punk ass Henry Winkler down, and if he were here he would be begging me for my autograph. Everything was much cooler than *Happy Days*. I can remember thinking that night, when we finally stopped to reorganize, orient, and take a few hours rest after destroying half of the Iraqi army, that everything was gonna be baby doll fine. As the bombs burst bright red Iraqi blood, the only thing that was on my mind was that Moms would be really proud now, my homies would throw me a big time celebration when I got back home, and one day my future kids would be able to say their daddy fought in the war. I'd come back home with gold medals on my hairless chest all the while knowing it hadn't been that bad. I felt guilty, but what could I do? I mean, the fuckers had given up. Worse yet, they'd literally turned their guns upside down and attacked me by kissing my feet.

That night, as we dug our makeshift fighting holes, I turned to my Brother in arms. "It'd be a damn shame if we came over all this way," I told my team leader, Corporal Montone, a down ass Texas country bumpkin, "and went through all this worst hell these past seven months and we wouldn't even see any hard core action."

"No shit, but it'd be ten times worse to have even one of us dead—except maybe him." Corporal Montone shoveled sand with his entrenching tool, grinned, and nodded towards Corporal Ramsey who was intensely picking his nose digging for hidden dry desert gold. I understood Corporal Montone's logic about the welfare of the troops, but the attraction of mythical and glorious combat sucked on my young buck skin like a leech. Blaspheming the Iraqi's cowardice, I fell asleep in my fighting hole that chilly night, body twisted and deformed.

I woke up to a thick black smoke that blanketed every grain of sand with an apocalyptic darkness. The oil wells set on fire by the retreating Iraqis set up a doomed scene from the Book of Revelation. In a stumbling daze, I gathered up my deuce gear, M60 ammo, and M16 rifle, and our whole squad of eighteen dirty Marines plus the fat little Navy Corpsman crammed together in our sardine can of an AAV. The shells from Iraqi artillery slam-bammed down in the soft sand, while we got settled in and curled up into little ball bugs inside of our cramped mobile beer can. There was hardly room to breathe with all of the gear around us.

We drove forward for an hour or two, jumped out, charged off with guns at the ready, took information and souvenirs from surrendering Iraqis, then got back in the beer can and kept on with our holy mission to liberate the God fearing people of Kuwait. As the hours passed in my stuffed, uncomfortable world, the bombs became more of a nuisance and the constant noise of gunfire and explosives began to make me tense. It was fucked up cause I couldn't see what was going on; all I could do was sit, shut up, and listen. The word from over the net was that we were engaged in some heavy armored vehicle fighting on our far left flank. We were useless as grunts, so all I could do was twist myself into a crumpled paper ball and wait.

I was gonna take advantage of the situation by catching up on some sweet slumber when a mad, operatic voice sang through the radio the words I had come to fear more than any Drill Instructor's harsh bark.

"GAS! GAS! GAS!"

In less than a second I had my gas mask donned and cleared and was sucking in filtered air to my startled lungs. I put my chemical protective gloves over my chemical suit and quickly stepped up on the bench that I was sitting on and closed the hatches on top of the track so that no chemicals would get inside. The bombs clamored, the track shook, and machine-gun fire rattled like a snake as we moved forward. At first I couldn't believe that Saddam had been stupid enough to gas us cause we'd been told that if we were to get gassed, the US would retaliate with strategic nuclear missiles. I thought of the Japanese's peeling skin after the atom bomb dropped on them. I sat stunned and tried to make magic.

"Ayy! I'm the Fonz!" I echoed over in my head. After I calmed down a bit, I looked around at my squad and wondered if they ever even believed in silly ass *Happy Days*. Everyone looked the same with gas masks on, their plastic eyes dead, devoid of all the fantasies we talked about a day earlier. Yesterday we had laughed, Iraqi officers had bowed down before us, we drank fuckin water! A day later, I brooded in the track, helpless to battle invisible enemies, and through the radio the cool Iraqi Fonz taunted me and whispered, "Sit on it, Jarhead!" I sat in the midst of the most fucked up experience of my life and silently asked God for forgiveness for my many young sins. I prayed I'd have the Sampson strength to stay a Marine.

But what the fuck is a Marine? He shits his pants just like you. He has regrets and fear and pain, and he cries too. See, if I learned anything on those dark days, it was how to suffer with class. That's what a Marine is: he's a professional sufferer; he suffers for you and me and he don't think about the shit. He suffers with a smile on his face. And I never wrote this down when I was going through it, couldn't put it on paper, wouldn't share my thoughts even with myself, didn't have the strength or courage to think, cause you gotta understand that thinking, thinking in all its grandness, in all its beauty, in all its fuckin enlightenment kills you. Fuck critical thinking. It sucks you into hesitation. It grabs your fucking throat and chokes the instinct out of you. I couldn't put my philosophy down on paper cause that would've meant I actually had such a thing; that I analyzed, pondered, meditated—but with bombs and black ash falling from heaven you die from the serenity of meditation. That shit is for the generals—for the fuckers sitting high and mighty chomping on cigars in little back rooms. They don't get their hands dirty. They don't sweat. That's what they got the fuckin grunts for, so that they can rush them machine-gun nests and sleep like moles in little holes—cause if a mighty Marine THINKS—he aint gonna do what he has to do. He aint gonna jump on that grenade or charge in front of the bullet.

It's beyond logic; that shit is beyond sense. What can make a man love that much? What force, what theory can give a man with a full life ahead of him the strength to fucking die on purpose? It's the theory of stupidity, the theory of lunacy, the theory that this is my Bro on my side, my deepest homeboy that gots my back, would never let me down, OR, with more profound thinking, maybe he aint got my back; maybe, just maybe, he'll leave me to die; maybe he'll fucking split when the time comes, maybe I should throw his ass on the grenade, maybe…

BOOM. Everyone fucking dies. Maybe, just maybe, with all of them grand schemes running through that big grape of ideology everyone fucking dies cause everyone is a fuckin genius, and your smart ass is left smelling the red roses and green grass for eternity.

We received the "all clear" signal an hour later and were then able to take off our gas masks. Looking at everyone's sweaty faces, I knew the previous atmosphere of confidence had changed. We sat silent. We drank our water reluctantly because we feared it had been chemically contaminated. I tried to find sustenance in a cold, old, dehydrated Omelet with Ham Meal Ready to Eat. Stuck in the track, no place to go, I gripped my rifle, and the cold, hard steel comforted me more than any kiss from Mama. After awhile, we all started organizing our ammo and making sure we knew exactly where everything was in case of an all out Iraqi assault. The word to attack would eventually come down and then we would only have a second to dismount the track and charge into the fortified Iraqi trenches.

"Toro, you been eatin beans?" Corporal Montone asked.

"Nah, that's my own deadly batch of gas," I smiled and let out another vicious fart. "That's what you call Omelet with Ham contamination."

"You're fuckin rotten." Corporal Montone punched me in the arm and the other Jugheads on the track cursed me out for polluting in close quarters.

Smiling and about to be relaxed, I was glad to have my gas

mask off when once again the words "GAS! GAS! GAS!" broke my heart. I made my instinctual reply to the profanity by donning and clearing my gas mask. I was high strung and stressed out but no longer scared; I was now mad, infuriated at the vermin who were trying to take away my glory and happiness, trying to kill me, scare me, and make me a coward. I wanted to charge out there with my thousand rounds of hard brass. I wanted to prove my valor; instead I just hunkered down in the AAV and silently cursed to myself.

"Confirmed Lewisite agent" was the word from over the net.

All of us were pissed off, but across the track, five feet away from me and to my right, sat the ultimate bitch, Corporal Ramsey.

"It's too fucking hot in this mask!" he garbled out. Corporal Ramsey was wired and rigid and noticeably fidgeting around. Earlier, he had told me that he had taken ten tablets of NoDoz stimulants because he said that he wasn't gonna get caught off guard in an attack. Now the stupid fucker was a hyped out base head, but it really didn't surprise me cause he always went to these kinds of extremes. The fucker talked extreme shit about everything and everyone behind their backs, constantly whined and bitched about any development out of the ordinary, and bullied around the fire team he was in charge of by threatening his Marines with extra duty if they didn't do the work he personally was supposed to have done. He was a tyrant who had spent his previous time in the Corps on stateside barracks duty worrying about the spit and polish of dress shoes and the sharp creases in uniforms. Then he came to the muddy grunts. He didn't have a clue about how to suffer with class, how to keep his mouth shut with a smile. His presence in this most fucked up situation left a sour milk stench floating in the already contaminated air.

Lance Corporal Totem, a rifleman who was part of Corporal

Ramsey's fire team, sat glued next to his leader and tried to kick back despite the latest gas attack. Totem nodded his head up and down as if trying to sleep, while right next to him Corporal Ramsey was going insane from a NoDoz overdose.

"I'd be fine if I only could've heated up my fuckin chow. It would've taken five fuckin minutes, and I wouldn't even care about this shit, but these fuckers can't even give me that much. Fuck the Suck!" He then started bitchin about the C-4 plastic explosive he had to run and hump around with in his already weighted down pack. "Once we finally get off, how am I supposed to run with this extra weight when I aint ate shit all day long? I should split this shit up to the fuckin new Boot Marines cause I've been in three years and shouldn't have to put up with this shit!" He thought he was too precious to carry an extra twenty pounds of life. Ramsey was angry we were all crammed like funky sweat socks in a boxing gym locker. "I can't fuckin breathe in this mask!" In his fury he found an easy patsy as the culprit of his dissatisfaction.

Totem had leaned his AT-4 tank and bunker destroyer, a mean, green, three foot, fifteen pound missile, on Corporal Ramsey's one square inch of private space. In our situation there was no way you could avoid touching on each other with something. The fuckin track was only about 100 square feet of space for eighteen grown men and a ton of hard steel. It was ten times worse than ship life, and ship life was cramped up for grunts. Now, though, according to Corporal Ramsey's distorted logic, Totem was the cause of all his unhappiness. "Motherfuckin AT-4. Bullshit. Shit aint mine. None of this is mine. Don't need this shit." Under Ramsey's rationale, Totem had taken him away from his beloved beer, his loved ones, and his family for seven miserable months. By the brutal look that seemed to jump out of his plastic eyes, it seemed that Totem had somehow singlehandedly caused Iraq to invade Kuwait and made the Bravo Company Marines come over to the Saudi hell-hole to take it back for them. Through sorcery Totem had caused the bombs to blast and the chattering machine-gun fire to roar, and now he was trying to take the one square of inch of bliss that belonged to Corporal Ramsey, the king.

"No fucking AT-4 on my side!" Corporal Ramsey rammed it into Totem's bent leg and woke him from his beauty sleep. Totem pushed it back. Corporal Ramsey pushed it back harder.

"All right, man, don't spaz out." Totem realized what was happening and tried to avert the problem with a compromise, placing it dead center in between them.

It was no good.

"Look, you fuckin Boot," Corporal Ramsey screamed, "if I give you this one little inch, you'll think its OK to take two giant inches later and then I'll be completely smothered. I'll be unprepared for combat. I'll fuckin die, motherfucker, and you'll have killed me with your AT-4!" Like a wild dog, he stood up and speared his finger into Totem's gas masked face.

Totem stepped up and reasoned, "Look, man, we're all in this thing together, just chill."

Ramsey stared at Totem.

"Yeah, chill," Corporal Ramsey chilled by placing his hands around Totem's throat. Totem reacted quickly by strangling Corporal Ramsey's wiry neck. They were Igor and Frankenstein in a horror movie rerun. Corporal Montone and Sergeant Accosted jumped up to break them up, and Corporal Ramsey, knowing he might not have this chance again, knowing this is what he came there for, became an individual: a human being of flesh and blood. He shrieked, "Fuck this shit! Fuck esprit de corps!" He grabbed

Totem's sealed gas mask by the nose apparatus and pulled it half-way over his head. Totem's protective seal against the invisible enemies in the air was broken. Five of us sprung on Corporal Ramsey and pasted him to the wall of the track.

I couldn't believe it. The little bitch took off Totem's gas mask in the middle of an attack. I would've put the fucker down, but Totem just put his gas mask back on. Sergeant Accosted split both of them up from their seating arrangements and told us all to forget it; there was too much else going on outside to get tangled up in a domestic dispute. We had to stay cool. The freak of nature, Ramsey, was now sitting directly in front and across from me. I loosened my bayonet from its sheath and was ready for this abomination if he tried an idiot move on me. But he just sat there and slumped down on the bench, and I stared into his untamed plastic eyes while he cursed and complained about everything under the sun.

We got the all clear signal about two hours later, and I took my gas mask off of my drenched face and gulped down water. I didn't care about contamination anymore. I opened up the hatches on top of the track, and with my rifle on "fire," I stood up on the bench of the track and watched the red/black sun set in a war torn desert. Fires and vehicles lined up uniformly just like a good Marine Corps outfit should. Blown up tanks, uneven sand, and full force forward. It was a perfect magnificent beauty in a satanically morbid situation. Hell, I thought, must be a beautiful place. The oil fires burned a thick black smoke that had made it a deep dusk in the daytime, and now that night came it was getting so dark I could literally not even see my hand in front of my face. I closed the hatches on top of the track so that I could put on a night light inside of our little AAV world and have at least a dim view of humanity.

We listened to the activity over the radio net. Our Task Force was killing multitudes of Iraqis and our commanding officers were giving each other high fives over the radio. But by now we'd also gotten our first amusing casualties. Someone in Charlie Company had blown off his foot with his trench shotgun, a First Sergeant in another battalion had a heart attack during the last gas attack, and by mistake some Tankers had destroyed one of our own vehicles. Through the net, our commanding officer, Lieutenant Colonel Crow, told us we were doing a great job but to calm down on the friendly fire.

We forgot about death around us by imagining and mimicking the First Sergeant who had the heart attack. We acted just like comedian Fred Sanford does when he has the BIG ONE. Corporal Ramsey did it best. And suddenly, through the cackle of laughter, blasts shook the ground and outside we engaged in close tank battles.

"Bravo, we need you on support of our left flank," some voice over the net commanded.

"This is it. Let's get ready to dismount," Sergeant Accosted ordered.

The time had come for us to get down to business, but I didn't know exactly what I was supposed to do in this situation. I had trained at night many times before, but this wasn't night; the outside was eight ball blackness. Due to burning oil wells coupled with the desert darkness, outside of the track there was no way we could see each other, let alone Iraqi enemies.

"Corporal Montone, what should we do when we get off the track?"

"Just stick by me no matter what and remember, I got your back and you've got mine." Corporal Montone smiled and half relaxed me with his certainty, but I knew that realistically if I had to fire it would be futile. How could I charge when I might even end up killing some of my Bravo Bros? Confusion and possibilities were killing my confidence, and to top it off, the vision of my future, Corporal Ramsey, sat in front and across from me, starry eyed, with his head tilted to the left and drooling uncontrollably. Then his head just froze, and he got stuck looking right in my eyes. Trancing with his eyes wide open, he started violently jerking his body up and down and side to side like a fish out of water. I stared in amazement at the floppy fish and realized how hungry I was. Then he started throwing up white liquid foam all over himself. The deafening silence of panic and mute missiles of chaos blowing up in his own head had turned the mighty pharaoh, Corporal Ramsey, into a dying, slimy trout. He was completely transmogrified.

The chubby Navy Corpsman jumped over me. "He's in shock!" he yelled.

"Punch him in the face!" Totem shouted.

Various likewise suggestions sprang up from around the track.

"Wake that tender pussy up!"

"Just slap that idiot and tell him it's going to be OK."

"Piss on the motherfucker!"

But the Corpsman and Sergeant Accosted didn't piss on him. They knifed open his chemical protective suit, injected him with some atropine and 2-PAM chloride, and forced water down him by shoving an IV through one of his collapsed veins. Ramsey was unconscious as we got the order to dismount the track. The Corpsman took care of him in the now comfortable track as we stumbled outside to an eerie blackout.

There was no longer an Earth. We used our night vision goggles to try to see something, but the burning oil wells' black smoke made the goggles useless. Sergeant Accosted assessed the situation and spit out sweet tobacco juice, unknowingly, all over my hand.

"Fall in where my voice is!" he shouted over scared thoughts and scattered rifle fire.

We scurried to our god and carried out his orders. "Corporal Montone up," he barked.

"Yes, Sergeant," Corporal Montone said.

"You position over on the right with your gun team. Spray a wall of lead all across our front in the attack. Once we settle in, keep it at fifty percent watch," Sergeant Accosted said.

"Aye, aye, Sergeant," Corporal Montone agreed.

"All right, ladies, hold fuckin hands, and let's get a movin."

Although we couldn't even see each other, we did just as Sergeant Accosted commanded; we grabbed at each other's hands like scared children and found our way to the front of the track by touching and feeling like blind boys. Once we reached the front of the track, we all got on line, and Sergeant Accosted yelled, "Forward, march!" We clutched each other's paws in a bizarre alien land and sauntered straight forward one hundred feet into the mystery of a black hole. We interlocked with the weight of many universes on our shoulders and our combined strength soaked into our bones. We were transformed into one giant Marine with one giant heart, all the same, scared fuckin shitless, yet controlling the fear; tired, yet controlling the exhaustion—no complaints, only faith: faith that Sergeant Accosted knew what the fuck he was doing.

"Squad, halt!" We simultaneously set down our gear and lay down, unsure of what the night and next dark day had in store for us, but we knew this: we were scared, we were united, and so we were hard. We were going to be fine no matter what happened.

Seventeen Marines faced their weapons outboard and flopped down on the soft sand to continue challenging themselves and more mere mortal men.

:: :: ::

Two days later the "Mother of all wars" was over. Headquarters put us in charge of securing Iraqi bunkers and armories in Kuwait City. We rolled in, broke down doors, and jumped into fighting holes looking for Iraqis who hadn't surrendered. When we stumbled across a giant armory of Iraqi weapons, we blew everything inside to kingdom come. We patrolled the city in daytime that was nighttime (because of the burning oil wells), and at night we stood around and bullshitted in blackness.

Then we got the word. Something that was unbelievable to most ears. "We're going home!" Since we were the first Marines to land in Saudi Arabia and the spear that went into Kuwait, we would be the first ones out. The government big boys back home wanted to show off the pride of the country and milk out this victory; we would make up for the Vietnam loss twenty years earlier. So, surprised, still in war mode, we rushed back over into the Saudi desert blowing shit up along the way. We bumped along inside the track boasting about all the beer we would drink and all the bitches we'd fuck. Doubting that we were normal again.

Once in Jubayl, we stayed there playing spades for a day and then hopped on a beautiful white and blue freedom bird. Military authorities didn't even do a strict search for contraband. It seemed like they just wanted us back in the States without any hassles. It was quick; it was too much, too easy. We made pit stops in France, Ireland, and New York. In New York, through the airport fence, we saw mobs of people welcoming us home, but we didn't have a chance to get close to them cause as soon as we touched down and kissed the ground, we had to get back on the plane and head over to Camp Pendleton. When we got off the plane in California, it was mayhem. Crowding the streets and sidewalks were mobs of people trying to touch us as if we were gods. At about three in the afternoon, we loaded up on white buses to get over to Camp Pendleton, which was about fifty miles away, but not without girls pushing their hands in the windows of the bus and old geezers handing us cases of Budweiser. I latched onto one girl's hand, and as we pulled off I didn't let go. The bus sped up, and I dragged her along the road for a little while. It was going to be over for the sweetheart that gave her *corazon* to me.

"Pass me a beer!" I shouted.

"How about a few, motherfuckin Toro?!"

"Let's do a shotgun!" someone yelled.

As everyone got ready to down their beer, Gunny Animo toasted, "First of all, lock the fuck up!" Our company Gunnery Sergeant lifted his beer up. "For the old timers, for the Dogs I was with over in Nam that didn't get no celebration but a spit in the face." He scanned the eyes on the bus. "We're winners now, and they love us. We're alive, and they didn't see what you all have seen. They're happy it was nice, simple, and clean. They're glad that they didn't have to suffer through your eyes. And I'm glad too cause I guess that's the way it's supposed to be. We did what we had to do and no one's gone. I'm here on this day I never expected, never asked for." And maybe there was a stutter in his voice. "Semper Fi." For a moment, we sat without drinking our beers. In that moment I knew we knew we would never be the same again. No one else would ever understand nothing or want to understand nothing except this homecoming, this parade, this good time—only we would be left with floppy fish, bombs dropping, burned bodies, and the memory of being scared like only Marines can be scared. Only we would live with the legacy of an experience that doesn't compare to anything else on Earth, that only few people have known. I downed my beer with a lump in my throat.

Outside, cars honked, people met us at every corner with "Welcome Home" signs, and lights flashed on and off. Now it was night, and we were bogged down in official red tape at the gates of Pendleton. Not even a week earlier we had been in a World War One–style war zone.

"Damn, I got to take a piss," I crossed my legs to dam up the ready river.

"Fuck, so do I," Corporal Montone concurred. No one had been used to drinking beer for the past seven months.

"We aint gonna get off this bitch for a while," Totem complained.

"Shit, I didn't piss my pants during the war, and I'll be damned if I'm gonna start being a punk now!" I said.

"Adapt and overcome," Sergeant Accosted said. He poured his water out the window and pissed inside his canteen. Everyone followed his lead.

The bus finally roared onto the road outside of Camp Pendleton's barracks. It was home. No transitions, just from one mission to the next. Front line fire to home.

"All right, settle the fuck down! Get off the bus and give me platoon formations. Make sure you got all your gear, and lock your asses up!" Gunny Animo shouted.

Still caked with desert dirt and dust, we filed off the bus. No one had showered in over three months. A memento of the chemical protective suits that we wore during the offensive, black charcoal soot clung to our desert camouflage uniforms. We clanked into formation with our immaculate rifles, machine guns, and SMAW's. No one spoke. My hands sweating, jaw tight, I was overcome with anticipation, happiness, fear, and longing; longing for a world that could offer me beer, bitches, and a warm bed to lie down in after seven months of living like a homeless bum. I almost wanted to get back on the bus, get back to the shit. "Paradise," Totem sighed.

But paradise was something else, wasn't it?

An orange. We had dug our makeshift-graves-slash-fighting-holes one night back in August, when we had first got there. Every day was so damn nasty, could hardly fuckin breathe cause the heat hurt my lungs so bad, and I thought that with my hole everything would get better. I dug it deep and wide and tried to make it as comfortable as possible. I molded a seat into the sand and even made a little table for my ammo. So I slept, woke up and ate chow, my neck and legs stiff, living in my hole. I gazed out at the eternal desert and opened up a book, *Marine Sniper.* By nine in the morning it was 120 degrees, and I couldn't read no more. I tried to lay as still as possible because every movement took away energy and made me sweat a bucket. By ten I'm singing songs in my head and lying in this barbeque pit. My water is like boiling coffee, but there's nothing I could do about it, so I imagine to pass the time. Thinking's the worst torture.

Medals, oh man, I thought, *if we get into the shit, I'll get a Combat Action Ribbon. OK, that's cool, a fuckin salad bowl on my chest just like Chesty Puller. I'm gonna have hella saved up money and buy me a bad ass lowrider—a 64 or a Monte Carlo. OK, I'm bad, cruising down* Montaña *jamming to the homeboy oldies, drinking a freezing fuckin forty, and blowing out O's from my cigarette. Yeah. Mom's gonna be proud. She's gonna give me a hug, and I'm gonna stand there hard core in my sharp uniform. Everything I've ever done will be forgiven, and she'll talk good about me and not insult me to all of her friends.*

OK, I feel dizzy. I aint sweating. That's not good. I'm fucking cold. That's bad. But man, I'm going to see all them bitches—Tricky Trina, Big Titty Bernadette, and See Saw Sally. All of em. All of em at the same time. Trina sucking the nuts, Sally on the head, and me making out with Bernadette's beautiful titties. On a comfortable ass waterbed. Aint never been on one, but I'll slice that shit up and drink all that water inside. Cold ass water and fine ass bitches. OK, my dick's hard, that's good, and my nut shoots off, but I've wasted too much energy. One hundred thirty degrees now and I'm cold, but I can't stand the heat. What the fuck is left out there?

Oh God, oh God, help me—just get me the fuck out of here—fuck all that shit. I don't want no glory, I don't want no pussy; give that lowrider to someone else. I'll be good. No more favors, no more fuckin favors—just this, just this, just leave me in the gutter in rags, just put me back on a street corner with no change in my pocket, and let me be. Just one drop of cold water. Just a slice of shade for my face. Do it now, God. Do it now, for Christ's sake.

I was in despair, human misery like I had never known—physical and mental torture, being cooked in a pit, *downed all my water and don't know when the water truck is coming, might as well be next year.* Loaded M16, *is that sweat streaming down my face?* And then there's something flying into my hole. Frag! I kicked it into my grenade sump and threw myself to the other side of my grave-hole waiting for a BOOM. And it must have been hours that I stayed balled up in the corner of that hole. Seconds or minutes it couldn't have been, cause my life flashed before my eyes, and I saw myself drowning at a lake as a kid, and damn if that wasn't heaven! All my happiness and all of my sadness and all the good and bad flashed through me, and there was nothing left but to jump on the frag and get it over with.

So I did, but nothing went off. I peeked into that grenade sump, and there was brightness that blinded, fluorescence that guided the way. An orange orange. Bright, bright, beautiful orange, fat like a grapefruit, round like the planet, plump like Trina's tits, heavy like a 64 Impala Super Sport, proud like my dress blues with medals on my chest, loving like my mother's touch. I embraced that orange, didn't rip it apart without respect. I was a good Marine. I snapped to attention for it, polished it shiny, and saluted it. I opened it up by the book, by the regulations under the *Code of Conduct*, and it was oh so cold, and there was no paradise except it; there was no perfection except each section, each juicy unit of hope. And God had answered my prayers.

"Right face!"

I was back in Camp Pendleton. Bravo Company was back in the USA, and we did a right face, tall and straight and no more fucking around, eyes alert to the next mission. "Forward, march!" And we stepped, stepped onto American soil on a beautiful night in March of 1991. "Left, right, left foot, right!" Gunny Animo shouted. And damn they were booming out the *Marines' Hymn:* "From the Halls of Montezuma to the shores of Tripoli…" And damn every Marine that was on that base made two columns for us to march through, and God bless them, they saluted us, saluted us fucking sand rats, us stinking ass pigs, me, a low down dirty bull. I marched forward, charged forward as always, and there is nothing that could ever compare to that feeling in my whole life, no million dollars that I would trade in for not being able to walk in that formation with all my fellow Devil Dogs on that star filled night.

After the welcome back speech from the commanding General,

crowds of civilians exploded with cheers.

"Battalion, dismissed!"

Wives and families searched for their loves. Girls along for the sideshow hugged and kissed Marines at random. Everywhere there was squeezing and slobbering. I got in some licks and kicks, but I ran into Corporal Montone and Deckdog and came up with a great idea.

"Let's go over to the Enlisted Club and tear up some whiskey and women!" I said.

"Aint got no money. We won't get checks until tomorrow. Hell, we aint even got a place to sleep, and we smell like shit," Corporal Montone had assessed the situation.

"Motherfuckin Marine combat leader!" I looked into Corporal Montone's expressionless face. "The fucking war's over! We'll bust some windows and sleep in some warm ass, cushioned cars. We'll wash our asses with whiskey, and I don't know about you, but I'm a have one of them bar bitches lick me clean!"

"Yeah, but what about cash?" Deckdog asked, scratching the stubble around his face.

"Man, cash is for country folks. We got authentic Marine Corps combat uniforms that will sell for millions! We better hurry before someone else gets the same bright idea."

Once we got into the crowded bar, we didn't need to sell our uniforms. There were hundreds of base Marines, Marines that hadn't gone to the war (mostly reservists), willing to poison us with as much liquor as we wanted. Everyone stood in line to talk to us and shake our hands and tell us what a great job we did. I kept hearing "Thanks" and "You guys kicked ass" all night long. We got trashed, danced with bar girls, and I threw up on the old Filipino lady that I was spinning around. Seven o'clock in the morning and we headed over to the company headquarters but didn't even bother walking in. We sprawled our asses out on the pavement and slept like babies. Savage ass babies.

The next afternoon I flew to the *varrio*. I didn't call or say nothing. Just went over to my mom's little hole in the wall and knocked on the door. Eight p.m. and no one was there. She and my little sister Letty must've still been working. My Dress Blues against my brown skin, I strolled down to Tip Top's, our corner bar, and ordered a healthy Bloody Mary. Sitting at the nearly empty bar, I realized that this was the *varrio* welcome. As I was firing up a Marlboro, the old washed up, bony homeboy Rusty walked through the double doors.

"Ay, homes, what's up? You join the navy or some shit?" Rusty's face was sucked in and his eyes seemed as if they were going to pop out of his head.

"It's the Marines. I just got back."

"From where? Where you been?"

"Living a king's life in biblical places. Kuwait City."

"Is that down south? I just got out one of them lousy pens my damn self."

"It's another country, Rusty, but fuck that shit. You seen any of the homies around?"

"Lobo's hustling some shit down at the park. Santo's kickin it with his lady, you know, that crazy broad."

"*Orale*, let's take a walk," I said.

As we walked to *Bajo* Park, I loosened up my collar and popped some buttons loose. I saw Lobo talking to some young white folks at the corner. I knew he had something going on the sly. I sat down at the bus stop and waited for him to finish. He handed over a fake ass gold chain and ring over to the white dude. The blondie that was with dude gave him a hug. Lobo snatched bills and looked over my way. He slid over with a smile on his face.

"Motherfucker! Can't believe my black eyes. Toro's looking like royalty with gold fuckin buttons. Hero and shit." When he put out his gold-ringed hand, I knew that he was genuinely happy to see me.

"It aint no old faded picture. In the flesh. Just come back from the war, Bro."

"No shit, which one?" Lobo asked.

"Man, I heard that shit was all over the news. Where the fuck you been?"

"Right here," Lobo, with hair greased back and handsome face blank, was serious.

"Enough said, caveman, where's *El Santo?*"

"Ah, Bro, that motherfucker's trippin. It's like he's all whupped on that bitch or some shit, you know, Maricela. He don't know how to keep his dick on check."

"What you been up to?" I put my arm around his thin shoulder.

"Same ol, same ol. You know how we do it. I just scored on some fare; we could go buy a *leño* or some shit, go kick it." He pulled out the crumpled cash he had just made.

"I don't smoke dust anymore, Bro. I'm in the Corps now, but we could go handle some beers and Bloody Marys if you're down."

"Where the fuck you say you been? Don't never question my ground, homes," Lobo looked at me hard.

"Shut the fuck up, bitch, before I backhand your punk ass."

Lobo grinned. "I always know I got a good homeboy in you, Bro. Sissy ass motherfucker. Why you all dressed up for, looking all sexy, aint no one out here but the con men and hookers."

"I just got back from the war, Lobo. In Kuwait with all the Iraqis."

"Did you kill anyone?" His chin tilted up.

"Didn't have to, Bro. They all gave up or were dead by the time we got there."

"That's cool. So you guys kicked ass then, eh? Yeah, that's cool, Toro. That's what counts," Lobo said this and patted me on my shoulders. I didn't like how it felt, like if he was patting a dog on his head. Even though Lobo was about three inches taller than me, I knew I could put his lanky ass down on the floor. But Lobo was my homeboy.

So we bought a jug full of tequila. After we were all wasted and puking out on the streets, the cops pulled up, shining their flashlights on us as if we were movie stars.

"Hey, buddy, you all right?" Buddy, that's right, the gray haired cop called me "buddy."

"Yes, sir. Fine as can be."

"Where you staying at, Jarhead, maybe we can help you out."

"You mean I'm not under arrest?"

The cops laughed. "No, buddy, looks like you got a Combat Action Ribbon on that uniform. You're straight with us. Figure you just got back from the scuffle in the Middle East."

"Yes, Sir. That's right."

"Great fucking job, Devil Dog. You guys kicked them fucking Ragheads asses up and down the block. Stuck it to em good. We're proud of you. We need more people like you to go and kick ass like that around here." The quarterback looking rookie said this smiling.

"That's my homeboy back from the days, homes," Lobo burped then fell back on the sidewalk. The cops looked at him as if he was the lowest slime on Earth.

"One word of advice there, Gyrene: Lose the dead weight," the potbellied cop said.

"Yeah, we need Marines, not bums," the rookie said as I pulled out a smoke.

"You got duty now. To everyone around here. They're gonna look up to you when you walk down the block, not look away cause they're scared, but they're gonna look to you for strength. You've proved it in the toughest outfit around. Don't let misinterpreted duty get you on the wrong path," the old cop said this as he massaged my shoulder with his right hand. I stood stiff and soaked in his words.

"You aint realized it yet, buddy, but you're gonna see you're different now," the rookie added. "You aint on the same level as these punks around here. You think they could've done what you've done? Discipline and shit? Hell no." The rookie spread his arms around the entire neighborhood. "You're different and you're changed, and I don't even know who you are. You probably don't even know who you are anymore. You're the American dream, straight up American champ-een, spick or not. One of us. A good guy." The rookie offered me a light.

"Yes, Sir," was all that I could say.

How wrong could that rookie be? The next day I lost my footing forever. The next day was the end of the world: a soft, sunny March afternoon in 1991. The next day came, and the three homeboys got together for old times sake, for sorrow's sake, to enjoy the day and reunite after over a year of not kicking it together. We got together to forget about war and violence, but we could never forget who we were or the pact of brotherhood that bonded us. How could we forget the pain that enveloped us? And so if one homeboy's hurtin, I got to hurt with him too. Aint that my duty? Santo, I aint looking down on him, cause he would never look down on me, he was hurting, and maybe he was strong too. Maybe the confusion of being both at the same time was just too much. Because he was unstable, we were all walking wobbly. Or maybe we had really lost balance the first time we ever took a step.

Even after that *familia* in the park shit, even after my heart was forever black; people, average Joes and straight aces, still only saw a good guy with a shiny uniform on; they couldn't see more than the outside. That rookie cop was right in a way. It hadn't hit me yet, but I wasn't the same anymore. I wasn't better than anyone else. The war taught me that, but I sure wasn't the same old Toro that didn't think at all anymore. That's what all the hugs and kisses, cheers, and hook ups were about. War heroes. We had kicked ass, trampled the enemy oh so bad. No, we hadn't suffered too damn much, hadn't bled for our countries like the Iraqis. We were the winners by a rout. Killing, straight up, no other word for what had happened over there; killing is what made us heroes. Half naked, starving men surrendering before us in the middle of a smoky desert made us big shots. Violence, force, brutal power made me a symbol of victory. But, damn, wasn't this the kind of shit I used to do before the Corps? Wasn't this the same kind of mentality that had *gente* locked up and getting executed?

Sure fucking was. Same fucking thing, no—worse. Worse or maybe, actually, better cause like the copper said, I was different now. Different cause I knew how to cause mass destruction—make people run and hide. Discipline gave me that gift. Discipline is the instant willing obedience to orders, respect for authority, and self reliance, Sir. Had that drilled into me a million times over, and it was a part of me now.

It would be part of the homeboys too cause I wasn't just gonna leave them to die. I would incorporate my new theories about what a good unit should be like to the homies. I'd be a *vato loco* Marine, a solid street soldier. Violence for the Corps made me accepted in all worlds, and there was no other way that I would have gotten that respect even with a million bucks. It would have to be violence that would give the *varrio* their proper respect. Violence was the universal key. Violence and death is what good guys were all about. With my experience and training, I would make sure we would be the best.

I'm glad I was able to get the fuck out of the hood after that *familia* beat down. I knew shit was getting out of control, yet I had a valid reason for running away. With fire in my soul, a substitution for the punishment I deserved, I went back to finish out the last six months in my active duty contract. Real deal loyalty and blood and guts bravery. That's what must be emulated. That's what must be taught. Corporal Montone, Sergeant Accosted, Gunny Animo—they all immediately got out of the Suck, while I pumped overseas for the last time. Straight up international troubler. I was put in charge of my own Fleet Marine Squad. Once again I was the leader, and once again I was a nutty bastard. Up in the morning before the rising sun and shouting my ass off—always motivated to wake up even though everyone else was bitching and moaning. Run a 10K at five in the morning, sit out in the pouring rain in the middle of dense jungles or rugged mountains: mainland Japan, Mount Fuji in late April, climbing to the tip of a holy volcano, stoned out guards all over the place, lions with menacing roars across their faces, and I thought to myself, some hard ass samurais had to hump all that shit up there.

And like it must have been for them, for us it was just another hump, another hill. That's the way it always is. You go up to reach the top, just to come down and go up another one. It never gets boring, never gets easy. It's always hard, always a bitch, always fucking singing on the flat lands. That's how it was that cold morning, idiots singing on the green flat land, talking shit about how this aint shit. But they didn't sing long. No, cause we start at the bottom, always start at the very heat of hell. We got to hump to the snow line. That's what Marines do. That's how we get to heaven; we walk there.

So the songs were loud and the melody was nice, but I know better—been through this a thousand times, and I aint opening my mouth for shit cause I'm conserving my energy, saving my huffing and puffing for the big tit that this mountain is. I'll be sucking on this hill as if I were a baby, and words don't fill my stomach with energy—words don't do shit but make me think I got it all knocked out—just like those fools that sang. Shit, the civilians walking on that Japanese treasure must have thought we were Boy Scouts. Some even smiled. But it turned into an hour straight up, then there were no more songs, only sorrow, only grunts and bitches, and hard core puppies, the new guys with illusions of painful beauty, talking bout "You got to love it" shit that some fool in Boot Camp brainwashed them with. But I tell em truth, "No, no." I open my mouth so they could learn, so that I could teach it to them before they die, "You aint got to love shit. You just got to hack it." We reach the second hour of straight up hill, and I'm a damn M60 gunner, humping the heaviest weapon in the outfit, humping and struggling cause it never gets easy, even for a salty dog like myself.

Flies falling out of the sky—that's what we were, but the skipper just keeps on chugging along cause he knows that time don't stop for no one. By now there's just the few and the true right in front—about ten of us—the rest of the company is straggling like bums up the mountain. But us ten, we kept it tight. Tight. And I'm just looking at the hard ground and my fast feet moving, sweat raining down on the deck, no thoughts cause thinking can only slow me down. I sing a song in my head for a second, imagine soft thighs the next, absorb the world around me the next, and it stays like that. Focus—that tree—get up to that tree, and I pass the tree, and then it's the next mark, the next goal, the only goal that matters—the right now—the right here—the eternal moment—cause the pain don't stop, and stopping makes it even harder.

A stop makes it hard cause it only teases; it only laughs at your battered bones and broken back. We stop, and I'm asking my Jugheads how's it goin on water, how's it feel on pride, steam rising off heads. I tell them not to sit down cause then it will be harder to get back up. We walk in place. We walk in place, and this is rest. I take the radio off a Boot's back cause can't no one make it up to the top with it except the little brown boy with the big tattoo on his back. And it feels good to hear whispers and praises that I'm the best humper in the platoon. It feels good that anywhere else I wouldn't be shit, but here I can carry a machine gun and a radio, and I got more respect than the President of the United States. The people straggling up the hill don't get no break cause once they reach us our break is over, and they're left behind again. Cause mission accomplishment is the name of the game. It's what gives us our fame. Marines.

He was a butter bar—a Boot lieutenant straight out of Officer Candidates School. White dove, hard pup. It doesn't matter he's only been in three months, doesn't matter cause he's in charge cause he gots a college degree; he's the leader, or so he thinks—he's the *gentleman*, the example to us all for some absurd reason—but I don't question it cause that's just the way it's been going for over two hundred fifteen years of Marine Corps history. But I glance to my side and see him gasping. I look at myself and remember how hard it was when I first tried—tried to fly. I stood on that cliff, put on my cape, and jumped. I tried, and I died. A horrible death, a beautiful beginning—the slaughter of innocence, the birth of brutality. The hard way. The only way. I looked at myself because I saw that butter bar wasn't gonna make it up that mountain and no one could help him cause he was the man, the shot caller, and it was just expected of him to make it up that bitch, unheard of that a man of "Sir" status would topple. Everyone else could be forgiven cause they were just dogs, damn grunts stuck in the shit.

I looked at him but couldn't kick him up his ass. I couldn't tell him what a punk he was or con him up with loud lures. No, it had to be soft. It had to be gentle; it had to be words between gentlemen. One human to another. Tears formed in his eyes as he was falling back, bridging a gap between Marines—the ultimate sin on a forced march, up a hill, cause space is disgrace. Tightness—unity—glued together fragments of men climbing up to heaven; that is perfection. But we were gonna lose him, and that was it. No one would say shit cause we all had enough problems of our own. Mission accomplishment—the first objective of any real Marine.

"*Corazon*," I murmur. "*Corazon*, Sir," I whisper.

"*Corazon!*" he responds. "*Corazon!*" He understands.

And there was more hill, and more mountain, and all around us no one else seemed to give a fuck cause everyone had to handle their own. All I had was one whisper to help that man. Cause loud shouts can only get you so far. The kicks in the ass only reach the stars. But heaven is above the stars. And if you're headed up, then you know the air is thin. There's no air to waste, no time to waste, no room to waste in this little sardine can we call the world. When every day you remember that you've seen shit happen before, you know that ultimately it's all up to one thing that can make any difference at all. It all depends on the master of the universe, or the destroyer of it. It's gonna happen only if there's one soul that smiles—the bull—cause you just do it. Somehow, someway, you just get the fuck up there—cause aint no one helping. Aint no one caring when they got the same problems you got, and if you give up, if you fall the fuck back, the team still gots to handle that mission. Each and every one of them.

Corazon. I think the sound of those words will make it up to heaven before I do.

Corazon.

And *corazon* seems to be that link when nothing else can make that difference. Butter bar made it, and it was unity, togetherness, the solution to all problems. Our problem is a mission, something to attain no matter what it is—a hill, a level, a new realm. No fucking analysis—just each man taking care of his business, doing what's expected. We didn't answer any profound questions that cold day climbing up Fuji, and we didn't solve the problems of the whole fuckin world. Cause we don't do that. We're not priests. We're not healers. We're destroyers of others. That makes us who we will always be, and I'll never be ashamed of it, never lose that pride. Cause no matter what else happens in life—highs or lows—I did something, and if it wasn't this it would have been the homeboy cause, the prison revolver; I'm glad it was this. I learned to love my fellow man, yet I never had to say it, never had to pretend—cause it was proven every morning I woke—sometimes shouting, sometimes miserable and homesick, but every morning I rose because we all needed to rise and get the shit done.

I can't even remember butter bar's name, but I know that on top of that snow covered volcano, we got just a little closer to heaven even though we were still a billion miles from it.

Always kicking people in their ass, and sometimes the elements trying to kick mine. Sometimes lonely, sometimes sad, sometimes losing my mind, but always with a straight face, never let anyone into my dreams or nightmares because let me tell you—the war haunted, but I always fought back with what I knew worked: sweat and solid drink.

Climbing the days and shrinking in height—before I knew it I was short enough to fit under the door crack. Single digit midget—Short Timer, the most sought after title in the Corps—four years of counting down comes to an end, so tiny that no one can even see me anymore. I was still a Lance Corporal cause of all the ass I had to kick, no raise in three and a half years for making sure my Marines were in line. But the sergeants would still come up to me for advice about the gun, how to employ it effectively, what should we do for PT today, Toro? Great time, fuckers. Tears and beers and won't forget it. Don't know what I've done. Everything is valid. All is moral and righteous as long as the shit gets accomplished, as long as we got time for beers and bitches afterwards. That's what I ask for—no, that's what I deserve—cause who the fuck else is gonna do it?

Little old ladies love driving their big old Cadillacs, but are they gonna take that nest for some gasoline; they gonna go live in the jungles? We all eat that shit sandwich that is this world. We all are to blame and question in the biggest wars ever fought and those biggest wars that we've always won. Lest we forget who we are. Lest we play ignorant about what this all means. Humanity goes out the window cause we all need more spaceships and rocket fuel and more chips and speed. In return, for my efforts, all I ask for is a glass of hops and a drop of pussy.

I got out on August 8, 1991. The Corps gave me some medals that I put in a glass case. It was my first night out, my first night back in the *varrio*, just in time for the attack. The medals were all shiny—gold and green and bronze and blue—and they were all fallen down cause I didn't pin them up, just did a half ass job with some tape. I didn't pretend that they were fancy or nice, and Lobo and Santo walks into Mom's spot, my old room, and Lobo gives me a hug and…

"Ay, you should hang those bad boys up, Bro, make them tight and pretty, straighten them the fuck up, homes."

I looked at Lobo and saw that he was serious. "No, Lobo," I said, "that's not how I earned em, Bro. They're not pinned right cause I wasn't pinned right. I earned em in the pits, and that's why they should dangle—always be twisted and fallen down cause that's the reality."

"Then you should just sell them fuckers, man. You aint gonna treasure em, let em go. Just like I got this sweet baby now, Sheila; but fuck her if I aint gonna enjoy her gorgeous face."

"It's true love, Bro, that's why I aint never gonna change em. How the fuck would it be if just cause I saw you lying in the gutter I sold you out? Just like if this bitch was your true love; would you pimp her out? Nah, they lay and they stay, *por vida*."

"Fucking dude," Lobo paused and tried to chuckle it off. "I think you took too many hits of that gas shit when you were in the war. You don't make no sense, but who gives a fuck, you still a silly ass sissy if I ever knew one, and I wants me some cow tonight, baby." Lobo blew me a kiss.

Reality check.

I knew something heavy was coming down. I felt it hard just like I felt it when we went into Kuwait, just like that *familia* shit. But I was prepared. I mean, I did the Corps for something, for all of them too. Cause I knew one day I'd have to come back, and there was no more safety of combat in another land to run to. I had to fight the demons that were in my own backyard; I knew that when I was seventeen years old—knew that I wasn't strong enough then to do anything to really help. I needed training for this moment that I knew would come, for the hell I knew I deserved.

I had infiltrated behind lines. I went to the Corps and learned all I could about the objectives of leadership: 1. Mission Accomplishment. Number fucking one priority of any true Devil Dog. 2. Troop Welfare—cause you just don't leave the homies to die. And I was back, just in time for the attack, and what was I gonna say, "See you later, Bros." Like some fuckin chump, and what the fuck would a Marine think about leaving his best friends in the heat of combat? But we would do this right. We would come out as winners, just like in the war, cause I was fuckin special now. I was one of the privileged of veteran status. I earned it. I carried my military ID everywhere I went, and the cops would pull me over yet let me go cause they thought I was one of them. They thought there was such a thing as brainwashing going on in this world, and they thought that a dumb little brown boy like me couldn't help but get brainwashed in the big bad Marine Corps. "Aye, aye, Sir," I say it louder and prouder, and I fool the whole world with my horns and my blank stare, and you can go ahead and stick me hard in the chops, and I won't do nothin but blow steam through my nose and fall flat at your feet.

Fool!

I was born to be killed, and we all got to go one way or another. Fool!

Do we live forever? You beat me, and I fall, but I rise. I rise because you always challenge me, always think you're gonna stick my heart. There's no getting away from it. But it's always me, always me. I never change. I never run away. And I'll be a damn idiot and a damn bore, not complicated at all. And still you challenge me, and think every time I'll fall, and like a fool you don't know that's when I rise and strike. I strike and you change—you change!

Fool!

Because I didn't take you for granted because I knew that your lust for life was unsure. You don't know if you can rise. You didn't and don't know where the fuck you're going or who the fuck you are, and shit, it's time to meet your maker, you...

Fool!

Time to look at that bull right in the mouth. And I'm there. And now you don't know if you're the matador or the meat, but I never have that problem cause I don't care if I'm eaten or worn, barbecued or boiled. I rise to the ring. And I don't ever run away. I just get stronger.

Lobo's kiss flew through the air but never made its mark. Instead, I turned to Santo.

"Santo, it's been awhile, but always good to see you." I said it, and there were no more formalities. We hugged and shook hands like always, and it was good to feel his grip was solid.

"I only know that with you here now there's nothing that can go wrong." Knowing our doom, Santo held his forty ounce up. "Most of all, toast to the strong. Here's to the bonds of homeboy ho-nor."

I looked at Santo funny cause the last word didn't sound right, and he knew.

"Cause ho-nor is with a loud H," Santo continued, "like Ha Ha, like Horror with a Loud H. The H shouts, and the word honor comes from the root word ho, like a bitch, like the finest bitch you've ever seen. Listen: HO-NOR, but maybe you can't hear it, Lobo," Santo said.

Lobo was laughing.

"Maybe you can't hear the noise cause you don't listen," Santo spoke softly. "Cause you got to live it to hear it, like this man right here," Santo put his hand on my back. "Listen loud and clear with no other choice but to listen to that bomb blast." Suddenly Santo started jumping up and down and going BOOM! BOOM! "See, Lobo, when you hear it like that there is only one thing to do but stop and calm the fuck down cause otherwise you're done for, I'm quite fuckin sure, cause to hear it like it's supposed to be heard means that you've learned more than and better than the dictionaries, and that is horror, and that is true ho-nor."

Lobo rolled around on the floor laughing, but he managed to say, "Sick Santo and the horse he rode in on! You aint never gonna change."

Santo stayed straight faced, and I helped Lobo up off the floor. Lobo helped me down.

Brown down. Almost a month later. Lying in a hospital bed after war with warriors. Before that night, Friday night, September 13, 1991, I'd been busy with infiltrating further in the hierarchy at a place called "School," a great cover, paid for by veterans' benefits. I'd started out the semester with a whole bunch of general education classes, and I wasn't doing too bad. I guess all those dime novels and war books that I'd read over the years in the Corps had

142

helped. Had to read them in order to prevent myself from going crazy in the reality of the Suck. That Friday afternoon, though, I had gone to the abandoned shack and found Santo living in his hole in the living room, a hole I helped him dig. We then went to get something to eat and saw Lobo in the welfare line. When I seen them both, all three of us together, I knew it was the moment that we had all dreaded, even though all of us acted as if we didn't know what was happening, as if that day was just another day given to us, that we wouldn't have to pay back anything on that day. Lobo had a plan, something about Chinatown.

Now I was down, incapacitated. And I was happy! Ecstatic! I wouldn't have to take part in the offensive, and it was justified! I couldn't move. My leg was broken split. I had charged and trampled and been trounced on by many matadors. There was nothing I could do for Lobo or against any Chinese. No one could expect anything of me now. I was safe lying down in that hospital bed, yet I was not safe lying down in that bed.

As I slept, the darkness overcame. Out of the black, there were flashes of light, shakes of the ground, a basketball bouncing—bing-bing—a shot being made—more than three points. Running and punching and gas masked men passing the ball to one another, and Ramsey had it, and he passed it to me, but I didn't want his ball, and I passed it off to someone else, but they were all me. We were all the same in the masks—all me and Ramsey—passing the ball back and forth to each other in gas masks, and it was time for the attack, and I grabbed my M60, and jumped out of the track and cut the corner, but there was nothing out there. I was the only man on the whole front line. Wiping the dust away from my gas mask lenses, I saw the stampede. The bulls charged out of the morning mist. I fired. Six to eight round bursts. And they came at me, a horde of bulls, so I free gunned it right there. I no longer controlled the ammunition—fully automatic. All in front of me they fell, but they kept coming harder and multiplying faster. As they got closer, I knew that they would win. I fired, but it was useless. I stood up and pulled out my KA-BAR knife for close combat. Strangely, they just passed me by. They ran right through me, to an orange ball bouncing in the sand—horns at the objective—the bulls moved in for the kill, and the ball bounced up and down, and then a great "Pssst" sounded from the air coming out.

I scattered for breath. I moved for life.

His halo shining, Santo was looking down at me, saying "Pssst." Abruptly, the face became Lobo's.

"Toro," Lobo whispered. "Come on."

And I still thought it was a dream cause I couldn't believe he would ask me to come on, as if all was fine, as if I didn't have a valid excuse for being knocked the fuck out of commission.

"What?" I said. And Lobo was a Drill Instructor playing jokes cause I could have sworn he said it was reveille. But I knew he'd never been in the Suck, so he didn't have the proper authority to kick me out of a nice warm bed.

"Yeah, that's right, snap the fuck to and get your ass up. We got a mission," Lobo said. Lobo always had these big old eyes, so he'd always seen really well. I could not figure out why he would insult me in such a way, why he wouldn't see that I could not move.

"Get the fuck out of here," I said. "I'm all fucked up. I'll be lucky if I ever even walk again." The room spun around ninety miles an hour, so I had to clutch onto the bedpost to keep from falling off. Smiling, Lobo spoke, but all I could decipher was his conviction that I was to go somewhere with him. "Lobo, I aint hearing shit. I'm out," I said. Santo's halo blinded me.

144

"Toro needs to be right here," Santo said.

Lobo's face dropped in defeat, his head down, his hands turned into balls, and then his chin rose in victory, a victory at all costs. "Toro needs to be with us, homes," Lobo did not smile, and he looked at my face. "What you gonna do, lay down and get better? Aint no better between us—aint no better since that day in the park, and we've been zombies walking the Earth since then—pretending this day would never come. You know that. All I've ever had is the chase; all you've ever had is the charge."

The charge. Who would I be without the charge, without the rush? I wasn't slick enough to be like Lobo, wasn't holy enough to be a saint. Namelessness, obscurity, no one. The charge defined me and gave me all the pleasures and notoriety I so dreamed of as a boy. It was the charge that would remain long after I was to be taken away from this place. With the charge as my only legacy, I couldn't turn my back just because the mission was impossible. The impossible had never stopped me before.

"What can I do?" I asked. Lobo's face lit up, and he was talking about gold in Chinatown, and the next thing I knew I was wheeling myself down the hall, and then I was on top of the mountain smoking my first *leño* since I got out the Corps. Best medicine in the world for battered bulls. Funny thing is, I was no longer a bull, but a cow staring out into green pastures and stupidly grazing in the grass, not knowing, not caring that the butcher was plotting what part of me he would have on his dinner table that night. Me, just mooing in and out of consciousness, hearing rumblings and grumblings between Santo and Lobo, but that didn't matter to me.

I only know that it was the darkest part of the morning when I heard Lobo ask, "Where can we get some heavy shit, shit that will stop and put us on top? These Chinamen don't play."

I was still high as a motherfucker, but I knew it was time to prepare for battle. Gunny Animo was a good old, down home loony tune who knew the end was coming soon. We had been through the war together and drank a few toasts to a very Merry Christmas and a chug a lug to the impending Apocalypse. The old toad didn't know where I was coming from as far as the street scene was concerned, but he knew I was down, and he respected me for my heart. Before he retired, he had given me some grid coordinates and a map and told me he had it all set up for the invasion. I could join his camp whenever I wanted, he said. He would always be there.

So, we loaded up in the car and drove, and I timed myself to sleep for an hour. I was now in combat mode. When I woke up, the wind was slapping my face and the new sunshine was baking my head. I pulled out the crumpled up map from my wallet. We were twenty miles from the first rally point. We hit that spot, and I told Lobo to pull over off the rough, unpaved road and drive between some trees. I told Santo and Lil Toon, our star runt and kidnap victim, to rip off some branches and bushes and cover up the car from the road as much as possible. Lobo hunted for some strong pieces of wood to use as part of a stretcher. We slipped Lil Toon and Santo's jackets through the long tree branches, and they placed me onto the makeshift stretcher. They fastened some rope around me to secure me from falling, and I held on tight.

Our journey began.

SEVEN

El Santo

Do not think I have come to bring peace to the earth;
I have not come to bring peace, but a sword.
For I have come to set a man
against his father,
and a daughter against her mother...
and one's foes will be members of one's own household...
Those who find their life will lose it, and those who lose their
life for my sake will find it.

MATTHEW 10: 34–39

I know nothing but repetition and nonsense and can tell you nothing you do not already know. I cannot tell you of magical experiences beyond the grave or of adventures in mythical Utopia. I can tell you only of the jokes I have played, the blood I have shed, the tears I have cried, and the many moons that have passed for me since I was brought into this existence. I cannot tell you of emotions you do not know. I can only give you words because there are still words left. Words endure; the power of memory haunts. When I have no words left, I will let you go—I shall set you free. I promise.

:: :: ::

Mine was not to question complications of a world dominated

by trifling matters. Mine was duty, honor, the battle with the illusion of beauty. I accepted blows to my face, pain to my pride because I had to be strong for family, strong for friends, powerful for the next generation. My rules, my laws, my private constitution meant sacrifice. Sacrifice was the epitome of success, and it is what put the smiles on everyone's faces. Don't get me wrong; I laughed and sometimes played jokes, but I was also the power to look for in bad times—because you could not trust your mama or your papa or your old lady that was probably out on the town, but you could call me up, and I would be there for you. I would come when you called because I loved you. Three o'clock in the morning, one hundred miles away, whatever crime or time—you knew there was love: homeboy love. And if you expected friendship, you knew there was no better friend to have. I would not argue with you. I would not give you advice. I would quench your thirst. I would do whatever needed to be done without hesitation because I was the friend you always dreamed of.

Homeboys shook my hand. They accepted the relationship because without us we were nothing. We, with no money and no honey; we, with brown faces and rude manners; we, the miserable, were kings because we had each other, and each other was all we needed. Homeboys took my love, and I expected the same in return. That was the cost of my friendship. What's fair is fair. If I could do it for homeboys, then they could do it for me. Is that not balance?

Balance was ultimately lost, but I also knew that losing balance was the price of our love. And no more screams out on busy streets, no more cries into the rainy black nights, because I give homeboys my life so that they could have something for later. *Take me, and give my people a place to smile, a place they could hold their heads up without being ashamed.* This is what I sacrifice myself for. Ah, I lost balance. Ah, I lost love and grace, yet I must go on and on.

What is that I hear—is it you crawling out of the dirt or swimming from the bottom of the ocean coming to get me? Is it you that I must guard against? Must I spend my nights expecting ghosts; can there never be peace? Then I accept your threats. Come and get me. I am the sinner. I am the evil. I accept the fate for everyone. I come outside now with nothing but dust in my hands. I AM HERE. I am outside. I am wherever you want me to be.

I am a little boy.

"Mama, can I follow you?"

"No, you must stay and take care of your brothers, *mijo.*" With Papa, Mama stumbled into their bedroom. I took care of my little brothers. We played Hot Wheels and Tonka trucks. Opening my parents' door later, I took care of them too. I put out her cigarette that was almost igniting the rug, and I pulled the needle out of his arm as he nodded his head up and down and drooled all over himself. I cooked up Top Ramen soup, boiled hot dogs, and the family was full.

And I am begging you please take this cup away from me. Take this cup away from me, and I will be a good kid and bless you every day of my life.

One Christmas we got presents. Mama and Papa surprised us. They woke us saying that Santa had come. I ripped open the red paper, and inside I found an Atari video game system with Pac-Man and Defender cartridges. Oh, there was joy, and oh, how my heart soared! And I believed that God had heard my prayers, and that day was truly holy. Laughing, we played the games all that day. Mama and Papa laughed too. Although we fought over turns, no one cried.

The next morning I took my brothers out to the school playground. We hit a tennis ball with a stick and ran around painted cement bases. Once the game got rained out, we raced back to our hut with smiles on our little boy faces.

"I'm first on Pac-Man!" Micho shouted.

"No, you hogged it all day yesterday. I'm first; tell him, Santo." Chico tugged at my shirt.

"Chico is first. The smallest is always first, you know the rules." I patted Chico on the head, and he smiled through his brown teeth.

We walked into the cramped up project apartment room, and there was only silence. There was no more TV, and there was no more Atari game.

"We got robbed! Call the police!" Micho commanded.

"Sit down, and shut up. Take out some Top Ramen and heat up some water." I walked into the bedroom, and Mama and Papa nodded their heads as if they were admitting to the crime.

"Oh, *mijo*, can you get your mama some Top Ramen?"

"It's already cooking." I looked into her. "Mama, was it worth it, are you better now?"

"Yes, *mijo*, I am much better now. I knew you would understand."

"But what are we to do now, Mama? What are we to play?"

"Play?" Papa mumbled, the tequila on his breath making me twist. "There is no time for children's play in this world. Busy yourselves with becoming men." Reaching behind his pillow, he grabbed a deck of cards and some dice. "But if you must play, play a man's game. Play a game that men die for, sell their souls for; play and learn now that you are a little boy so that when you get older you will have mastered the game." He shoved the cards and dice in my hands and asked me to fetch his lighter and cigarettes.

"Yes, Papa," I murmured as I handed him the Marlboros and naked lady lighter. I walked out to my brothers and rolled the dice against the wall. Craps. Before they could open their mouths, I told them, "This game is better than Pac-Man."

I helped if I could. When I met Toro in the sixth grade, back in 81, I helped. As my friends and I were walking down to the bus stop after school, we noticed that there were two boys ready to tangle. Fifty middle-schoolers gathered around them. I pushed my way to the center of the crowd. Toro and this other boy, an eighth grade fat boy, began pushing each other. With his head to the ground, Toro charged at the boy. Fat boy simply stepped to his left and punched Toro's head down to the floor. Toro rose instantly, and they began pushing each other again. The fat boy shouted, "Come on! I'll fuck you up!" Puffing, Toro about to charge again, I grabbed him and told him, "When you get close to him, let go like a windmill, but don't start punching until he's in your reach. He's bigger than you, so spit on him so he gets mad and charges you." Toro nodded his head, but when I let him go, he rushed with his head to the ground, and once again he was punched down. I grabbed him, "Don't you understand what I told you? *Let him charge you.*" I looked into him. He did not understand. He knew no other way. And after I gazed into his heart, after I knew that Toro's courage alone could not win the fight, I took off my jacket, stretched out my neck, and told the other boy, "Now you must fight me."

The fat boy laughed as I kicked his kneecap. He threw a windmill right. I ducked, swooped my leg behind both of his, and tripped him. Mounting him, I punched his face three times. As he turned his body around to avoid getting hit directly in the nose, I straddled him from behind, put my arms around his neck like a vise, and squeezed. His body became limp, and he fell asleep like a big snoring baby. I left him lying in the street as the crowd of boys and girls looked on in silence, stunned from the sheer ferocity of a young man with the power of love.

With thanks in his eyes, without a word to be said, Toro walked away. I knew that one day he would return because we were, from that moment, eternal brothers.

Brotherhood is the deepest love I know; it is my life. And my brothers, the ones who are worthy, know how to prove. Because, after all, is that not what it is all about? Proving love is not for anyone else unless he treasures pain and defeat. I am willing to accept those consequences because I have a duty to make sure that in these worst times my brothers have my love.

With my special gift, I knew when things would get too deep. When I was sixteen, I felt a funny feeling, and I knew that that day would mark my existence like no other. My body tingled; my eyes would not blink. I tried to relax with Lobo and Toro that day, a showery April day in 1986, but I felt the blessing or curse upon me, but told no one. We drank malt liquor and smoked a joint of angel dust, but towards the end of that afternoon we went our separate ways. I did not want anyone to come looking for me that night because I knew the power of fate would be tested. Shaking uncontrollably, I walked into my little room at my *abuelita*'s house. I got down on my knees. I always trusted in the Lord Almighty, but I never got down on my knees, not even in my most horrible times, but on that night that I knew would mean so much sacrifice, I knelt down close to my bed, clasped my two hands in a ball, and bowed my head for mercy.

"Lord, if it is possible, please, please take this cup away from me."

Afterwards, I ironed my Bens and white T-shirt and waited for the knock on the door.

Knock, knock.

"Monica's throwin a party, Bro. Beers and bitches." Lobo smiled.

"I've been *listo* for this one all my life." I put my arms around Lobo. Toro, Lobo, and I scooted down the street. We splashed through flooded dark streets and reached the party without a scratch. Monica came up, gave me a hug, and her boyfriend, Lucky, a drug dealing *vato* dressed in money green, gazed at me with disdain. He did not like that she hugged me. I shined this off, but kept him within sight as I drank my beers. For some strange reason, I kept having to spit. I couldn't help it. At first I began spitting into an empty cup. When I felt eyes upon me, I refilled my beer and walked out to the porch. The night cold, I breathed in the freshness that comes with the pitter-patter cleansing of the streets. I felt good; perhaps I had been letting my intuition run away with my common sense; perhaps instead of a bad omen upon me, I actually, for once, predicted a good benevolent grace. I downed my beer.

I spit. I caught my breath again and spit more. The rain fell and so did the saliva from my mouth. I could not swallow. I could not swallow my saliva, so I spit.

"What's up, Santo? Come in and have another beer." Lobo, in a puffy white Starter jacket, lead the way. I stepped back inside the house. As people danced and strutted, laughed and bullshitted, I kept my mouth closed for fear that I would slobber all over the place. I went into the bathroom and emptied out my cup of saliva, flushed the toilet, and quickly walked back out. I told myself that another beer downed as quickly as possible would stop me from this spitting insanity. I downed Lobo's beer. I caught my breath and felt the saliva build up in the back of my throat. I trotted towards Toro and downed his beer too. This was my tenth or eleventh beer, and the spitting sickness, I felt, was being cured. I went around the living room and grabbed people's cups and drank them. I got caught up with homeboys I didn't know and hit on their weed. I talked with Monica and drank two shots of her Cuervo tequila.

The world was becoming lovely again. I went up to Lucky and put my arms around his neck, "How's it goin, Brother?" I asked.

"It's cool. What the fuck, you aint gotta lay on me, though." He brushed his shoulder off.

"Nah, Bro, *dispensa*. Just feeling good is all. I feel good to be around good people."

"Yeah, whatever, homes. Why don't you post up next to the toilet? You're probably going to be needing it soon." Lucky stroked the five gold chains around his neck.

"You think I'm fucked up? I aint fucked up. You think I can't hold my dignity?" I pulled out the dark brown wooden cross on a leather lace that I had on underneath my T-shirt.

"Whatever, homes," he said as I slobbered all over my cross and T-shirt. He turned around to his Bro. "This *leva* needs a fuckin bib," he giggled. Toro and Lobo looked on without saying a word. They knew that nobody ever had to stand up for *El Santo*.

I looked myself up and down, all fucked up and slobbering, and straightened up quickly. I needed another drink. I snatched the beer out of Lucky's hand and downed it in front of his face. He stood there for a moment dumbfounded at my action. I grabbed him around the neck and whispered so that only he could hear, "Many try, many die. Few succeed in the life I lead."

He punched me in the mouth, but I came forward anyway. I

grabbed his head with both of my hands and brought it down as I kicked my knee up as hard as I could. I tackled him to the floor. As his Bro jumped me from behind, Lobo and Toro commenced on whipping him up. The party went into panic, but then Monica's mother came out and implored us to please calm down. I stopped and told my homeboys to calm down too.

Lucky and his homeboys did not want to get down. They knew they were outclassed, but one of us had to leave the party. After looking at me, Monica's mother felt I was to blame. I accepted this but as we were leaving she began to lose her mind. She shouted, "Don't you come around here no more." I made sure that Toro and Lobo were leaving nicely. "You're no good for shit." They were out on the sidewalk, and I skipped down the stairs to join them. "You fuckin wetback!" On those words I turned back. She had her hands on her broad hips as if she had the right to tell the truth. I spit on her happy face. I walked down to the street.

"Fuck them bitches," Lobo said, "let's go kick it at Chavez schoolyard; they got a cool spot under a roof." Lobo knew the strange *varrio* pretty well because he also used to fuck Monica, kicked it, and got to know the homeboys around there well. At the corner liquor store, we spotted an old bum panhandling for change and told him to go buy us a case. After I gave the bum a beer as a tip, we marched to the schoolyard to drink and bullshit.

A half hour later, we heard whistles in the distance.

"Check out, someone's comin down," Toro said. Silent, we mad dogged two silhouettes.

"Nah," Lobo said peering closely, "it's cool. I know these fools." Lobo raised his arms up and said, "What's up!"

"Is that Lobo's bullshittin ass down there?" someone shouted.

"And my homeboys too." It was two dudes named Chavo and

Dodo from this neighborhood. We gave greetings, shared beer, and bullshitted. Before long the young night became gray haired. At two in the morning, after Toro threw up all over the place, I thought it best to call it a night. Lobo said he wanted to kick it some more, and the two strangers said they knew of a cool party. Even though Toro was all fucked up, I knew he could get home all right, knew that he probably wanted to go home and sleep; but I couldn't let Lobo go into this darkness with two strangers who really didn't give a fuck about him.

"Toro, you just threw up, so you should be feelin better. Get to your *canton*. I'm gonna go to this party with Lobo," I said.

"All right, Bro," Toro said. We gave the homeboy handshake and hug and split up.

"They got bitches over there?" Lobo asked Chavo as we walked in calm, wet blackness.

"A gang of em. This is some *veterano*'s getting out party, dude Sky. It's in the cuts, but I kinda know this broad, so we *should* be cool." A mile into *Varrio Pueblo,* we reached a house with a giant staircase. "This is it." We climbed. Chavo rang the doorbell. Maricela answered.

"Hey! The party just started! Come on in," the thunderbolt said. Confidently, we strolled.

"*Q-VO.*" Some guy standing in a dark corner said.

"*Y-Que?*" Someone else asked us as if we were intruding on some sacred event.

"Bang, bang." Heads turning, eyes became fierce. Perhaps this was not such a good idea.

"Hey, you're Java's *carnal* aren't you?" A buffed out giant looked at my face and thought he knew someone else. I didn't know who Java was, but I suddenly felt a close kinship with him.

"*See-mon*," I nodded.

"That's a down ass homeboy. I was locked up with him." This stranger put his hand out to me. I grabbed it and looked in his eyes. "These little *vatos* are cool," he said. Everyone resumed their bullshit, and the stranger offered me a beer. "Yeah, what's Java been up to?"

"He's still locked up," I lied.

"He's a down ass homeboy!" he repeated and thrust me a Black Label beer. "So what's your *placa*, homes?"

"Santo. They call me Santo."

"They call me Sky." I tilted my head up to positively affirm his status. We gave the homeboy handshake and listened to soul oldies blast from the boom box. Lobo stood over a girl and pressed her for her phone number. Homeboys and homegirls grabassed. Smoke blurred the air, but through it all I embraced Maricela's smile. Her eyes invaded my silence. Sky emphasized jailhouse war stories, but it was pure gibberish to me. Her eyes were what shouted—

"I do not know you, but I want to know. I want to more than know; I want to feel you. I want to know why I admire your eyes, your face, your unknown soul. I want to be part of it."

Or maybe she just wanted to fuck.

We stared at each other, and I did not nod my head or move my lips, but I told her, with my eyes, through my mind, with a telepathic connection, "Great love is great pain."

And Sky saw that she loved me. But this was his love. This was the woman that he claimed, the woman who waited for him while he was in jail, or so he thought. And it was my fault that she loved me. It was my fault that this woman, who could have remained silent with her eyes, screamed to me through the room that she loved me or at least wanted to.

"That's my lady, Maricela, homes," Sky said.

"Beautiful girl," I said.

"Beautiful? What the fuck you trying to say? Fuck that bitch. You want to fuck her?" He added bass to his voice. I looked at him, and he did not look away.

"Nah, Bro, I don't want no problems."

"That's what I thought," he said with unbreakable pride.

"But she might. She might want some problem," I said this as she and I looked into each other's eyes, as she affirmed my statement.

"Get the fuck out of here, *puto!*" All of the homeboys that had been statues turned into human beings. "What's up!? Fuck these punks!" Sky added.

"Not in the house!" Maricela screamed. We were escorted out by angry shouts and jeers. Chavo and Dodo shot out first. I grabbed Lobo and pushed him out the door. Behind me, the armies of the night crowded the door. Lobo jumped down the stairs in two quick motions and ran to his right. I fumbled down holding onto the railing and dashed to my left.

I splashed down the street as fast as I could and heard giant stomps become weak, distant steps. A block away, I looked back. A blur, perhaps nothing at all, but a blur of figures bunched up on the sidewalk, and I thought of Lobo. "Lobo!" I screamed, and for whatever reason that went through my head as I was completely safe from danger a whole block away; perhaps out of peer pressure, or concern for a friend, or perhaps because I did not know exactly where I was running to, I stopped. I stopped, and because I saw the bunch I figured that Lobo was down on the ground and was getting beaten to a pulp. I ran back, perhaps out of a concept only heard about in poetry or the movies, but maybe, even though

I cannot define the word, I returned and ran back into hell's fiery flames on a stormy rainy night out of love: pure unselfish die for love.

Or maybe not.

I ran back to the scene of ugly Indians, and the rain had not quenched their thirst. Sky threw off his shirt and revealed green tattoos all across his giant chest. He reached into the trunk of a car. One of his homeboys followed.

"I'm gonna kill you, *puto!*" Sky shouted, swinging a tire iron at my head. I ducked and stepped to my right. His friend jabbed at me with an ice pick, and I skipped to my left.

"Lobo!" I shouted and looked around. There was no more bunch. He was nowhere in sight. I ran back to be killed. I ran back out of stupidity.

"Motherfucker!" Sky swung, so I ducked, mumbled "God," and put my hand to the wet earth. And God answered my prayers. Yes, it was a dirty neighborhood; yes, bums drank and littered the streets; yes, perhaps the next day was garbage recycling day. But God, I tell you, God Almighty, put a bottle on the street for me, and as I reached down for I don't know what, by the grace of God, I felt smooth glass become part of my hand. Then it was a jagged shank as I looked into Sky's furious eyes and broke the bottle on the cement.

Sky, a man of about twenty-two, charged me screaming "Ahhhhwrrr!" and I stabbed the broken bottle into his Adam's apple. He gargled as if trying to clean his mouth. Sky's half naked homeboy charged from my right side, and I swung around and stuck his chest. I screwed the glass inside and heard him grunt "Ummph." For a moment I stood there looking at the beauty of the masterpiece I had just created. Then I ran away as fast as I could. After many blocks, I tired, but I would not stop because Sky's voice was right behind me, even though the last thing I saw was Sky lying down in the street clutching at his throat. I ran and no longer heard any pitter patter of raindrops, but instead the water spoke "Mo-ther-Fuck-er-I-am-kill-you." His voice surrounded me. There was no escape.

At *Bajo* Park I saw some of my homeboys kickin it.

"Lobo, he's in *Pueblo*'s *varrio*. Lobo, he needs us," I managed to say. Packed into two cars, we went back to the scene of the crime. The ambulance's orange and white lights spun around. On stretchers lay the bodies of two men. As we pulled up close, I saw Sky's still face.

"Let's go; cops are gonna trip," the OG, Duster, said. "Fuck, Santo, what happened?"

I did not answer as the paramedics pulled the white sheet over Sky's head.

I try not to answer when I hear the voices. I stay silent. In a room full of people who are laughing and happy, the invisible voices intrude. The invisible voices persist. I am always strapped, always on watch, but they never leave me in peace. "Your whole *familia,* all of your homeboys—dead. Your mother—I'm coming in with my disciples, and we're going to kill everyone except you. I'm gonna let you live, sucker. I'm gonna force you to burn in living hell."

I coolly excuse myself from the room. I go to the bathroom and lock the door.

"Okay," I whisper. "Let's do this, one on one. No one else needs to be involved."

"Bullshit! Everyone has to be involved. Everyone is involved. They got to pay because I know what hurts you. We could kill you right now. We could snuff you out *orita,* but it would give us no pleasure. It wouldn't be revenge because we know—we know that you don't hurt for yourself. You hurt for everyone else, and that's why everyone else must go."

"So you know me. I will admit that, but why not simply do what you say? Why tell me if there is nothing I can do about it? No, I know you too. You want something; you need something from me. That's why you speak." In the mirror there is the reflection of the dark brown wavy hair, the scattered beard across the face, the wooden cross dangling from neck.

"You are special! I knew I did not waste my time with you! I cherish your insight and power. I demand your strength. Bow down before me, and all will be forgiven, all forgotten. All that will remain is our *carnalismo*." The tan face is semi-handsome, but the features and twitches that shine the eyes are feared, misunderstood, not of the norm, and that makes the face ugly.

A knock on the door. "Santo, hurry up, homes. I got to take a piss."

"No, I will not."

"What? I'll break the damn door down. Quit fucking around."

"Even if I accept your terms, there will never be peace. You will still destroy *La Familia*. Do not insult me with fake friendship. You know nothing about it." He is tall for a homeboy, about 5'10", solid weight of ready, young muscle—180 pounds. He looks into the reflection.

More thumps. "Fuck this. Stink that motherfucker up, I'm going to piss out front."

"Your family, your friends—they will all die horrible deaths. You will be unable to save them. You will not know when the hour comes."

So I waited for the unknown hour. I waited for other *vatos* from other *varrios* who had contracts out on me. Ready, I waited, hoping that someone would challenge my misery, but the big time shot callers like Rey and Duster, main *chignons,* saw something in me, and they called all dogs off. They had swaggered up to me with sharp knives in their hands, yet I did not run, nor did I hesitate to declare to them that it would be an honor and a privilege to die for love. Stunned, instead of stabbing me, they embraced me. They put their powerful names on the line for me because in me they saw a future. I could not be touched by my own *gente's* hands. I walked fearlessly into *Pueblo,* all around the Swamp, and even in the back alleys downtown. It was then that I could have changed. At that point in my life, having reached street stardom, completely untouchable, I was intelligent enough to realize I was fighting a futile fight and could have started what is considered a "good" life, a crusade to holiness. But I could not. In my heart I did not feel moral to start anew only because I could. If I were to be good and wholesome, I would first have to battle my invisible enemies and win or die. Then, when I could look into myself and feel no shame, I would be good.

The day came—the unknown hour was known to me. It was a soft, sunny March afternoon in 1991. The family, the voices, confronted me. They told me it was time to choose either happiness or destructiveness. They tried to fool me with the illusions of laughs and songs and a game in the park. I saw then that our destiny was pain and humiliation. Only complete and utter madness and sadness could help us weather the voices. A giant step into reality is what was needed, so I smashed the fantasy of family. Taking initiative, I shattered the lie. But exposing the lie would not set us free but sink us in deeper to our just desert.

Each incident causes more awareness. Each battle imprints

deeply. Is it wrong for me to be aware? I cannot believe so, that I suffer in this way only for my sufferings to be incorrect. I must be aware of smiling faces, for they are the ones that carry knives. Pretty lips lie.

"I love you, Santo." Maricela loved me. She said so.

"I love you too." I loved her because I knew that she would have to pay for her words. We had been together on and off for five years now, grown up together.

"We should go somewhere, Santo. Leave this *kaka* and move to some beautiful place."

"Where should we go, darling?" I said as I sat down on her beat up flowered couch.

"Florida. I heard Florida is hella pretty. It's always nice weather, and there is all kind of work. No fucking gangs and shit. I could go to beauty school; you could work construction. Places are cheap there. We could buy a house one day. We could get married if only, if only…"

"If only what, *mi amor?*"

"If only we had enough money. I've been looking into it. There's this place I called up, and they said if we had ten thousand dollars we would be guaranteed work and a beautiful little place by the ocean. By the warm ocean! Only ten thousand dollars."

"Ten thousand dollars, that's not a problem. Your dreams can come true. You'll get that money for us." She would lead me to where they hid. I would find out where they were.

"No, Santo, I was thinking that you could do this." She puckered her lips at me. "There's an armored truck that my *primo* works for as a security guard. They make a cash delivery every Thursday night." She scooted closer to me. "You could stick it up. My cousin would be in on it too. He would make sure his partner didn't press the silent alarm or try to get brave. There's twenty-five grand in two bags. We'd split it up, and we'd go down to Florida, baby. We'd get away from all of this garbage, and nobody will get busted." Mari was excited.

"You are the most beautiful woman I've ever known," I pet her.

"I know. I know." Her hair shone even though the lights were off. "Now, will you do it?" Her body curved like an hourglass through her tight cotton dress. Her feet…

"How beautiful are your feet in sandals, oh prince's daughter!" I grabbed her foot and brought it to my lips.

"Come on, Santo," she kicked away. "How about it?"

"Let your will be done."

"Oh, Santo, we're going to be so happy!" She kissed my lips as I looked into her dark eyes. I grabbed her around her soft neck.

"Is it with a kiss that you show me you love me? Is it with a kiss that you think you could convince *El Señor Santo* to sell his soul?" She would not look at me or answer my questions. Instead, she pulled up my shirt and kissed the wooden cross, then my chest. Instead, I stroked her hair as she bobbed her head up and down and tried to convince me how much she loved me.

At six p.m., on that Thursday night, just about a month ago, on August 18, I showed up to her house dressed all in black. She was waiting for me in her living room with pink polish on her toes and a tight pink mini-skirt wrapped around her beautiful ass. She greeted me with a kiss.

"Are you ready?" she asked.

"I stole a Caprice, you know, the kind of cars the cops drive."

"Yeah, that's nice, but do you have a gun and a mask to make it look legit just in case something goes wrong?"

164

"I got this .38 from my homeboy." I caressed its snub nose. "Locked and loaded."

"Yeah, but did you get a mask? Did you get a mask to cover up your face?"

I looked into her.

"Here," she said, "use this then." She tried to hand me one of her leg stockings.

"Mari," I grabbed both of her arms, "I will never wear a mask. This is who I am."

"What's wrong with you, stupid? You need a mask to cover your face and make it look legit, so no one gets wise." Mari pulled her arms away from me.

"Exactly. I need you, wise one. You'd never let me down, would you? You love me."

"We better forget the whole thing. I'm not going anywhere with your crazy stupid ass." She plopped herself down on the couch.

"What about your dreams, Mari? What about your beautiful house by the blue ocean? What about eternal happiness?" She shifted around in her seat.

"Fuck that shit!" she screamed. "I'm not gonna get busted and go to prison! If you really loved me, you would have done what I said."

"If you love yourself, you will get up." I placed the .38 on her lips. "I need to know where they're at. You must show the way."

"You're crazy. I'm not going anywhere."

"I could hurt you, Mari. I could truly hurt you. I will kill you right now if that's what needs to happen, and then you will have no more dreams. Then you will return from whence you came. I tell you now to show the way or return to the scorching fire." I pulled back the hammer.

"All right, motherfucker. But after this there aint shit between us."

"Was there ever?"

She drove on the dark freeway, and I looked in the rearview mirror as the city lights became dim. I kept my mouth shut and tried to memorize exactly where we were going.

"You are very clever, Santo. You're coming to get us—coming right into our trap."

"Shut the fuck up."

"What? I didn't say nothing," Mari said.

"Keep your mouth closed." Her mouth. What a precious mouth. She could never keep it closed. Full, thick, ruby red lips that were not afraid to stretch. She was the most physically beautiful woman I had ever known, or would ever know. Her smooth tan legs sat spread in the driver's seat, and she wiped her right hand on her thigh and made it juicy with her palm's sweat. She wiggled trying to get comfortable, and I remembered many nights when she wiggled around on me with her perfectly round cluster of grapes in my face. I'd take her any time, any place, and she had no shame or hesitation to perform during any of our endless nights of fornication.

"Pull over," I said.

"What? I'm driving," licking her lips, she said this as if she did not know what I wanted.

We jumped into the back seat. The match was lit, and it burned slow and steady. The passion of our bodies' nectar wet the match, but the fire, instead of going out, ignited like gasoline and became even fiercer. A sparkler started off the festivities, small pops and the clamor of thunder followed, and then fast and hard the real fireworks went off. All the colors of the brightest rainbow shot out

166

high into the dark sky. All the happiness of the Fourth of July filled the thick air. All the love of an apple pie stained the seat.

Afterwards, I relaxed as she drove on the dark country roads. She made left turns and right turns, but I no longer gave a fuck. Slowly, I smoked a cigarette and let the smoke out of my mouth in a yawn and watched the fumes run out the open window. I wished that this drive would last forever. I did not want to reach our goal. It felt as if I was not even really going to meet them, as if this was not the mission I had expected. What exactly was I going to do when I saw them, when I confronted them? Plans and wishes are always pleasant but now, so close to the reality of my worst fears, I did not see glory. Perhaps Mari was right. Perhaps Florida was a fun place. Perhaps there was no such thing as shame and honor, perhaps I could find a new life, without pain and degradation, in a little white cottage by the blue ocean beach.

"There it is." Mari pointed to a truck backed up to a warehouse in an empty black lot. I snapped out of Disney World and looked the mean truck in its face.

"You found me. Now come and get me—if you dare." The truck bullshitted just as I had expected it to. It wanted me to expose myself without thought.

"It's twelve thirty. Perfect. My cousin told me that between twelve thirty and one would be perfect. He said that he would take a break at twelve thirty, and he would make sure his partner did too." Mari was excited. She could already taste the marlins.

"I bet if I went out there right now everything would be just *firme, que no?*"

"Santo, we're going to be so happy!"

"Your dreams will come true, Mari." I pulled out my .38 and pointed it at her head. "You must create truth. Dreams don't come true without a whole lot of sacrifice. Get out of the car."

"You're tripping. I'm not going. That's not the plan. You're going to fuck up my whole plan. You have to go out there. *You* have to take the money. That's how I have you set up."

"Your plans have changed. My plan is in effect: you get out and rush the truck."

"No way! I'll beep this horn right now, I'll scream bloody murder. I'll…"

I grabbed a clump full of her long curly brown hair, stepped out of the car, and dragged her out onto the concrete. "Get your ass up." I forced her to a stance and pushed her body in front of mine. We jogged up to the dull black and white armored truck. No one was in the driver seat. Nor were there voices of two partners on a break. There was nothing. In one quick motion I, dragging her in front of me, leaped out in front of the rear entrance of the armored truck.

"Mari?" A man asked with his shotgun already pointed out through the gun hole.

"Put the gun down, Pato! He'll kill me!"

"Open the door if you value your love's life." I knew right away.

"No, Pato! He's crazy!"

"And what about your dreams, Mari? I told you that you'd make your money. I didn't lie to you. Open the door," I said and looked into caged eyes. "Now."

The door opened. A bright light parted the darkness. Inside the truck the partner lay, tied up, gagged, face first to the ground. From inside the truck Pato pointed a twelve gauge double barreled shotgun at Mari and me.

"Okay," I said, "now put the shotgun down, and take the gag out of his mouth."

"You'll kill me," Pato said.

"I will not."

He put the shotgun on the deck of the truck, bent down close to his partner and took the gag out of his mouth. I pushed Mari into the truck and jumped in.

"Thank you," the old man lying on the floor said. "Now push that red button over there, and we'll be fine." He was happy.

"Tell me," I said to the wrinkled old man, "did you think you could fool a fool so easily? Did you think I would walk blindly into hell's bright fiery flames?"

"What you talking about, boy? You off your damn rocker? Push that red button, and quit fucking around before Pato gets brave."

"So we finally meet face to face, and you still must play your silly games. Fuck Pato."

"Pato's crazy, boy! He tied me up here, and he was gonna shoot you when you walked up. He was gonna use that gun you brought and shoot me as if you had shot me. He was gonna make it look real. He was gonna say your partner ran off with the loot, and then he was gonna cry about me to the boss man, run off with that young lady, and laugh all the way to the bank."

"Pato is just a pawn. You are who I came to see. Do not insult my intelligence by blaming one of your idiots." I pointed the gun to Pato's head. "Your master aint talking. Tell me, is he the one? Is he the main one, or are there others who are higher?"

"He's the one," Pato said, "the head dude, the master planner, the head honcho. Now kill his ass cause he's gonna snitch and tell the cops everything."

"The cops! I should have known! It's so obvious—they're the ones."

"Damn, boy. Damn, you're lost, boy. Look into my eyes," the

169

old man pleaded. "I aint done shit to you. I don't deserve this. I got a wife and kids—shit, grandkids."

"You've got to go, just as we all got to go," I said. "Did you think you could live in this world forever? This place is not your home. Your place is in the next world, but even though I must snuff you out, I know you'll come back in a new shape or form and try to convince me you care about *familia* or something else profound, something I should have pity on you for, set you free for so that you could kill and torture more of my innocent people. No, I will not fall into your trap. I am *listo*." I looked into his dark red eyes and saw that he proudly feared the next life.

"You are only postponing the inevitable pain. I will return with a vengeance," the old man calmly said. Giving up his worldly role, he now spoke as a true prince should. In horror, Mari moved close to Pato. She used his shoulder as support for her head. I pulled the trigger slowly, and green ooze from the prince's head splashed all over the inside of the truck.

I looked down for a moment, for only one moment at my green hands, and Pato immediately kicked the gun out of my hand. His head a ram, he slammed me against the wall. I elbowed the back of his head, but he, with face to the floor, punched full force upper-cuts on my dick and nuts. In the heat of the moment it did not hurt me. In the heat of the moment I continued bringing elbow upon elbow down on top of his hard head. Which pain would be more intense? The pain of brain damage or the pain of dick damage? Who would give up first?

Blam! Pato fell to my feet. Blam! I slumped down beside him. I was shot, but in the heat of the moment it did not hurt, in the heat of the moment I put out the fire. There was no other way to win this one. I shut my eyes and pretended death. Mari's feet rustled over our bodies, over to where the bags full of money were at, and then her sandaled feet trotted back over us, and she jumped off the truck. A moment later I heard the Caprice's engine rev up mightily, and I smelled the rubber from the skidding of tires. Mari was gone.

In agony, I rose, stumbled, cleaned off my prints, and jumped out of the truck. I heard the moon shine and saw crickets chirp brightly. Thousands of little white lights flashed on and off and on and off, and the full moon screamed loudly. I was lost. I had let my dick think for me back in the Caprice and now I had no idea which way the *varrio* was. In the middle of nowhere, I walked, in a state of both confusion and clarity; I followed the scent of the burning rubber of the Caprice's tires. The burning rubber threw off a mighty bitter smell, so I no longer needed my eyes that were blinded by the flashing lights of crickets' voices everywhere I turned. Nor could I think clearly because of the raving madness that the moon screamed and shouted about, but I took air into my lungs, and the smell, the power of rubber stink led me to total clarity. When the day's darkness came, I jumped in the bushes along the freeway, and when the crickets' lights once again flashed, I continued my journey. I walked with one hand pressing my ripped up T-shirt against my bloody shoulder hole. The next night, after hours of walking and jogging, and hitching rides on the backs of trucks, the crickets' lights were replaced by city lights, and I knew I was home. I walked into the shack.

"Fuck, Santo, what happened?" Toro asked. Playing Spades, he, Lobo, Sucio, and Sleepy were sitting on turned up buckets in our abandoned house. Lobo was keeping score on a yellow note pad.

"It aint *nada*, but I know it needs attention. Who got a smoke?"

Lobo handed me a cigarette, and I plopped down on the

mattress in the middle of the floor. "Check out: in the morning, go to the community college and get to one of those nursing classes. Wait out there until you see someone who looks halfway cool, a black or Latin person, tell them that they got to come with you. Go pull some 211's tonight, and get some cash so you could really convince them, but if they still got a hard head, knock their ass out and bring em anyway. We'll get their address afterwards so that they don't try to snitch, *entiendes?*" I tilted my head to Toro.

"Loud and clear, Sir Santo." He saluted me.

At noon the next day, they brought a Vietnamese dude because they said they couldn't find any Latins or blacks. The Vietnamese kid knew what time it was, though. He studied me as I sweated on the floor mattress, and he knew what I needed. He cleaned, dug and picked, burned, and patched my left shoulder up the best he could. He told me that I should get a hold of some infection drugs and painkillers. Toro gave him a hundred bucks.

"Go get a half gram of dust from Maton, and then go to the county hospital pharmacy and ask someone if they're waiting for penicillin. Give em a few bucks for a bottle. Bring Zig Zags and parsley," I said. Lobo shot off, and I downed Wild Turkey.

When I woke up, it was a new night. The dust and penicillin were centered for me on a turned up bucket. No one was there. My head throbbed; my body shook. I staggered outside to the chilly night and reflected about what had happened. The cops—that was my main concern. They were watching; they were plotting against us. I had watched the news and heard nothing about any robbery or murders. No police had broken down any doors, and there was only one possible explanation for that: the cops had to be in on it. They must have covered up the scene of the crime when they saw their master was dead. They would eventually find out who did it unless they already knew then, unless they were just torturing me more by not immediately exposing me. The cops wanted me so bad they had not even come looking! It made sense. I needed a new gun. I'd have to lay low until the heat blew over. I needed to relax anyway. Yes, relax—because even the hardest homeboy needs R&R after a good battle.

Mari. She had gotten away. Good for her. I wasn't angry at her. She did what she needed to do to make her dreams come true. She was in Florida, and I missed her. I missed her pussy and fake smile so, so much; how she could make me feel supreme. I missed the lies now that I was confronted with the truth. How dreadful knowledge of the truth can be when there is no comfort in the truth! The truth was that Mari did not give a fuck about me, a sucker. The truth was I wanted to flow down the river of love and forget the world. I wanted her high voice and sweet, sweaty body funk. I wanted to hear how much she loved me if even just one last time.

And so, alone and blue, three o'clock in the morning, with her picture in my hand, I pulled out a piece of paper and a pen, and I wrote down words, images, disturbed poetry. I imagined all of the beautiful things she would tell me and added things that no one would ever say to anyone:

> Dear Santo,
>
> I love you so very much, more than I can begin to express. I will not insult you with words—but if you were here now now now you would know the meaning of love. For I would stroke your hair and kiss your hands, and wash your feet with my happy tears. And afterwards I would no longer cry as the wind does on this loneliest of nights. I would no longer punish myself with your precious memory: of days walking and talking, of nights moaning and groan-

ing, of time between dusk and dawn when you held me tight in your strong arms. For you would be here, and nothing more would be needed. No dreams of green grass and red roses, no fantasies of roaring rivers on a rainy day, no hallucinations of a place called paradise. For you would be here, and we would be there. For you would be here, and one moment, one breath, one damning kiss and heaven would shatter into a billion tiny pieces, and God would damn us eternally because no people, no beings should feel so good, so pure, so much love as we would. Together.

Por Vida,

Maricela

I wrote with the finest penmanship: beautiful penitentiary style calligraphy handwriting with wide fine loops. On the envelope I drew a giant heart with a knife running through it. Blood dripped down the knife's point. I put a stamp on the envelope and walked down to the corner mailbox and mailed it to myself. I went to my *abuelita*'s house and waited. When the letter came the next afternoon, a tear strolled down my face as I thought about how much Mari loved me.

I walked to Mari's spot at eleven o'clock at night. I didn't expect her there, but when I peeked in the window, I saw her sitting in the corner of her dark living room with a glass pipe in her hand. She was not in Florida. Maricela was in another world. On the table beside her lay a giant white planet of crack cocaine. Sitting wide legged, her pussy hairs peeking out, she chipped off pieces of crack every few minutes. She wrapped her lips around the glass dick and inhaled deeply. She stared straight at me yet did not acknowledge my presence. She simply looked into me, kept hacking at her titanic, twenty-five thousand dollar shot that she had probably gotten down at the Alamo housing projects, and she blasted off to another planet.

Mesmerized by her, I stood there that whole night, but when the darkness of day came I left and went to sleep. When the night's lights woke me again, I went back to Mari's. She sat in that same corner, in the same wide legged position, and she chopped away at her work. Squinting my eyes, I noticed that underneath her on the floor was a huge puddle of piss and a tall pile of shit—flies flew fast—for she did not move from her chair for anything. The planet of crack on the table had now become a meteor. I left to buy a twelve pack of beer, and when I came back, she smiled, but, still, I stayed outside. I stayed outside and looked at her through the window.

After I hammered the twelve pack, I walked in and sat down on her couch. The rotten egg stench was horribly thick and musty. Almost vomiting, I didn't think I could handle it, but as I watched her calmly sit, chip away, put fire to the crack, and inhale deeply, I knew if she could tolerate it, then I had to. Maricela did not look at me. Her eyes wide open, she stared at the window that I had stood at the night before. She saw where my nose had implanted its mark, and she remembered. Maricela recalled green ooze, and her cheeks sunk down low into her face, and she sucked her stomach in deep, and then she exhaled china white crack smoke through her nose.

On that night, five nights after she saw the fate of man, her meteor was now a pebble. She stuffed her tiny pebble into her pipe, and she spoke for the first time.

"Ask me the way to the sky, and I might say down. Ask me the shape of this room, and I might tell you round. But ask me what man is, ask me what a human is, and I can't tell a lie; there is no such thing." Maricela did not say this to me. She said it to the other presence, the presence that was with us since the beginning.

When the last flame of fire was extinguished from her pipe, she let the pipe roll out of her hands. It landed in the big pile of shit beneath her. Hundreds, perhaps thousands of flies buzzed around her, covered her entire face, and she looked over at me. Panic swept across her. She realized she was not in Florida. She was here with me, and she knew about green ooze and other planets, and Maricela inhaled the air in the room, flies invading her orifice, and her face twisted in horror from the sour putrid stink.

She needed another planet. Another planet would take away all her worries and kill all uncertainties. She looked down between her legs, dug the pipe out of her huge sun of shit, and scooped up a healthy pipe full. She molded that shit between her fingers and stuffed it into the pipe. She turned her head away from me, and she lit the brown shit bright.

That next night, when I returned, all of the shit had vanished from the floor. The entire room was spotless. Maricela stood up for the first time in six days. She put makeup on her sweet face and lifted her skirt up almost to the crack of her ass. She graced past me, opened the door, and all the flies followed their queen. I watched from the window as Maricela walked down to the street corner and posed for cars passing by. A Chevy Blazer stopped, and she was certainly the most beautiful woman I would ever know.

EIGHT

Prayer

"Pray, my child, pray! You'll feel better!... Yes, really, it'll make you better," he whispered, pointing to the icon and looking at me rather strangely. "Say your prayers," he said in an imploring voice.

I went down on my knees and clasped my hands. I was once more filled with horror and despair, which completely overwhelmed me. I sank to the floor where I lay for some minutes like a dying person. I concentrated all my thoughts and feelings in prayer, but was overcome with fear.

FYODOR DOSTOYEVSKY, *Netochka Nezvanova*

Because there was nothing else left, Sheila prayed. Even though God had never answered her before, she knew praying could not hurt her. Afterwards, she started praying to Lobo because he was a living concrete being. She thought that maybe he could actually hear her if she prayed hard enough. But he was no God, and even love had its limits. She realized the only person she had ever known and would ever know in her life was herself. And then it sledge-hammered her with a shocking simplicity. She should and would pray to herself. With a faith in her own power and strength, Sheila, as her own God, squeezed her eyes shut. She did not want black-ness, but the redness and stars that come when one concentrates on the internal darkness. For some reason, she thought that in the purple and blue darkness, she could find a link to another world, somewhere buried inside of her.

She clenched her fists, pleading to herself: "I pray to me." Frightened, she stopped. But as time was not stopping, she knew she had to continue: "Sheila, I pray to me. Whoever you are, here, here is my prayer: I am not locked up but am free. I own the air." She calmed and remained in nothingness for a couple of minutes. "Sheila, with your might command that man. You know the times you spent together, the joy you shared. You know your power; you are the one. Tell him what you want him to do." Inside of herself, she had control. By going inside, she had entered Lobo's spirit. With this great power, she found elation and a peace, but she was still unsure of what she should do. Perhaps she should command him to save her. Her selfishness haunted her. Then she decided. "Be free. Whatever you do, Mr. Lobo, do it because you love me. Because you love me. You love me. Lobo, you love me."

Sasquatch was amused by her strained silence.

"Do you have to go to the bathroom?" He laughed.

Her eyes closed, her lips pursed, she did not hear. In the zone, she had contacted Lobo, helped him get ready for what needed to be done. And even though she charged Lobo to love her, she now also knew that Lobo would never come. Standing over her, Sasquatch kept laughing. If Lobo had been stupid enough to try, he would have been disappointed. Sheila grasped that the Sasquatch was not going to allow her to live. So even if Lobo had been an "honorable" man, he would have been stupid for his effort. Sasquatch did not care about balance.

The Sasquatch was not a man of his word or of tradition. The Chinese tradition had only caused him shame and had abandoned him when he needed it most. The Chinese were weak, he thought. As a child he had fancied the extravagant Chinese rituals, but as he

178

grew he knew the rituals were really a cover for a scared people's superstitions. Why couldn't you clean your house on New Year's Day? Why so many ghosts? The traditions were so poisoned that they corrupted even the corrupt! Sasquatch thought that the entire traditional Triad structure was obsolete and counterproductive for progress and capital. Members were supposed to make believe they were in the 1700's, still wearing ponytails and believing in fire breathing dragons. They forbid you to have a political stance beyond that of the Triads' stance. The Chinese, Sasquatch thought, were living in the Chinese past.

The Dragon Head Mountain Master forced everyone to lie. On Sundays, gangsters were supposed to act like monks. On Sundays there was tribute to pay. Purposely, although it made no sense now that they were living in the white man's world, the Dragon Head boss, an old peasant looking man, would compel the Blue Lanterns, or ordinary members, to show their faces to the community. On Sundays, big bad gangsters had to come with hat in hand to publicly pay tribute to a feeble old shot caller. And it had to be in public because the Dragon Head wanted everyone to think in the old ways with the old terror.

As always, Kwai Chung would come dutifully, but Sasquatch knew this was all an act. Kwai had set him up, betrayed him, and Kwai was skimming off the top, starting his own bullshit. Sasquatch, himself, knew he could not snitch to anyone because he was not in good standing. His time in the penitentiary and association with non-Chinese others had branded him as an outlaw. Still, Sasquatch had a few followers, but even they were scared to desire more, to completely break from their Chinese heritage. On Sundays, the people bowed and kissed. They thought they were back in China. Sasquatch predicted that their world would soon be evaporating, hence the diminishing numbers of American born Chinese gangsters. Instead of desiring to be men of "honor," they all went into accounting, engineering, and computer science. He, Sasquatch the giant, was the new face of the Chinese mafia. And the new face had to know how to deal with different peoples and goals.

Blacks, Mexicans, Vietnamese, Japanese. Dealing with any one of these others was a blasphemy, and adopting anything Japanese was especially taboo. But Sasquatch liked the Japanese, especially because he was supposed to hate them for their cruelty to the Chinese. The Japanese had raped Nan King and had unashamedly begun genocide against his grandmother and grandfather. But the Japanese uttered sensual *sayonara,* and at the same time had also invented the Samurai, those fat headed brutal but noble savages. The Japanese did not make such a big deal of magic, nor did they show weakness by forever praying to ghosts. Sasquatch admired the Japanese so much that one of the first things he did when he was released from prison was to buy himself a Samurai sword. Sasquatch imagined himself as a true *Ronin.*

So stupid, Sheila did not seem to hear Sasquatch take the weapon out of its sheath. Studying his sword, he admired its shiny steel beauty and strength. Iron ready to fire. On the couch, Sheila sat silent, bending her neck naturally for him, ready for him it seemed, as if she knew this was supposed to be her destiny. The sword had also known that it was created for this precise moment. Standing over her, Sasquatch thought she looked like she was praying as he raised the blade in front of him. The room was silent.

NINE

El Santo

I choose to be a singer of songs. I know this is where I belong. I've been up and down the mountain, around the block a few times, and side to side on these psycho streets. There is no other place for me. And so it's not paradise—I've been cold, wet, and hungry, but, I must admit, it's good to be hungry sometimes. It's good not to have bread for the belly. Night Train wine, fat joints of parsley sprinkled with magical dust, and homeboy *carnalismo*. That was what gave me nourishment more than any cow, pig, or little bird topped off with chocolate cake and soda. Little seasoned birds actually made me weaker. Those things made me lazy for the times I needed to be awake. But the serenity of hunger, the pain of a growling stomach, the bitter beauty of starving gave me hope. I was hopeful because I was on my toes. When you're hungry, you don't fall asleep. When you're hungry, you conserve your strength. When you're hungry, you don't waste your power crying. When you're hungry, you're alive because you are so close to death.

And then there were two, few and true, who savored hunger, made hunger an art. They came to me after not having eaten for years. In baggy khakis, creased up T-shirts, and hard smiles, these *vatos* bowed their heads, and in reciprocity, I bowed mine. They showed me the way, and for me they took off their masquerades; they revealed their sins and—Behold! They were so thin I could see the bones about to pop through their skin, and these two gods, who hungered so nobly, never put their hands out. So I gave them more than just the satisfaction of animal flesh. I gave them the food of my heart, the food of my soul. To serve and protect them, I became the most savage beast in the concrete jungle: a man with a cause, a *cholo* with duty.

When I left Maricela's that night, I dazed around the city streets all night long. I talked with pigeons and laughed with rats down at the pier. I bent down, lapped water from a puddle, met the morning sun and praised its infinite glory. My shoulder not feeling so bad, I went into Safeway and stole ham and crackers. In a pet store, I meditated through the afternoon. At night, I hunted down the homeboys. Toro had recently been discharged from the Marines and he was sitting with Lobo drinking fine wine up on top of the cement stairs leading to Tweak Peak, looking out at the view of the city lights.

"I went to the pet store on 29th today," I said as I put my hand out for some wine.

"Yeah," Toro said handing me the bottle. "For what?" Clean, healthy, brawny baby bull.

"I don't know. I just walked in and started looking around."

"I been there before; they got bad ass snakes," Lobo stuck out his tongue and hissed.

"I checked out the fish," I said. "The fish are beautiful. I stayed there looking at all the colors, the tiger stripes, staring into their bubble eyes. I've decided, Bros. I'm gonna get some fare together and buy a nice ass fish tank."

"You're trippin, homes," Toro smirked. "What you gonna do with a damn fish tank?"

"I'm gonna keep fish in it. I'm gonna watch them and figure out the answers. I think they got answers. Fish float with their eyes wide open, never blinking."

Lobo laughed while with his fingers he followed the sharp creases on his black Bens, "You always gotta start going off like that aint you?"

"Going off like what? I want a fish tank. Is it wrong?"

"Man, you got a cigarette?" Lobo took out a palm-comb and combed his black hair back.

"I heard fish make you more peaceful," Toro joined in.

I had not considered that and felt ashamed of myself. "Toro, I get what you're saying, but peace can't be the answer I'm looking for. Peace! Man, what the fuck is that?"

"You don't know what peace is?" Lobo asked, rubbing his thick, but trimmed goatee. "I mean, I heard of it. It's supposed to be like kicking back with the finest bitch twenty-four seven, getting your dick sucked all the time. Like being with my shorty Sheila. Peace is like a sunny day every day and the flowers blooming hella different colors. Lemme get a drink." After soaking in his words, I handed Lobo the bottle.

"Where them fuckin flowers come from?" I asked pointing down to the ground. "They come from mud, and we're in mud up to our necks. If this were peacetime, then you could talk to me of nonsense, but motherfuckers been fightin since time began. I mean, aint never been a time on Earth when there hasn't been murder, and, shit, we been here millions of years, and in all that time there aint never been a time when a Bro aint killing another Bro." I turned and faced Toro. "You can relate cause you've been in the shit with the baddest motherfuckers in America, so you know we can't get caught up in fantasies. The war drums bang, and I hear them clear. They command the day and rule over the night."

"Yeah," Toro nodded and opened up the cliché: "Only the strong survive."

"To me it aint the strong that's gonna survive," I preached. "The strong are fucking all this shit up. The strong smart fucks are gonna get everyone obliterated. It aint the strong that's gonna be here when it all comes to an end. It's gonna be the roaches and little shit bugs. It's gonna be the hardy ones that make it to the finish line, the *vatos* at the bottom of the barrel." I wanted a *leño* because my shoulder was still hurting a bit. "That's where we come in; we can't give a fuck about what's happening out there. That shit gots nothing to do with us. What we got to do is make ourselves hardy—make ourselves ready to accept the doom. And that's when we're gonna be on top, and, Bro, shit's been going down. I know that it's only a matter of time before they find me, and once they got me they got all of us. Right now it's pretty cool. I don't hear shit. I got rid of them, but it aint gonna last forever. They're gonna come back with a vengeance. We got to be prepared for that fact."

Lobo shook his head. "You are really fucking gone, Santo. I mean, you know I love you, Bro, but this shit has gone too far. Somebody's got to tell you you're losing your damn marbles." He looked me in my eyes. I put my hand on his shoulder.

"Don't worry, I got it under control. I'm gonna have it all under control. All I need is time. Time," I said as Lobo looked down at the ground.

"You call the shots," Toro answered. "I'm with you always." Head shaved, standing straight as a hard on, Toro said this and looked about ten feet tall. I smiled.

"Orale." I responded.

After our trek back to the shack, I searched around for pen and paper. Exhausted, I knew I still had lots of work to do. *Yes,* I thought, *all I need to do is make time. I can make time, and we will make it through this storm,* so I started writing down goals and giant lists of things I needed to do. The plans for fortification—and I knocked on the next door neighbor's at three in the morning and asked for a shovel and pick. I woke up Toro, who was sleeping on the floor, and we dug what he called a regulation Marine Corps fighting hole in the living room, the only room besides the bathroom, of our abandoned shack, and we went outside and dug a makeshift moat and filled it up with water. I did all these things to be prepared and to save my sanity because, of course, these are all things that a truly sane man does. Then I crawled down into my little fighting hole and made more lists and more plans, and the sun rose and the sun set, and days passed, and the homeboys came by and said, "What's up, Santo?" but I had no time to give answers. Lobo came by and told me, "Ay, there's always tomorrow." But tomorrow was right now, and I was letting it slip away. And I heard the bells chime a new day every minute. Bong! Gong! There was no time for anything but strategies because I could not let life pass me by without a plan, without a hope for tomorrow.

I rose from the Earth's depths when my list was done. I had been in that hole over two weeks, only leaving to use the head and re-supply. Now there were a hundred pages of plans in all, but as I started thinking, I could not conceive of carrying a book with me. It could be found and used against us. There were too many plans! Sitting on the bathroom's throne, reading my genius, I realized I needed to compress it. On a single sheet of toilet paper, I summarized the main ideas: *I know nothing but repetition and nonsense and can tell you nothing you do not already know...* That is all that was needed; everything else I decided to burn; for my epiphany was that true plans could never be put into words. They must be embedded in the soul. Fuck the rainbow at the end of the storm and the pot of gold at the end of the colorful rainbow! The top secret plans for the future of the *gente* was on a sheet of Charmin toilet paper. I squished the sheet into a tiny ball, and put it in the folds of my sock. After my flush, I opened the door to face the world.

"It's been a while, Bro. You hungry?" Toro was waiting.

"Yeah, food. I need some food."

"Check out, I got five bucks. Let's go get some 99 cent burgers."

"That sounds like a plan."

As we walked the streets to the burger joint, Toro told me that he had started college and was listening to some wild theories about something called "Education." Then we saw Lobo in a line that stretched around the block.

"What you doin, Lobo?" I asked.

"Hey, what's up? Long time, homes." He seemed nervous. "They're giving away cheese, big blocks of it."

"We're about to get some burgers," Toro said.

"Fuck that," Lobo said, "keep your money in your pocket. Save that fare for some beers. Let's cut up to the front and get some free cheese."

186

Each of us grabbed a block of cheese, and when we got to the liquor store, Lobo sold two of them to an old lady coming out of the store. We then went in and bought some beers and bread with the hustled and saved money. We walked to the park and settled down to enjoy our meal.

"Damn, this is some good ass cheese, aint it?" Lobo said.

"Yeah, but why the fuck they give us cheese? Why can't they give us steaks or some shit?" Toro asked.

The cheese tasted too good. "They know what mice like," I said. "They want to kill the mice with poison cheese." I realized that I had already swallowed it. "I ate the fuckin poison, homes. I ate their fuckin poison!"

"We got you now, sucker!"

"Fuck you!"

"Be cool, Santo."

Yes, yes, I had to be cool. For the homeboys' sake, can't trip out. Just keep my mouth closed, just keep my eyes open in this darkness.

"You took the bait and now no one can help you!" There was ringing in my ears. *"We got you now, sucker!"*

Can't trip, can't trip. All right, Lobo's mouth is open, he's talking, telling me something.

"We got you now, sucker!"

Lobo—he's got a point.

"So I've been thinking about it. As a matter of fact, I got this master plan to make some killer fare, but I need some solid *gente*. Just you and Toro and we aint got to trip off nothin for a few centuries. Chinatown: pajama gangsters got bank." Lobo spoke with his mouth open and the orange cheese in his mouth reflected shiny off the sun.

No, no! Not Lobo! "I always knew you were the smartest." Be cool. I looked into Lobo and saw emptiness. "The only thing I can give you is what I got." My heart broke, my soul sank. "All I got is right here." And I pounded my heart, and I pounded my heart, and I gave him all that was inside of me because that was all I had, and I knew it meant my life.

"*Orale!* Then it's all set to jet. Let's go get a deck and a *leño* to celebrate." Lobo put his skinny arm around me.

We walked the city *calles,* broke a few cars' windows, grabbed a few Alpine stereos and six by nine speakers, and sold them at Tip Top's bar. Then with crisp lettuce, we strolled down to the Swamp and hunted for Maton because he had the best prices on dust. In the heart of the Swamp, ten old time junkie vet gangsters stood around still as statues, as if there was a problem.

"What's up, Bro?" I asked Bug, a *vato* I used to look up to when I was a runt.

"Them fuckin Bananas took this *vato*'s jacket. Went straight up to him, threw him to the floor, and took that shit." He pointed to some little *mojado* who was shivering in the cold.

"Fuck them *putos!* This is the Swamp, the original monsters!" Another OG shouted.

Lobo tapped me from behind and talked softly. "Santo, fuck these washed up motherfuckers. This aint our *varrio,* so this aint our problem, let them handle this shit." I looked at the little *mojado* who hadn't done shit to no one, probably just walking home after bustin his ass washing dishes for some bullshit wage under the table.

"Let's see if they need backup. If they don't make the first move, then we'll go." The *veteranos* were deep as we walked across the street to where all the Samoans were kicking it.

The *veteranos* stopped, stood on the street, and mad dogged the Samoans. It was just about even numbers. The Samoans laughed and bullshitted and paid us no mind. "Fuck these punks," Bug finally said, so only we could hear. "Let's go." We all walked back across the street.

"All right, Santo, enough is enough. Let's get a *leño*," Lobo said. I was about to say OK when Big Bird, a *vato* from old times, came out of the cuts.

"Hey, what you *vatos* doin? I seen you all walk from across the street."

"Them fuckin Samoans took this *mojado*'s jacket," Bug said.

"So what's up! You dudes didn't fuck them up?" Big Bird's beak was big. "What's the fuckin world comin to!? This is the original *varrio*! This is Swamp *varrio, por vida!*" I felt nothing at the words, but suddenly Toro began marching across to the other side of the street where two lone Samoan crack dealers sat down on a bench. I joined his side. Everyone followed. Across the street, the Samoans stood watched closely. Even numbers, and the time was ripe.

Toro's little ass walked straight up to the bigger Samoan sitting on the bench. No words. Just punched him in the face. "Where's the fucking jacket, homes!" The other Samoan made a move to get up, and I grabbed his shirt collar and threw him to the floor. "Where's the fuckin jacket!" Toro asked as he pounded the Samoan's head, and Lobo and I stomped the other Samoan on the ground. The Samoans across the street just watched, perhaps figuring if they should go to all out war with even numbers, perhaps wondering if they were really bad. Our Samoan knocked unconscious, I looked up and one, only one giant of a man marched from across the street, threw his jacket to the street, and as he walked, he repeated, "I aint no punk." I ran up to meet him and did a beautiful left, right, left, right combination on his face. He happily accepted the blows, bent down, grabbed both of my legs and slammed me to the pavement. And suddenly there was a swarm of Samoans on top of me, and they were kicking, stomping, and batting my arms with makeshift clubs they broke off from trees. I covered up good, and they finally got off me to stomp someone else, but the Sam that Lobo and I had first knocked out was on top of me with a passion. As he swung a stick at me, I timed his swing and yanked the stick out of his hands. I kicked, jumped up, and scared him away by batting the stick.

Running around a car, Lobo was boxing two Samoans. When he saw me get up, he yelled over for us to get the hell out of there. I looked around for the *veteranos,* who were nowhere to be found. Toro was in the middle of the street getting stomped on by about ten Samoans.

"Let's go!" Lobo yelled. I moved close to the bunch of them and started swinging the stick. "Fuck you Bananas!" I hit a dude on his back and danced away, but still they paid me no mind. While Toro lay unconscious, they practiced daredevil acrobatics on him. "*Putos!* Ya'll can't fuck with me!" I twirled the stick around like a baton. Lobo yelled, "Cops!" And then they charged after me. I ran around cars on the street and Lobo yelled "Cops!" once more and they must have considered it because they ran to their rides and burned out. Lobo and I then sprinted over to Toro. He was out cold, and we ran with him into the closest taco shop, Taco Loco. I jumped over the counter and grabbed the cook by his shirt. "I need a *filero!*" He handed me a giant butcher knife. Lobo laid Toro on top of a booth, and groggily, he woke.

"Ay, homes, I fucked them *putos* up." These were Toro's first bloody words.

"Yeah, you fucked them up with your face and head." Lobo said.

"I can't feel my body," Toro said as I knifed open his pants. He had a nasty open bone sticking out of his left leg. His head was a planet full of pockmarks.

"We got to get him to a hospital," I said. And then our saviors, the cops, pulled up on a shining horse. Chewing gum, emerging cool and complete, they took command.

"What's going on here?" A young Latino cop said.

"Homeboy fell down," Lobo said.

The cop came over to Toro and inspected him. "Did he fall out of an airplane? Hey, Dick, call up an ambulance for this crippled." Dick got on his radio and called in.

"Hey, dude," Lobo said scrutinizing the Latin cop, "I remember you from the days! It's me—Lobo. Remember, homes, we used to kick it—drink that nasty ass liquor down at the school park, smoke that skunk weed on top of the mountain, and mack on all the finest honeys."

"Yeah, yeah. You two clowns turn around and assume the position."

"I know who you are," I said as we turned around, legs spread, hands behind our heads.

"Yeah, I remember you knuckleheads," the Latin cop said patting us down. "Yeah, we used to kick it, but that was many moons ago. I'm in the force now and those days are long gone," he said this as he put handcuffs around our wrists.

"For you they're over. For me it's business as usual," Lobo said. "Man, why you gotta put the cuffs on so tight? We aint done shit. Why you actin like we aint cool? Is it cause of your boyfriend?" Chuckling, Lobo nodded his head towards his partner Dick. "Fuck it. I guess it's your fuckin job, *que no?* But hey, remember we'd box up at the Boys Club? I used to help you off the canvas. Remember Johnny; man, he was a cool old man, you still keep in touch with him?"

The cop confronted Lobo: "Johnny. He's dead. I went to see him at the hospital last month and you know what, I can't believe it, but he asked about you. He asked about *El Lobo* and said how you were one of the best raw fighters he ever saw. What a shame! He wanted you to be there, but there was only me." Lobo's head dropped. "So if I remember right seems as if you had a kid on the way the last time we hung around, you ever take care of him?"

"One kid?" Lobo's head rose, and he mad dogged that cop. "Man, I got lots of em—every street I turned. One here, one there. So many different bitches I don't even know how many fuckin kids I got."

The cop looked away from Lobo and said, "What a worthless waste. May God have mercy on you." The cop shook his head.

"Mercy on me?" Lobo said with his arms shackled behind him. "Listen, homes, where we came from you could either be a good guy or a bad guy. You chose your way; I chose mine. My way was tougher. I remember you. You were a little older than me, and we would box together at the gym, and sometimes we would go and fuck around afterwards. And then you left. You went to college or some shit, and you left the *varrio;* but I stayed, homes. I fuckin stayed and put up with all the *kaka* and all the tears and all the waste, me fucking included. And let me tell you something: you think you're all high and mighty now, with a tin star on your chest, you think you're better than I am, but let me tell you to your face that you left because you were too much of a pussy to do what I do now. You left because you could never do what I do now."

The cop slapped Lobo across the face, proving the wolf's point.

"Let's get these suspects in the car," Dick said winking.

"Yeah, the ambulance is outside for idiot." The Latin cop pointed at Toro's mashed body.

They pushed us outside and stuffed us into the back seat. The Latin cop drove to Tweak Peak and parked. "You are a disgrace to my race," he said to Lobo. "You aren't involved," he pointed at me. Dick grabbed my head and turned it so that I could not see, as if I could not hear.

Knock, knock. Is anyone home?

Afterwards they let us go on that mountain because they knew they didn't have nothing on us. The cops sped off. I started to pick Lobo up off the ground, but he brushed me away and got up solo. It was a full moon, and I knew what he needed. He rose, and we climbed to the top of the mountain. We walked to the edge of the highest cliff, and the wind swayed us around, making it hard for us to stand, but *El Lobo* did not care. He pushed forward and let go at the bright blue moon. He lamented his soul. Never could he release this emotion on the streets. On the streets he had to calm his urges. On the streets he was never completely the wolf. He was forced to remain silent in his agony. But on this night on the mountaintop, his howl would no longer be suppressed. He let it go at the top of his lungs. On the highest cliff, while the wind pushed him around like a rag doll and the moon made his heart flame out, he howled.

He talked with that moon. He conversed with all who had passed and all of those billions of creatures that went to their fate before time started. Yet they all reunited once a month, they who could not talk with words, they who could only scream with light.

They communicated with those who howled, communicated with the power of flash, glow, red, and sometimes they shouted with the power of blue, as on this night, with the power that only the few that have been chosen can hear, the few that walk on four legs and devour livestock and kill innocent sheep, the ones who eat Grandma and Little Red and the ones who must be removed if the world is to survive because they take and take, and never give back. They come at night and do not ask. They steal the food out of children's mouths. And Lobo howled louder, and he howled as mighty as his voice, his soul, his destiny, his immortality allowed. For he would not make it to the next age. The Lobo would not steal away eternity. The Lobo knew that he would one day have to pay.

"OWOOOOOWOOOWOHOOO I will ask for penance later, OWOOOOOWOOOWOHOOO I will shout with light when I die. One day I will light your way on the darkest day, my friends, my dear precious best friends, and *El Lobo* will always be with OWOOOOOOOWOOOHOOO you as long as the moon does glow. My Sheila, my treasure, my love. "

I listened clearly. That pain, that noise, that gift gave him power. For just as he howled out all the evil and degradation within him, he also howled out my own consciousness. It lamented my own fate and lies. His pure moment cleansed me because it revealed to me bitter truth, the deepest depth, the highest space. It told me of billions of years that passed and billions of years that must still come to pass. All I ever understood would be gone one day, but the stones would stand, the sun would shine, and the moon would continue to glow.

After Lobo was done, we walked down the mountain and headed to the gas station. Lobo scoped out broads and asked for numbers. I went to the liquor store, scrambled some change, and grabbed a forty ounce. When I came back, Lobo was pumping gas for two fine *hynas*. They were cruising the *varrio* top down in a new Mustang convertible. As Lobo talked to the driver, I walked over to the passenger and looked into her blue eyes.

"What's up." Not a question, but a statement, a hard quick sentence to size her up.

"Just cruising." And nothing more.

"Yeah, that's my good Bro, Santo," Lobo said pointing to me. "He's a boxer, too."

"Really!" The passenger inspected me, and even though I hadn't eaten very well for the past few weeks, I knew I had a naturally solid one hundred eighty pound frame.

"So you go all around the country too?" The voice of a baby.

Lobo winked at me. "Yeah, everywhere." I had nothing more to say.

"Hey listen, since I just won my bout tonight, let's go out and celebrate," Lobo said.

"What do you want to do?" The driver asked her friend.

"I don't know," the other girl replied.

"I know a spot," Lobo said, "but it's hard for me to explain how to get there. It might be best if I drive." Lobo smiled and stroked the back of his hand softly against the driver's caked face. She liked it. "You sit shotgun, and let my homeboy and your homegirl hog up the back."

"OK." She smiled at her friend, my new backseat partner.

In the back seat of this new car, I asked my girl her name. "Diana," she said.

"Let's get some drink," Lobo said.

"That sounds cool, get us some wine coolers," Diana said.

"Ah, you all are the sophisticated type, eh? Hey, Santo, we're with high class now," Lobo chuckled and turned to his date, "but check out, me and my partner don't get our fare until they count up the gate money, so you know what time it is, right?"

"Huh?" she said.

"Just give me a twenty, honey." Lobo put his hand on her thigh. She hesitantly pulled a twenty out of her purse and handed it to Lobo. Lobo took her hand and held onto it. She tried to pull it away and Lobo yanked on it harder. He bowed his head down and kissed her polished red fingernails. He parked the car at the bus stop across the street from the store and told his lady, "I'll be back in a second, love." Lobo and I jumped out of the car and walked into the store. He asked the man for a fifth of Jose Cuervo tequila and a pack of GPC cigarettes. As we waited for the change, Lobo looked over at me, "Ay, Bro, don't get weird on me, cool?"

"Come on, homes, I know what time it is."

Lobo smiled.

"They didn't have any wine coolers," Lobo lied as we got back into the ride, knowing that only the hard stuff would do the job.

"Oh, that's OK," his lady said.

"I got a fifth instead." As he drove, he stroked his hand on her thigh, and she scooted close. Once on the mountain, we walked to the top where we had been just an hour earlier.

"Look, it's a full moon!" his girl said.

"Really?" Lobo said, "How nice." Lobo grabbed her hand and they walked to a tree.

Diana and I stood around taking turns swigging on the bottle. She broke the silence.

"Do you have a girlfriend?" Bold baby.

"No," I said, "do you?"

"No, I don't have a girlfriend," she laughed, "or a boyfriend."

"You look good. I mean, you got some nice tits and ass." A bolder big boy.

Her cheeks blushed cherry red in the glow of the giant moonlight. "Thank you."

"So what do you do?" I asked.

"I'm working at a doctor's office right now, and I go to school part time."

"Really, that's cool."

"Is all you guys do box?"

"Nah, I kick it."

"What do you mean?"

"I kick it with the homeboys, get into shit, and do what we're doin now. This is my life."

"You mean you do this all the time?"

"Yeah, pretty much, except for a few days here and there when I need R&R."

She did not understand. "Do you have any plans, though, I mean, what do you want?"

"You mean what do I want to do when I grow up?" I laughed. "I grew up when I was two years old. I've been doing this for a while now and it's more than just my job, it's an adventure—except there aint no retirement plan here."

She giggled and handed me the bottle. Our fingers touched.

"Look over your shoulder, you'll find me waiting. I'm everywhere, always for the long haul, through thick and thin, and until the sun don't shine no more. That's what I am. That's what I do." I looked away from her.

"But don't you know you're headed for destruction?"

"I got duty."

"It's sad to me, but your eyes seem genuine. It seems as if I know you from somewhere, somewhere deep inside. I don't know you, but it looks as if you're an honest guy."

"I may be a Saint, but don't let me fool you! Don't think I'm better than you."

"It looks like you know where you're headed, and that's scary to me. You believe in something that much. Sometimes I feel empty." Her head down, Diana swigged off the bottle.

"I understand, Diana. I understand how hard life is, and that's why I'm not going to try to give you quick solutions." I moved closer to her. "Look, tonight is tonight, and I'm gonna laugh with you if you want to laugh, and I'm gonna mourn with you if you want to mourn, but for now, let me put a smile on your face." I let go with some teeth. "But you should know I got sins, and I'm cursed. Nothing will ever make it better, but I got to live and keep going and if you aint with what I do, I understand, cause we all have our own set of values and perspective about how this world turns. I understand that, and I won't insult you with easy weasel words."

She took my hand. "You have a beautiful heart."

"OK," I frowned, "maybe you shouldn't touch me. You don't see my heart is black."

"No, I completely understand," she said. I kissed her mouth hard yet held her soft.

"Do you want to go down to the car?" she asked sweetly, with the voice of an angel.

"We're cool right here. Get down on your knees."

"I'm sorry, I don't do that," she half-smiled.

"Just get on your knees."

"I had a bad experience when I was younger." She snuggled to me. I pushed her back.

"YOU had a bad experience when you were young? Are we children? Can you give up that role?" I got down on my own knees and looked up at her. "Understand I didn't ask you for shit. Understand I didn't ask you to suck my dick or jack me off, I didn't cum in your face. I understand that you can't get down on your knees. That's an abomination to you." I looked up at her fixed hair and nice clothes. "You aint used to bruising your knees for shit." I rose.

She began to cry, "You heartless bastard. You don't know anything about me."

"You could never compare to my true love. You were about to sling me that pussy. You were about to lie down on your back like a lazy bitch and praise the Saint, but to get on your knees was too hard for you, to show me that you could do it with faith was too much. I know what I deserve, so I aint gonna try to convince you to give me heaven when I know I ought to have hell."

"BASTARD!" she yelled out. I heard the rustling of grass by the tree and then I saw Lobo run over to us pulling up his pants and buckling his belt.

"What's up?" Lobo asked.

"This asshole is a fucking bastard." Pointing, Diana lunged at me. Lobo grabbed her.

Lobo controlled her and then looked back over at me. I stood silent and looked in his face. "Bitch, that's my homeboy. You better calm the fuck down before I let you go," he said. Lobo's lady came trotting up trying to fix her hair that was all smashed and tousled.

"What's happening?" she asked with no lipstick on her mouth.

"This asshole is talking shit," Diana said.

"Aint no need for insults," Lobo said, "Let's just walk this off." As we walked, before Lobo even asked anything, I told him, "She doesn't know how to get on her knees." He laughed.

Enveloped in silence and meditation, we walked back to the car while the girls chattered. Lobo opened the driver's door and looked tenderly at his girl.

She stood there with a silly smile on her face, knowing she was fine and that all guys were privileged to be with her. But as they met eyes, she seemed to know Lobo's job.

"What do you think you are doing?" she asked confidently.

"It's like this. There's a phone booth a few blocks down. Give me your shit."

"Huh? You're not serious," she said this as Lobo gently slid the purse out of her hand. "Get in, Santo." I walked over to the passenger's side, got in, and shut the door. Lobo put the key in the ignition, started the car, and we rolled on down the mountain. He turned up the radio. "Hey, Bro, we got a bad ass system. Let's go get Toro."

TEN

Lights Out

The lights out, it was the end of their world. The great morning sun died as they drove into the dirt roads of the bushy brown and green mountainous growth. They went from the power that brightens, driving on the freeway in a top-down convertible being splashed with rays of early morning sunshine, to the darkness and cold of unforgiving forest. Two hundred foot tall redwoods covering them completely in shade, they found themselves in a unique situation that they had never anticipated—none except Toro. He understood first hand the jungle darkness in daytime, so it was he who took charge of the situation. Biting back his pain and anger, he commanded from the back seat of the car. He took off the hospital gown and put on his clothes, cutting off a leg from his baggy blue jeans so his big bandaged leg could fit through the pants hole opening. He sweated and his heart beat fast; he knew it was truly life at last, what he had both yearned for and dreaded since that day so many years past when he had fallen out of the project window.

Toro did not know the area, but the Marines had taught him the power of symbols. According to the map he had once received from the old Devil Dog, Animo, they were at the point for departure. Toro had Lobo pull the car off the winding dirt road into the middle of closely bunched trees. They then camouflaged the car with branches and sticks. Toro commanded them to find two strong pieces of long timber. When Lil Toon came back with sturdy redwood branches, Toro told them to zip up their jackets and slip the jackets' sleeves into the wooden poles. Lobo and Santo then placed Toro onto the makeshift stretcher and fastened him securely with rope from the trunk. Santo emptied the radiator coolant container so they could place water inside of it at some stream.

At seven a.m. on Saturday, September 14, 1991, Toro piloted from the prone—laying on his stomach with his head peering up and out, handwritten map in hand, without a compass—just from the lay of the land and the certainty of north. *As long as I know where north is,* Toro thought, *I know where we're going.* North, he knew, was the side where the moss grows on tree trunks.

They pretended they understood. And so Lobo, at Toro's feet, and Santo, at Toro's head and leading, squatted down, picked up the poles, and moved. Since Toro could not constantly keep his head up and see everything clearly, he would look down at the map and then tell Lil Toon to run up to a reference point in the woods, a tree with a strange hole or bent at a peculiar angle, or a giant, discolored, or beaten up rock; in this way he made sure they were walking a straight line—the positive azimuth. The three would then catch up to Lil Toon. This slow, painstaking process is how they maneuvered and broke through brush and thickets.

The terrain was treacherous, with its steep hills and abrupt, rocky declines. And after a half hour, everything started to look the same. This made Toro question his instincts. *What if this aint the way?* he thought. *What if I don't know where I'm headed? I've got these homies on a mission, but maybe I don't even know the objective. But this is really for Chinatown, for the glory of Lobo's dollar, I guess.* Although these thoughts irritated Toro, he grasped that uncertainty was defeat in this atmosphere. They had to keep going even if it was in the wrong direction, for there was no time to stand still.

The only sounds that escaped Toro's big lipped and dark purple mouth were the few words it took to command "Here" "Over there" "That tree at twelve o'clock." Even though Toro was exhausted, he felt proud that he continued. Glancing at Lobo, he knew that Lobo wasn't worth all this agony. But because Lobo was his homeboy, Toro had obligation and duty. Toro didn't mind bumping up and down for minutes or years if it meant being part of something greater than himself.

Behind Toro, Lobo huffed and puffed as the green grass grew slowly and the red fire ants roared. Having started off too quickly, he had now expended his energy. His pace slowed, and this made Santo work harder because Santo was trying to lead.

They struggled up the highest hill in the forest. Santo kept his head down, and Lobo allowed Santo to pull most of the weight for him. Although the lush greenness overhead kept them cool, sweat rained down their faces. Quickly skipping down the other side of the hill, Lobo grinned. Then as they pushed up another short incline, Santo noticed that the pace was dragging, and he asked Lobo what was up. When Santo glanced back at him, he saw Lobo's unashamed smirk. Although Santo could not see the clouds, he knew the rain was certain.

Santo, however, could not worry; he had to show strength. He had accepted the rules before the game ever began, and he would live and die by the rules that he had freely chosen. To live, you see, after the deaths of so many would have been outside of the rules, outside of the law. *No*, Santo thought. He would flower in death—he would grasp the intensity of the life he had chosen. Santo would follow the letters that were written down, the words and ideas that constituted both death and life, he would rise to meet his fate, and in the end he would be true—so true to all that ever mattered to him, to all that he had ever made of himself. Although he was a sinner, in the end he would make things right. He could only pray that at that last moment homeboys, the world, would know that he was always trying for them—that they would figure it out—that they would see his intentions were always noble. Yet he did not trust their vision.

Only Santo knew the sky was falling, but he did not shout for help to anyone, for only he could see it. *They believe in hope,* Santo thought as he adjusted his grip and looked back and down at Toro twisting his face, trying to ignore his pain, trying to be hopeful and optimistic in this total despair. Santo shook his head and continued thinking, as the first drops of a humid September shower wet them all, *they fool themselves into believing that if there is such a thing as hope, then they are the ones who are hopeful. They mask fears and conform to standards and believe that one day they will be rewarded for their faith.*

I, though, live without that luxury. I've gone through life smiling, crying, and living day by day, and I never looked into any crystal ball because there is no such thing. The now, the present time and forever that is this memory, is what I put all my money on, and nothing can be erased so what good is penance for? I probably am the same as many, but if the holy allow it to show, despair would abound. I put my faith in the power of the homeboy ideal, whatever that is.

All throughout my childhood, I remember Mama and Papa taking me to the drug addict and convict hallelujah church. Whenever they were coming down off a high, they would tell me there was such a thing as a savior. The body, they confidently proclaimed, never rots, but I saw both Mama and Papa in that funeral home, in cardboard boxes because no one could afford real wood, and they were both stinking and rotting and vanishing forever before my very eyes.

Santo focused on Lil Toon, black baseball hat on backwards, dancing his way through the forest, blindly leading the blind. Lil Toon thought of this all as entertainment, and Santo knew that it would all write itself out. There would be an end to the story, and no power could stop it. Santo looked down at his red and swollen hands gripping the makeshift poles. He stared straight at the forest's blackness.

Even in this blackness, I must move because I won't get caught in lies. Once upon a time I fooled myself into believing that the picture would be clear. I strove to create reasons for my insanity and solemnity. I studied the Bible, read the stars. An honor student in junior high, placed in gifted classes, I would challenge the teacher. Then, I strove to find wisdom in the streets, in the dark corners of dungeons, in the red hell of the sun. It was a waste of time, but it comforted me to run around in circles. It is worthwhile and pleasurable to waste my time with theories.

"Achoo!" Toro sneezed.

"God bless you," Santo said. The brief rainstorm had passed, and now the dirt that they kicked up contained the freshest ingredients to disturb allergies.

Toro had held the sneezes in as long as he could, his eyes watering and his nose stuffing up, but something in the air or in the bush was torturing him. Toro was once again on the front lines, crashing through shrubs and downed trees. Like a good Marine, he had held in his sneezes for the sake of silence.

To him, the situation was ludicrous, but he knew why he had joined them. *I got to get up all the damn time cause one victory don't mean shit. I constantly prove myself cause motherfuckers forget too easily. I rise and charge. Aint nothin real unless I can feel the flesh hit my horns.*

"My pain's real, Bro. Let me get another hit off that water," Toro said to Lobo, who huffed and puffed hard.

It had been an hour and a half of up and down hill mud and dirt. Santo's tense hands cramped, yet he held onto the poles that sustained Toro the rock. Santo struggled to master the pain—he meditated that his hands were soaking in warm water. He closed his eyes, trusted his fantasy, and walked forward; and he told himself he would not trip, but he did. Santo's grasp gave way when he stumbled over a foot-long crack in the earth, and Toro fell on his face. Lobo scrambled to retain his footing and did not let go of the poles. Lobo laughed, placed Toro down, put out his hand, and lifted Santo off the ground. Santo wiped the dirt off of his knees. He realized that he had fucked up and busted his homeboy's gourd. To remove the cobwebs, Toro shook his head a few times, then was the first one to shout for them to march on.

With the scraggly beard of a bum, Santo mumbled out loud as if no one could hear him. Toro's body tightened. Lobo smiled. He knew Santo was on one of his trips. The reality of who Lobo had called up to help him hit him hard: Purple headed little Toro. Nut job Santo. Baby faced Cartoon. Lobo laughed.

His laughter made him nostalgic for the rotten piss in the back alleys of *Varrio Montaña*. Lobo thought, *When we get back, we'll come as champs and make sure we hog the bread we deserve. Aint just Chinamen who can be gangsters.* Lobo reflected on his position in life and tried to understand at least a bit of Santo's audible inarticulation.

Like him, Lobo shook his head, *I'm a fucking schizo; it's that paranoia keeps me going.*

But just cause I'm nutty don't mean I can risk losing all the cards I've stuck up under my sleeve and stacked up and built up—cause a strong wind's blowing, and this house gots no foundation. I'm afraid that it'll all just blow away, and then I'll be left with nothing, nothin after so many years hustling. The only property I got is a castle of cards, all aces and big jokers, and I can't afford to have it destroyed just cause Sheila blew me a kiss, so I don't want no more of her kisses, no more tender breaths under the covers cause it all threatens who I am and the home I've built. Like I said, the house aint got no foundation, but what can I do about that now? It's home. All I can do is be very careful and love what I've got cause without it I'm a homeless bum. And I can't have her be a homeless bum with me; she deserves better. The next world's gotta be better.

The squirrels in their trees, moles in their holes, snakes slithering in the grass looked at and listened to Lobo parading through their home. *My haunted castle of ghosts and goblins. We laugh all day and party all damn night and nothing is ever left for imagination. Every day was fun and crazy, daring and dangerous, sad and painful, tragic or terrible and happy faces and hard looks. Everything was true and proper and real forever.*

"We're gettin close," Toro stated. He realized that he had said it more for himself than for any of them. He had spoken just to hear a voice—to get away from the scattering of squirrels and Santo mumbling to himself. Bombs burst from the pain and tragedy of his leg. Still, Toro was pleased. He knew he could tell the homeboys nothing they would want to hear, but in his heart he knew that they were collectively in this game. *We're gettin to the destination together*, he smiled, *mission accomplishment, together, whatever that mission may be*—juntos. It was Toro's Marine ideal for the homeboys, so he smiled even happier, was utterly inspired. *You guys got to be my reason for life, cause I don't matter. And this may be self pity or a lack of self esteem. Maybe it's even downright wrong—wrong as the red sky, the left hand, the black night, the world that surrounds us. But we have to be right for each other, no doubt about it, fully automatic machine gun on full blast—free gun all around—right like the might of love at first sight.*

We pick each other up off the ground, never abandon each other until death comes around and snatches us up, and then we're stopped, but the legacy continues—stronger—the myths, traditions of barbecue and beer, the walk and talk with new words, the eyes with fresh faces—cause while we're here, while we got the world in our grasp, we gotta do what we gotta do to live without regrets, to live without fear, to place our heads up and be filled with dignity even if we know we've fucked it all up. Cause what the fuck do I know about this or that? I spent my whole life on that wire, homes, all my life with a big ass stick for balance. All my life I'm teetering and tottering on the brink of destruction, but now I'm comfortable wakin up on the high wire. I walk to take a piss in the mornin, heavy and hungover, and a fall aint gonna make me any less of a man cause we proved ourselves for way too long—that loaded as fuck we could keep our asses up on that string. I never had nothin but a string of thread for security.

If this is all the same bullshit, then it's all the same bullshit cause I'm looking for strength, the will to power. Toro bit on his bottom lip to make himself feel better.

No one cared about Lil Toon. No one paid him any mind—he was the point, but no one realized it until they were already there.

"This is it," Toro said as they skipped him down into the lowest ravine in the area. Santo and Lobo placed Toro on the ground and kept silent as the oceans of what this meant overcame them. For ten minutes, they waited.

A man rose from the depths to meet them. His face was painted green, gray, black and brown, and a streak of silver dotted what were his eyes. He was the mud and the roots, and he was the underground.

"Animo," Toro muttered. "It's the biggest bullshitter you've ever known."

"Torito," Animo whispered and bent down to shake his friend's hand. "You have remembered the good Corps teachings." He looked at Toro's bloody bandaged leg and inspected the make-shift stretcher that the homeboys had created. Looking at the other three men, Animo said, "You must pay close attention to my steps. Where I go, you must go also." Animo then holstered his standard issue nine millimeter Beretta. "Come, and say nothing," and Animo revealed a manhole in the earth and stooped forward through a maze of tight tunnels. He pointed out camouflaged pits with feces covered stakes, with Claymore mines and "Bouncing Betties" hiding in corners of turns; booby-trapped fish wire ran across the lanes. The homeboys dragged and lifted Toro and had to follow Animo's exact steps or they might jeopardize everyone's life.

When they finally reached HQ, Santo noticed there was no God in the room. Guns and ammunition were scattered everywhere. Shelves of books surrounded the room. Strewn around on tables and the ground everywhere, open books revealed highlighted passages. On one wall there was a big sign that stated the following: Commit an act of worship: STUDY.

Heavy but hard, forty-year-old Animo noticed that Santo stared at this sign.

"You've come because the end is near," Animo said as he picked Toro up and propped him into a cold metal chair.

Toro patted the dirt off of his shaved head. "I've come cause it's time, and if that means that the end is near, then it also means there's a new beginning to be met."

"What's mine is yours," Animo said. He looked at Lobo's and Santo's hard unforgiving faces. Lobo's skinny fingers massaged one of the M249 machine guns that was piled in a corner. "This's gonna be for Chinatown fireworks and homeboy gold," Lobo said.

"This is the age I expected, when no one would abide by any rules." Animo scratched his thick salt and pepper beard. "Well then, I understand revolution: new rules must be made, and you will be the creators. I only wish I could be a part of it, but my duty keeps me holding down the fort." Animo stretched his bent back and stood proud.

Looking around at the basement bunker, Lobo could not help but think of stupidity. "If a motherfucker gots to live like this, then there aint no point for me bein here," Lobo responded. "If everything were already completely gone, I'd be the first to swallow a bullet, but you fool yourself, fool, cause it may come to what you're thinkin; radiation, fallout, and anarchy all over the damn place; but right now there's still pussy, still dope. Out there they got music and noise, and it may only be for a little while longer, but that's cool with me cause I figure that the end is gonna come quick anyway, and I aint even gonna know it's comin, so what the fuck should I be afraid of? Ten minutes? I'll get my dick sucked while them nuclear warning sirens blast. Let me be extinct if I can't bust a nut. And I'm gonna bust me many nuts after Chinatown."

"You are a quick thinker, friend of my friend." Animo put his two hands on the imaginary lapels of his standard Marine Corps camouflage shirt, as if he were a statesman addressing his country, "But I will continue, slow and sharp—unraveling my confusion—and I tell you that it was because of me—and the like—that you can speak those words so frankly!" Animo's right fist hit the table hard. "It will be because of me, in the times to come, that we will travel without spaceships—like the light. And I will be here frozen in my freezer, and maybe one moment in the future, I will be thawed out of heaven or hell and be sent back to this body on Earth because the legacy of my struggles have unlocked the mysteries of the universe. Perhaps you cannot understand that, perhaps that is blasphemy to your ears."

When Santo heard these words, he wanted to kneel; he felt he had met his guru, his soul mate, at last.

"Just like you said it, pops," Lobo responded. Lobo did not care to get into any further waste of time. "You got the answers. All I know is I need some of your heat."

"So who is your god?" Completely enthralled, Santo turned and faced Animo.

"As if you had to ask." Animo stole Santo's energy and used it for his speech. "That struggle to live, even though you know you'd be better off dead, is more powerful than the sun. It shines all around, and you convince yourself that this thing we call life is better than complete annihilation because you just don't know if myths are true." Animo emphatically shook his jar-head from side to side. "You've been convinced of so much pain, and have been told that this place is nothing compared to the other side, that over the rainbow there is no sky and no air—only truth, and Truth—let me be the first to help you see clearly—Truth is only an absurdity, nonsense; for how the hell can you be honest with the truth?! You imagine you can be, but that imagination is greater than any cartoon or science fiction movie—and so you are left only with imagination—perhaps cursed with imagination, and only imagination can create the dread that you see before you." Animo waved his painted green Frankenstein hands over his room, and they all looked around at missiles stacked up, cans of ammo, rats in cages with a barbecue pit near them, and big books with little print. Animo stepped into Santo's face.

"Now is this imagination?" Animo asked, pointing to his own forehead with his middle finger. "I tell you it is fiction—make believe—and I tell you it is more powerful than any reality. For only you know that truth—naked, hypothermic truth shivers and shakes like a coward at the power of imagination.

"For you have imagined that there are such things as emotions and feelings, songs and beats, colors and streams, clouds and speed, fire and words.

"This is your planet, your god," Animo poked Santo's brain with his middle finger. Toro slouched and rested his eyes. Lobo tried to pick the best weapons available. Lil Toon read from the books on the table. Animo continued. "It controls who you are in this world. This planet that you are has prioritized value—and these are words you believe exist in this outside world:

"Words such as life.

"Words such as death.

"Only you know the definition of these words. And is this fact or fiction? Only you know.

"So, friend of a friend," Animo put his hand on Santo's stiff shoulder, "if you can let your heart pump for life the way it once did as a child, if you can release the pressure that the dam can no longer hold, then I beseech you to submit to your *corazon*," Animo stood strong.

"Or can it be that we have become too intelligent, too serious, too enlightened to believe in red hearts?" Animo looked up at the ground above them.

Santo could only look at his feet and question his entire identity, the meaning of independence. Did he believe there could be such a thing redder than the lava of a volcano, fiercer than the fire in the barbecue pit? He was afraid to make that decision, afraid to judge if red hearts truly were real—afraid to judge because he knew he was the worst sinner of all. It was then that the voice that was always growing inside of him spoke, and Santo no longer knew himself. Yes, there was the outside man of Santo, but that man was simply a face for the collage. It was then Santo knew there could be no control of agony in hell; there could be no bearing in total chaos. It was then that Santo remembered that God had turned away the sacrifice of green grass and yellow corn, and the red tomatoes were not red enough. God had specifically asked Abraham for red hearts, and God had loved Abel much more than Cain because blood was pure and clean, and the ground's harvest was dirty and filthy. Yes, Santo believed in red hearts, and he would offer only the best to his lord. He knew what he would have to do. And Santo must have truly been a saint, for he did not tremble. His hairs did not stand, nor did his flesh swell. His holy instincts took over, and he accepted the fate he controlled.

Once they packed up the arms in two duffel bags, Animo led them back out to the forest.

They did not stop for long goodbyes, for time could not stop. The ultimate hour had arrived, and they must have realized it, for none asked for a break or a rest. Toro used Animo's compass and they soon reached their hidden Mustang, which was off the side of the road. Once they swept the leaves and branches off of it, they laid Toro in the back seat. Both Santo and Lil Toon sat crammed in the passenger seat while Lobo started up the car and peeled out.

Lobo, oh, what grand meals he envisioned. Toro, what pain he bit back. Santo twisted and turned with no dreams and no pain, nothing but the horror of certainty. Lil Toon bumped his head from side to side, lip synching the raps on the radio, his hands flying up and down as if he were trying to fly.

They made it back to the shack as two o'clock chimed. Lobo knew that they all needed rest and relaxation or else they would not be able to function effectively for the next day.

"No matter what anyone does, let's get back together over here at noon tomorrow. I'll have it all figured out by then. All you guys should do now is chill to the fullest—make it count."

Still bleeding and spinning from the concussion, Toro told Lil Toon to get him a duster. After a run, Lil Toon came back and Toro took a few puffs. He nightmared through unbearable agony.

Lobo shut his eyes and set his plastic alarm watch for five o'clock in the afternoon. At five, he knew he would still have enough daylight in Chinatown to set up the whole plan. Questions set him to sleep: *How much money did runners drop off on Sundays? What kind of gangster security did they have? Would good old-fashioned citizens try to save the day? Where was Sheila? How was Sheila?* And then Lobo was snoring.

Listening to Lobo's gargling, Santo could not sit still. He tried to sleep because that's what his body told him to do, but it was

214

impossible to sleep when this might be the last time he independently felt life. His hands shook, and his face poured down sweat. His thoughts shuffled around at one hundred miles an hour. Santo got up and ran.

He sprinted down Army Street, dodging in between couples walking, people talking, little babies being strolled down the sidewalk. He ran through red lights and the ruckus of beeping horns. He was faster than a messenger boy on his bike, able to leap fire hydrants in a single bound, and stronger than the branches of a red rose bush he trampled through. He didn't know where he was going, but he wanted to just keep on running so that he could tire out his uncontrollable body and think with his head.

After thirty minutes, Santo reached the bay. He looked out at the murky brown waters and started running in place. He was a perfectly healthy young man, yet in approximately thirty hours, he was committed to breathe no more. So Santo, who was still shaking, jumped into the dirty, cold water and started swimming. And all the piss, shit, diapers, and tampons floated in the water beside him. He swam fast and breathed deeply, with all of the vigor in his lungs he breathed more and more deeply.

Santo swam far out into the middle of nowhere. When he finally tired, he stopped. Looking back at the dock, he realized that he was at least a half mile from shore. Because he did not think he would be able to make it back, he began to panic and started to sink. When he realized it did not matter if he made it back or not, he became absolutely spastic. When all was seemingly lost, a calm spirit flew over him.

A seagull flew down and landed in the water next to him. The bird briefly looked at him flailing, and then started gliding to shore. Santo sank and struggled: kicking, swallowing water, and punching slow feeble fists into water that could not be hurt. The bird swam to the shoreline while Santo went into convulsions in the water. A strong, virile, young man that could bench press three hundred pounds could not beat the ugly, big faced bird. So Santo, a human being since birth, became the bird. He started flapping his wings, and he soared through the water. Spreading out his feathers, he floated to shore.

When Santo made it to shore, he took off everything except his boxer shorts, socks, and Converse All Stars. He balled up the rest of his wet clothes, threw them as far as he could into the water, and jogged back to the shack.

As he jogged, he thought about his life: the beautiful moments of meeting Mari, winning a fight, hogging on a humongous pizza pie. But now his mortality beckoned, and he considered his mistakes. Where had he gone wrong? At what point had he made that irreversible left turn into Fucked Up Alley? What was the hour and exact minute of the point of no return?

It was going to be in one second. For in one second, at exactly four fourteen p.m., he reached the liquor store down the block from the shack and an obscene thought overcame him.

He would write it down.

He would die; to him, there was no doubt about that, but he would leave his legacy so that others could learn. He would write it so that it had to be true. Santo would research the furthest depths of his soul. Because he had to leave a legacy behind him, he would write what should never be written or spoken about. And he would not burn it this time. He would not repeat a manifesto of the mind; he would, instead, weave a history for his people who had no history. He would write it; then he would force himself to die.

Santo did not know what mattered—he questioned the world,

what truly counted, and then he pulled out the short summary of life that he had kept from his previous manifesto. He meditated and then began something new: *Mine was not to question…*

His hours numbered, Santo knew that only the true story needed to be told. It was his voice, and then it wasn't. Then everything became a blur, and he did not know whether he was writing the story or whether the story was writing him. Santo did not know if it was past, present, or future—only that it was, perhaps, eternal—forever—never ending—never before—never again. It calmed him. It helped him accept what would happen because after it was written it could never be taken back—for writing from the heart required a dedication, a pact, an oath that could in no way be broken.

:: :: ::

Toro knew he was awake when the sweat almost drowned him. His body spilled streams and his shivering flesh was ice cold blue. He had not realized that this was the worst case scenario. Unsalvageable, his leg was leaving him. *Maybe, maybe,* Toro thought, *if I go to the hospital right now, they could stop the pus from spreading to my heart,* but then he looked down at his ragged bandages soaked with his wet blood—*no chance for him.*

His hard head spun with ideas and emotions that overwhelmed him—*I'm tired; it takes so much from me to know I'm forced up outta a warm bed, and I'm still supposed to keep going. A simple nap can't energize me for this one. Lobo's still sleeping like a baby. He needs strength for tomorrow. Me, too, and I want to square everything the fuck away and not leave any loose ends or sad faces. I don't want no one to mourn for me cause I want it to be known that it should be a celebration. I deserve what I get for that fucked up shit we did.* He released the ideal. *Ah, who ever gave a fuck about me anyway?*

217

Mama. But by going and showing her his suffering, he would only cause her worse pain. Still, he had to notify her somehow that she did not birth him, raise him, cry for him for nothing—for he knew that's what they would brainwash her with, and she would believe it because she was a simple lady that believed in the goodness and logic of the masses. They would tell her he was a despicable criminal, unfit to live and breathe. Looking at her in disgust, they would say he was a monster. Yet she would still love him—still have given her life for him and worked sixteen hours a day for him; nonetheless, she would feel betrayed.

She would love Judas, but he did not want to be Judas. Guilty of hurting the innocent, he had to accept his guilt. He did not want that for her; she did not deserve it. He propped himself onto the wheelchair, his leg throbbing, eyes watering from the pain. He looked over at Santo in his hole, frantically writing on a notepad. Toro asked Santo for a page and a pen, and Toro began to make magic with his love, a magic that was not English or Spanish, a combination of the two that could only be deciphered with years of growing up in the *varrio*—

> *Mi Madre Querida,*
>
> *Nunca pare porque tu tampoco nunca te paraste. Solo tengo la disciplina que tu me diste, y si yo no escuche y no conforme a las reglas fue porque quice hacer alguien mas para ti. Te van a decir que fui monstro, salvage. Quedete con orgullo cuando oyes esas palabras, porque significa que tu hiciste tu trabajo bien.*
>
> *Con todo amor, sinceridad, y humildad,*
> Sonny Boy

He signed the letter, and then asked Lil Toon to roll him outside. Toro placed twigs and branches in an empty steel garbage can.

Lighting a match and breathing in the smoke's fumes, he fanned the flames high and hard. He tossed the letter in and covered up the fire with his hospital gown. Then he let out the smoke high into the sky, sending the message to heaven.

The smoke signals reached the house with the little chubby woman making her *frijoles* and *caldo de pollo*. She smelled the smoke first, then looked out the window and stepped outside onto the sidewalk, wiping her *gordita* fingers on her apron. Neck stretching, looking at smoke in the heavens, she was filled with the presence of her son whom she had lost many hard years before. She saw him floating away and sank down to her knees in the middle of the potholed street. She understood, yet the understanding could not console her, for she cried and shouted royal words, "Toro, Toro, *mi hijo, mi hijo*."

Toro stayed outside even after the smoke was gone. Head bowed low, he remembered his mama in a beautiful way. She had always been absolute in her traditional peasant ways. She had never trusted America to give opportunity; therefore, she milked America for opportunity. She did it with hard work, persistence, and an intentional ignorance of discrimination. She knew that nothing would be given without a cost, even the free welfare and food stamps. They cost dignity, or at least they tried to charge, but she never accepted that price. She hustled the entire time she collected welfare. She worked under the table jobs cleaning houses and saving her money, while others who had been brainwashed by illusions of funny money, lay down and died, only to rise twice a month on the first and fifteenth, welfare paydays. Toro's mama kept all the junk, making them cramped in their project apartment—but Toro did not want junk. He wanted to be new. He wanted to be fresh and clean and Latinized in the American sense. He wanted to be that stereotypical American gangster *cholo* he saw all over his neighborhood, and he dreamed he could be cool as he watched the homeboys kick back under the corner street lights.

But Toro's mama did not know what cool was—except for the dark at night when the wind slapped the windows hard, which was cool enough for her. Chillin with fillin, dukin and dancin, hittin high and hard was pure nonsense, the most absurd play game. Could coolness pay the water bill? Could the sidewalk shuffle and mad dog stare fill the belly? Only shame could do that; only knee bruising scrubbing and grape picking strutting could bring the fulfillment of a hot plate to their table.

But Toro could not imagine her ideal any more than his mama could understand his. She would look at Toro when he was ten, with the thick bandana on his head, the shiny spit shines, and his spiked black hair greased back with Crisco cooking oil, and she saw a *puro pendejo*. He looked into the broken mirror and saw a prince. His royalty, however, didn't count in the outside kingdom, for he had no gang. He was torn between the world of his mother and that of the streets. He did not want to abandon his mother, but he also did not want to be a punk. Toro wanted intelligence and significance, but smart in the *varrio* was not calculus and astronomy. He could not plot stars to show his worthiness as the generations of his ancestors had.

Toro was solo. He never accepted that his mother always agreed with the people at school, when she believed in their authority to raise him. Feeling they had the answers, she thought they could help Toro because they were professionals. She sold herself short, believing that her opinions and beliefs were second class—and she became so brainwashed with this mentality in the land of opportunity that she did not realize she did not even have a mind of her own anymore—democracy mattered; the majority ruled! So when she saw the boys from around the neighborhood dying, killing, and walking *con dolor*, she came to tell Toro, "Don't be a *pendejo* and get your ass killed—run away!" Toro tried to block this terrible noise from his ears. He would get so angry at the words and confused at the meaning, because maybe, he would think, *maybe she's right*, but it hurt him too much to think that, and so he would want to disown his blood and run far, far away where no one would ever know who he was.

That's also why he chose to charge. To show his mother. That's how he eventually made his mark. Toro, understand this, had been whipped up and down the block, round and round the fence. A mama's boy. He was a spectacle, a fool among fools, not even strong enough to be a runt. Only pretending to understand mean faces, he was the sideshow in a circus.

Toro was alone. He wanted the ideal, but that was dangerous, might mean scars and time, life and death. Up to that point he had sat safely on the outskirts and watched life as a movie. After school, he would go home talking to imaginary Bros. The leader, Toro had fun.

He had played by himself for too long, mastered his mask of machismo very well with the hours he spent in the prison that was his room. Whether he believed who he could be or he was simply tired of seclusion is not certain, but what is certain is that Toro chose to charge.

Seventh grade, 1982, dressed in baggy brown Bens, white sneakers, he took a piss in the boys' bathroom, unafraid of the gang there. He hoped someone would start with him, but he was unknown. Toro prayed to be challenged, but the gang messed with a lamb, and the lamb laid down. Though he was outnumbered and he didn't even like sheep, he attacked and made the lamb's problem the bull's problem. Toro headlocked one of the homeboys, any homeboy, and did not let go. More than anything he had ever desired, he wanted to kill, and with every second of squeeze, he grew happier. It was a one-on-one and respected as such, but finally the homeboy Santo scrambled out of the lock and caught his breath. Having charged blindly, Toro now saw that he had attacked the only homeboy who had ever stood up for him: the Saint who had saved him one year earlier.

When Dean Murphy and two security guards walked in, the boys automatically assumed innocent expressions and started combing their hair.

"What's goin on here?" Dean Murphy asked.

"Huh?" Everyone answered dumbly.

"Quit pulling my pud. I know when something's up. Is it you, rat boy?" Dean Murphy grabbed Lobo by the shirt collar and dangled him by his feet.

"Man, you best get your hands off me, Murph," Lobo kicked Dean Murphy in the shin. The bathroom roared with laughter.

"All right, fucker, you just caught another suspension," Dean Murphy said.

"I enjoy vacations," the young, skinny Lobo said as a security guard dragged him out.

"Let's clear this up," Dean Murphy ordered. The crowd in the bathroom dispersed. It was going to be ended just like that, and maybe Toro could have gained some respect just by his show, but he knew the proper etiquette for seventh grade drama. With the most serious face he could muster, he advanced up to Santo.

"After school," Toro told Santo. Santo looked surprised, as if he did not understand this challenge. Santo thought that it must simply be a bad joke from a wannabe comedian.

"*Bajo* Park," Santo smiled and walked away at the lead of the homeboys. He did not think twice about it because he did not consider Toro a very serious threat.

Toro, however, knew exactly what this meant. Throughout the day, he remained silent, lonely as always, yet strangely happy. When the school bell rang, he walked through the back streets where no one would see him. He knew that this would be the last time doing it this way. He knew that this day marked a beginning. As with all new experiences, there was sadness, anticipation, and fear. He did not know whether he was making the best choice. The homeboys might jump him. The fight might mean embarrassment beyond belief, especially if he were to lose severely. The homeboys did not care about getting into trouble.

Toro knew only that the loneliness he endured and the shame he carried around in his heart were too much to bear. He would either break out of despair or die trying. No one else would fight his battle or force him to cross the street in fear. No one would snatch honor's imagination away from him, for he saw himself as not so cool and not so quick with slick words and fine rhymes, but he saw himself accepted, and he imagined the noblest of words from other *vatos locos'* mouths: "Toro, he's crazy, a down homeboy." And crazy was the best compliment he could ever hope for. For crazy meant he was sick with it and out of his mind: insane, no brain, one of the few and true. He knew that in the *varrio* a brain would not get you where you wanted to go, a mind made you a fool, perfect health meant you were worried about death—but crazy meant independence: life, liberty, and the pursuit of pain—because Toro knew crazy had consequences. That's what made crazy so complete and fulfilling; because it could never be mistaken for a fairy tale.

All of the homeboys could believe in it. And a crazy homeboy only feared one thing: living too long. And a crazy homeboy would go up and meet the challenge without the security of confidence. A crazy homeboy was always unsure about every little movement and sound, but a crazy homeboy knew his insanity would never abandon him. As Toro closed in on the park and saw homeboys passing around a bottle of Mad Dog 20/20 wine, Toro knew that showing up for the fight was sheer lunacy, yet he continued sure and steady.

He looked around at the scattered oak trees of *Bajo* Park, the empty basketball courts. Santo was nowhere. For one second, he knew it was not too late to turn back. Santo must have not taken the challenge seriously. Toro could return back to whence he came without any loss of face, but Toro, instead, walked up to one of the homeboys and asked, "Where's Santo?"

"He's kickin it at the house," the homeboy said.

"Go tell him that it's time to fight," Toro said.

The homeboy's head retreated, confused at the audacity of such a person. "Who should I tell him's here?" The young homie asked.

"He'll know." Toro folded his arms and postured himself against the wire gate. The homeboy took off. And Toro had never learned how to fight nor box. In his head, all Toro could do was go over Bruce Lee and Rocky movies because he had no game plan whatsoever.

After approximately five minutes, Santo ran up with a gang of homeboys behind him. He threw off his shirt in grand display and let the wind take it to where it wanted to go. Santo put his dukes up. Charging, Toro caught two knocks on the head. Toro threw wild fists out and hit empty air. Santo backed up, stepped to the side, and aimed at the X's that were Toro's eyes. Toro blinked as he felt the bee's stings, but he reached out and grabbed onto Santo's pants and took him to the ground. Toro was on top, and he pushed his fists right into Santo's smile. Toro was then flipped over by the momentum of Santo scrambling. Santo got back up on his feet.

Santo landed six, seven while Toro landed one. Still, Toro would not tire or quit. He maintained his forward movement. When Santo bent down for air, Toro allowed him to break. Every now and then, the homeboys shouted out words of encouragement and praise to Santo. Toro stood alone and let Santo get some water. They boxed more, and now it was only four to every one shot for Toro. When Toro landed a right on the dot, Santo turned his head and walked away. Toro allowed him to regain his senses and catch his breath; then they started from the top with Santo connecting a beautiful volley of five on Toro's head. Toro bent forward and grabbed Santo by his tank top, and then they were on dirt and rocks rolling and tumbling, and Santo fish hooked Toro and tried to tear out his jaw. Toro squeezed the lock that he had on Santo's neck. Toro heard the homeboys' silence. With this hushed support, Toro squeezed harder. But Santo would never give up. He would let his life go, and now Toro was uncertain, for now he truly had that power in his arms—to kill and be crazy. This uncertainty caused Toro to speak.

"I won," he said.

"Nah," Santo said in a faint voice.

"I could kill you," Toro said.

"Go head," Santo whispered. Toro was scared by these words for he knew that Santo meant it. Toro would not continue then, but he would not have done all this to lose face either.

"I'm gonna let go, but you didn't win," Toro said.

"Nah," Santo muttered.

"I get up, then, and we both walk away."

"Yeah," Santo gasped.

Toro let his grip go, and he helped Santo up. The homeboys hugged and praised Santo. They walked away, and Toro was left battered and bruised, double black eyes, tendered meat for supper. He hung around the park for a while and thought about what he would tell his mother. His mother would say she was right, that he was an idiot for trying to be a *cholo*. So Toro would not tell her. Alone, he cried, and no one heard.

He walked home and slipped in the door. The mama called for him to eat some food. Toro yelled back that he was sleeping. He woke at two in the morning, crept out of his room, and found his plate was covered with a cloth to keep it warm, but by then the food was cold. He ate because he needed strength. Toro heard his mother leave for work early the next morning. He lay awhile in bed without sleeping, then got up and left the house. He cut school and rode the bus around the city. He wore dark shades and looked out the bus's window all day long. When darkness overcame the land, Toro marched to *Bajo* Park and waited. The homeboys came blasting a boom box. They looked at Toro and knew that he was of fine stock, bred to battle.

"Look at this crazy fool!" Lobo smiled pointing at Toro. Proud, Toro stood silent. He was one of them forever.

:: :: ::

Lobo woke to Santo scratching on paper in his hole. Without shaking his head, he dressed himself in black, went outside, and saw Toro asleep in his wheelchair, dim smoke drifting out of the metal garbage can that they sometimes used as a barbeque pit. At

5:15 p.m., he sped off to Chinatown in the girls' stolen Mustang. After finally giving up trying to find legal parking in overcrowded Chinatown, he parked in a parking spot reserved for the disabled. Lobo then looked up towards the puffy pillowed sky and saw his ultimate objective: the largest, most dynamic golden cross he had ever seen before in his life. *There's Christianity in Chinatown,* Lobo thought, but the true religion, Lobo realized after walking in a trance for five minutes, was in the hustle and bustle of the marketplace where natives, not tourists, abounded. Chinese men, women, and little kids shoved along the streets of the overcrowded fish and vegetable stands, as windows displayed greasy brown ducks hanging by their necks. The smell of fresh fish and salty seasonings entered his nostrils, and the chopped tonal language invaded his ears. The squawk and bock of chickens challenged Lobo at every turn. He was happy when he finally crossed into the souvenir streets. Although he was not looking for gifts, he could not help but notice the happy fat golden Buddhas and ivory elephants' tusks, the bouncing rabbits and the fierce dragons breathing fire onto the cold, narrow, over-populated streets. On side alleys, shirts and underwear hung out on lines from the windows of run down tenements.

The skyscrapers surrounded the area and protected the land. Bums on street corners listened to radios, yet did not even ask for change. In a store window, Lobo saw a rendition of Jesus Christ nailed to a thick tree, no cross. Pretty women walked with their heads down, and he marveled at a man in a blue business suit walking with his two sons who were proudly shooting off toy space-ship guns. Construction hammers and drills pounded new ideas into the dirt, and there was red, red, red everywhere he looked. Lobo felt lucky.

No fireworks or Kung Fu kings. No fighting, kicking, and

punching Bruce Lee style; it was simply business as usual—180 degrees away from the myths he saw on TV and the movies. Lobo looked at the names of the streets and saw some were named after American presidents. Then he looked at the community's inhabitants, who were mostly Chinese. To the Chinatown natives, their own streets' names were merely funny titles that had no significance in their lives. These people were making their own America. They were brown and yellow just like him; he thought their language sounded a lot like his Indian grandmother's native tongue.

About to reach the church with the great cross on top, he halted to look at a beautifully crafted ornament of gold and ivory outside of a store window. This Buddha was unique, at peace. Underneath it, in English, a note explained the sculpture: The heavenly kingdom is free from all the frustrations of the five senses. *Man,* Lobo thought, *a heaven where you can't feel it sink in and pull out, a heaven without whips on the back or nails in the hand, huh, pretty wild.* He felt better for Sheila. Crossing the street, Lobo then almost tripped over an ugly young lady sitting on the sidewalk selling shiny pieces of jade. On the cement, she sat Indian style while old ladies squatted down to inspect the jade's quality. Looking down into her face, Lobo wanted to call her a stupid bitch, but then he realized he was now in front of the monster church he had seen from his parking spot. He made the sign of the cross in front of the grand Gothic construction that was ornamented with sharp statues and a giant golden cross on top of its bell tower. On the front of the church was the command: *Son, observe the time and fly from evil.* Instead of cursing at the pimple-faced hag, Lobo handed her a dollar bill and gave her a smile. Lobo would not let despair enter his heart.

Almost forgetting he was actually supposed to be looking for the park, he saw that the park was right down the block from the church. He knew a reconnaissance of the park had to be made, but he quickly turned around and walked away. First he would get himself a drink and a smoke. That way he could think clearly. He walked to the nearest liquor store and bought himself a twenty-four ounce can of Budweiser to wrap in a brown paper bag and a pack of Marlboro Reds. He did this so that he would not be completely overwhelmed by the foreign land. His vices also gave him a sense of serenity and security, for he was used to parks, had been kicking back in them all his life. How could he chill with open sky and green grass without a drink and a smoke? Heading up to the park, Lobo thought it was an illusion when he first saw the sloping red matchbox rooftops and little children climbing on top of them and swinging out of the windows. It was, in fact, a beautifully designed children's play structure.

There was no green grass. Rat infested bushes surrounded the innards of the park. One section was filled with sand and miniature Chinese structures for the children's play area. As Lobo walked through it, he knew that this was something to consider and remember because of all the firepower involved. He sauntered through the rest of the square, as incognito as possible, looking no one directly in the eye, but not looking away from anyone either. The square was mostly for the pigeons begging for scraps, a tourists' shortcut, and people out on an afternoon stroll. Along the boundaries of the square were benches where old men sat silently. Lobo picked out an empty bench, sat down, popped opened up his tall can, and fired up a cigarette. He saw that there was a small covered area. Inside of it there were tables where Chinese men sat bunched up looking in on the action. *They're playing mah jong,* Lobo thought, *figuring out new strategies. That's where they do the Sunday drop offs. That's where we take their money.*

Sitting on park benches, little old Chinese men wearing baseball caps quietly fed the scrambling, half baldheaded filthy pigeons. *There gotta be a shot caller around here somewhere, though,* Lobo thought, *but these guys all look the same.* The leader truly was indistinguishable from the rest, and Lobo thought, *man these fuckers got it going on! They know how to keep shut the fuck up and keep the ship moving tight, but,* Lobo wondered as he dragged on his cigarette, *why they even have this shit in public then?* Lobo thought that Sasquatch might be sending him on a wild goose chase and remembered the ducks hanging in the windows.

Lobo drank some more and realized that this set up made sense. It had to be public because the whole community had to be involved. It was only public because the public that mattered had to be reminded, warned, and threatened. The community had to know how to keep secrets with the whole lot of everyone passing by. Everyone had to be in on the underworld so that everyone was guilty; there could be no snitches or revolutionaries because everyone knew their duty. One lapse of that duty implicated not just the person, but the entire community. Shame was the common denominator. No one wanted to break tradition and disgrace his family and culture.

In the middle of this epiphany, Lobo peeped out an argument between two old men.

"You cannot eat there," an old man in an olive green hunting vest and baseball cap commanded to a business suit and tie man. "There are only certain places you can throw bread."

"Who are you to stand up in my face?" the businessman shouted. The old man in the hunting vest took out his stumps from his pants pocket and brandished his mutilated fingers of authority. The man in the suit and tie stood up, gathered his bread, and mumbled to himself. The other men sitting on the benches listened and laughed at the businessman's tantrum. With smiles, they told Stumpy to "Kill him." The businessman walked away.

Lobo saw that the fingerless chieftain was upset that he had had to show who he was, and he seemed to blame one of the other men sitting down in the area for not taking care of the rules and regulations of that section of the park. This traditionally ponytailed man in his black pajamas responded by lighting an ultra-thin cigarette. He listened to the fingerless man's complaint. When he finished his argument, pajama man blew out puffs of smoke into Stumpy's face. Still sitting, pajama man raised his left hand high above his head and brought it steadily down lower and lower. With that, the fingerless man calmed down and returned to his bench.

That's fuckin leadership, Lobo thought as he hit on the beer. *But that can't be the main* vato, Lobo knew, *cause Stumps wouldn't even show himself like that.* Perplexed, Lobo looked around. *Maybe the main* vato *aint comin around till tomorrow,* he thought, *but I bet he aint gonna be nothin to look at, so I got to be ready for this fool. I might not even know who the fuck he is till I see Kwai come around to make the weekly tribute.*

When Lobo downed the last drops of his beer, a smiling old toothless man stopped in front of him. Toothless looked down at the can Lobo was going to throw away. As Lobo handed it to him he noticed that the man slyly stared at him; Lobo was being observed. *These fools got my number,* he thought. *They know I'm here, but don't know why.* He looked around at the entrances on both sides and saw two men at each entrance keeping tabs on all people who entered. Lobo could tell that they dismissed some while they concentrated on others. The park, however, was still like any park he had ever known. It was populated with its crew of straggling bums, and Lobo realized that that would be their ticket for undercover admission tomorrow. He covertly looked around for an ideal place to be concealed and yet still be able to view the entire square.

Lobo had to piss. About to piss in a tall bush, he instead entered a small concrete restroom. It was the foulest smelling thing he had encountered in a long time. While he pinched his nose and held his breath, he took his piss. When he walked out, he noticed that there were no eyes on him. No one paid any attention to the filthy shit house—everyone stayed away. *That's the mark,* Lobo thought. The homeboys would form up next to the shit house.

Lobo thought about how he could make a slick retreat out of the park without being marked in their memory banks. Checking his zipper, he aimed towards a slightly overweight white woman in tennis shoes and faded blue jeans who was walking briskly through the square. As if he knew her, with a warm smile, he shouted "Annie!" The red headed woman looked startled but smiled back broadly at Lobo's shiny teeth. She shook her head at Lobo, and he shook his too. Lobo said as he jogged up to her, "I know, I know it's been a million years. I can't believe it's been so long," and he made steps with her and asked her where she was going. Gentle as a lamb, he did not want to alarm her, did not want her to show any displeasure or hint of unknowingness. Thirty awkward seconds passed, and Lobo knew that the charade would not work. To her, he softly admitted that she was not the person he thought she was, that she must be the twin of someone he once knew, but that he could not think of any other way of knowing who she was if he did not try, that his dream would be gone forever if he did not get up and do something and take the chance of making a fool out of himself or being rejected or having his heart broken or, maybe, perhaps, catching a smile. The freckle faced woman grinned at this. Lobo invited her to sit down and talk, talk please for a moment so that this was not all just to be forgotten and thrown away. What school did she go to, what book was she holding, what was her business in Chinatown? What was her name and her place of birth and what did she love and long for? Her eyes opening wide, she smiled. And they had seemed to know each other for more than just five minutes. They were old friends that had met up and reminisced about old times. As she declared her beliefs and ambitions, Lobo peered around and noticed that no one seemed to care about him any longer—he was simply a man to be forgotten, a man meeting an old friend, so he asked her to get up and for them to walk out. Lobo pulled her phone number in front of the church. As he offered her his hand, as she put out her hand to shake his, he brought her hand up to his lips, not in any overzealous way, but softly, gently, tenderly and sincerely. He bent his head over and kissed her hand, brushing his jet black goatee whiskers against the back of her plump fingers. He caught her trusting eyes as he rose. Lobo walked away.

He looked up at the open church bell tower as it chimed. With that alarm, he instantly knew that that was the ideal place for him to make out the whole scene. Tomorrow Lobo would stay there and snipe while Toro and Santo scooped up the loot.

Race walking back to the car, he noticed a ticket on the windshield wiper for parking in the handicapped zone. He saw a white tow truck turn the corner and knew it had been called up for his car. He cursed because he could not think of any other place to park in all of overcrowded Chinatown. Tomorrow they would need to wait yet be able to pull out quick and hard. They could not risk being towed. The only places to park were the few spots with blue curbs—*handicapped parking for disabled homeboys.* Lobo giggled. *Disabled homeboys like Toro.* Lobo would steal a disabled placard. *Their fuckin gangster security aint never gonna expect no bum ass savages to be gangsters. We gonna shock em. With the engine running, Lil Toon's gonna wait in front of the park's handicapped zone for the heist to be complete.*

Lobo's blood surged. He was eager yet anxious to steal the at least fifty thousand dollars cash envelope payments from all over the city. He knew Kwai paid at least a G every Sunday.

Although his mind had allowed for the details, Lobo knew it was the heart that would provide the will. Lobo blasted the car's radio and lit a cigarette. The immediate payoff and even more. *Kill Sasquatch and have it seem that Sasquatch killed Kwai. Yeah,* he thought, *then I'll take over the gambling operation without any trace of craziness leading back to me. And I know this shit aint gonna get me no security, that aint the long term, but that's why I'll invest my money right, get into stocks or bonds of crack or some other really maniac shit with a big ass payoff. After taking over Kwai's gambling operation, in memory of Sheila, I'll live so large, just like the Chinos, doing all the things I've ever wanted to do, and I'll suffer for awhile, but the wolf is versatile.*

He would return back to the Chinese park to wreak fulfillment. There was no more turning back. Lobo laughed at this, but he also died and tried to hide it by stepping hard on the gas on the freeway. He thought—*going to set it all up now. I've got to be strong and smart and, goddamn it, safe—cause what does it matter if it don't work well? I'll go straight to hell for all my sins, but maybe that's just another hustle, another gamble, but I don't know cause I can't fix that game. I don't even know those stakes: the stakes of hell.*

Don't matter, though, cause I know that even if I lose the devil'll reward me for playing a good game, and if that aint taken as merit then I'm stronger than hell. I don't give a fuck if it's el diablo himself— I'll check his ass cause I play a good game even when I lose. It's time to make my name again. A bitch gotta relax me now, he thought of Sheila, but instead pulled out the chubby girl's number. He looked at the digits then threw them out of the window.

Nah, a motherfucker's gotta be straight minded. Just for this one time I got to deal with reality. Close to the *varrio*, Lobo parked, went into a liquor store, lifted a Bic razor and cheap shaving cream, and shaved in a Thai restaurant's restroom. In the mirror, he admired himself: *I'm as clean as a baby's bottom, crisp as the lettuce in a sandwich, straight as a soldier. My thoughts may be wavering, but my soul's solid, and my mind's got its juices flowing.*

I got to sacrifice bullshit and put all that shit on pause for a minute. No, he battled within himself, with his urges for drugs and sex, with his urge to call the whole thing off and simply surrender himself for Sheila's sake. *I got to just lay low and maybe get me some more shut eye, be tidy for this next day that comes, and let me figure. It's seven thirty now, and it goes down at five tomorrow. I've been wide awake for the past three days, so I need to be sane for tomorrow. Fuck going back to that madhouse.* Instead, Lobo picked out the *varrio's* hallelujah church, the one congregated by winos, junkies, recently released convicts, the church where he had first met Santo as a kid. Inside, there was no anxiety. He knelt down, crossed himself, then crawled into one of the pews and shut his eyes. *It's cold.*

Ok, Toro's gonna be in his wheelchair with shades on, a baseball cap low, his camouflage uniform unbuttoned with his chest puffed out, them war medals pinned all across the blouse, ripped up shorts with his bandaged leg drenched in blood. I'll write USMC on a cardboard sign for donations, and he'll hold out a tin cup and jiggle around quarters inside.

Santo'll stand beside him and smoke. I aint gonna be able to make him change. He'll be dressed like he always is, but it'll be known by anyone that gives a fuck that he's takin care of Toro. Santo'll have a sea bag on his back with two M16s in it, and Toro'll have two .45s and all the magazines full of ammo lying underneath the blanket on his lap. I'll be squatted down above them in that giant church's bell tower, rifle in hand, waiting for Kwai and Sasquatch to show up, and the loot to be hogged. Lil Toon'll be in the handicapped zone with the engine running.

Lobo rubbed the muck out of his eyes and rustled around on the wooden bench. He thought of the TV show *Lifestyles of the Rich and Famous. Yeah, I'll show America what America's about. I'll be more American than an albino white boy, and I'll slave so hard that the Africanos will laugh. After this lick, I'm gonna study days and nights, and the Chinese'll be left with their mouths open. I'm gonna make shit happen with all odds against me, and I'll persevere with all them bullets aimed right at my head. But in doin this shit, it'll also be for them. And I aint talkin bout the color of my skin or the language I speak, and I aint talkin bout the blood that's flowin through my veins or the flag that's slappin in the air—it's all for any motherfucker who got the sense to appreciate the finer things in life, motherfuckin connoisseurs of existence. And I'll show em just cause a* vato*'s got three strikes against him don't mean he's out. I'll prove that just cause it can't be done don't mean I can't do it. What a damn shame the fuckin big boys couldn't give me my props unless I put a gun to their throats; I got to clip Kwai. Sasquatch is terminated. They'll all respect me after that. Fuckin broad daylight. Fuck it. I see that logic to the fullest.* Lobo thought of Lil Toon. *Hustle, fool! I'm getting mine, and aint no reason you can't get yours either. Get up off your ass, and do some shit and work like a wolf at everything you do whether you're lying in the sack or workin that corner or, motherfucker, if you gonna just lay down and die, do that shit with zest, and do it bet-*

236

ter than anyone before, and don't waste your time cause that makes the
shit boring. Do it now, and do it to screw it. Cause I'm America whether
motherfuckers like it or not, and I'm America when it gets down to rot.

Ding! Dong! Ding! Dong!

Bells rang as Lobo felt his slobber slither onto the cold wooden bench. He turned over to his other side and sleep overcame him.

Rising from her dank cardboard coffin, Sheila spoke directly to Lobo, forced him to look directly at her. More beautiful than the sunrise, she sang:

"You'll go because I want you to go. But at the hour that I want you, I will have you. I know that without my love you are lost, because whether you admit it or not, I own your heart.

"I want you to go around the world, and I want you to meet many people. I want other lips to kiss you so that you can compare them with mine, with always. And if you ever find a love who you feel understands you, who you feel loves you more than I, then on that day I will truly disappear with the sun when it dies in the evening.

"Go because I want you to go."

Lobo reached out his arms to Sheila. With all his muscles tense, Lobo squeezed her and accepted the farewell.

The kiss was sweeter than wine, softer than clouds in the sky, tender as veal on the plate. It was more than Lobo could ever have hoped for, more than his imagination could comprehend. It was only a fairy-tale dream, yet it was happening to him right there at that moment, and he felt it with all the intensity of a million pinches on his skin. Yet Lobo knew he would have to leave, though he did not want to. He wanted to stay and die with her and live with her and forget all that had happened. When Lobo looked into Sheila's sharp eyes, he knew it was worth it—all of it—the exact way it turned out, because without the crazy incident, without the master plan, he would have never known; Lobo would have always doubted that such a lady could exist, and he would have doubted the homeboys, his own convictions, the power of endurance, the human heart in its most beautiful form—in the form that can only be tested and challenged with the most severe moment. The logic, the faith proved, could not comfort him. It only proved him wrong, and his skepticism was a failure of his sight. For Lobo had demanded a sign, and he had received an anointed angel from heaven, yet he had still refused to believe. Now it was too late.

Now Lobo would have to wander the lush valleys and the rocky mountains and the dead end alleys, and all the sparrows in the sky or all the gold in Chinatown could never take him back to what he had, but let go. Without Sheila, he would be in fire and brimstone, and the coals underneath him would burn forever, and the emptiness inside of him would envelop his whole world. Yet it was his torture to have to go on and on and turn away and doubt that this ever took place, and Lobo would believe a man selling him a fake ass platinum Rolex, and he would trust the sun to rise from the East, but he would never ever believe that there could ever be such human beings as these, such ladies with the title Queen, such homeboys as Kings. *Bitches and hos forever!* Lobo tried with arms grasped around himself and crackling around on the cold, flat bench, half asleep, half awake. *Bitches and hos and no fuckin world after.*

ELEVEN

Little Cartoon

Few are made for independence—it is a privilege of the strong. And he who attempts it, having the completest right to it but without being compelled to, thereby proves that he is probably not only strong but also daring to the point of recklessness. He ventures into a labyrinth, he multiplies by a thousand the dangers which life as such already brings with it, not the smallest of which is that no one can behold how and where he goes astray, is cut off from others, and is torn to pieces limb from limb by some cave-minotaur of conscience. If such a one is destroyed, it takes place so far from the understanding of men that they neither feel it nor sympathize—and he can no longer go back! He can no longer go back even to the pity of men!

FRIEDRICH NIETZSCHE, *Beyond Good and Evil*

We went all the way
Until the tires tumbled off
Rough ride on wrecked rim
Sparks flying off asphalt. High speed chase with no one behind us. Still, I was floorin it anyway. Santo was shotgun. Toro was laid out in the back. The front passenger side tire had burst, but no one even gave a fuck. We were snapped out—double lined fat one—lit that *leño* up right after the lick, cause I was ready and prepared to celebrate after that lunatic shit. Even though PCP was a washed up old timer's high, this time, though, it didn't matter that we got

all twisted cause we were clean out the scene. It hurt to feel so high—like if my head was about to burst from the altitude, but fuck it; that was the life of strife.

It was eight at night on Sunday, September 15, 1991. When we got back to the shack, only we were there to cut up the cash. After Santo shot up the park, we didn't wait around for Lobo. He was up in the church's bell tower and started shootin just to keep motherfuckers off us, from chasin or following us. Everyone in the park was plastered to the concrete except us. I had the passenger seat of the stolen Mustang already laid back so that Toro could just throw himself in. Sliding in his wheelchair, Toro rolled himself down to the ride and crashed into it. He fell on the ground, face first. Santo, who was right behind him, grabbed him by the ass and back of his desert camouflage shirt and heaved him into the running car. The car door still open and the wheelchair's wheels still on the sidewalk spinning, Santo jumped on top of Toro. That's when I peeled out fast and hard. I heard sirens, but I kept calm and went with my plan to drive the straightest and quickest way to the shack. When I thought we were clear, I fired up the *maton*.

Once we got to the shack, I was sweatin, still in a space daze. Sat there for a minute in silence. Then we divvied up the loot, a pile of cash leftovers for Lobo. Santo threw his share into the hole that was in the middle of the room. Toro smiled. I don't know how. I grabbed my cut and told them homeboys later days. I was about to jam when Lobo showed up. He had his own sack with him, but I knew that that was kinda crazy cause I was pretty sure we had broken them Chinos to the fullest. Lobo's bag was fat and full, like with a bowling ball, and he slung it around his head like Santa would—

"Motherfuckers, we got gold from Fort Knox! I got heaven

in my hands." Brokenhearted, he passed his sack to Santo. Santo palmed it and then dunked it into his hole in the ground. I said, "Later on, niggaz," to them boys and was about to book, but Lobo grabbed me by the back of the collar.

"This is all been for you, Bro—how the fuck you gonna leave your own party?"

I didn't understand what he was talkin, only that he was strapped. I had ditched my shit in the gutter once we fired up the fat one cause I knew we were in the clear, and I didn't wantta get busted with no evidence. Now, cause I didn't have a gat, I had no way to be convincing, but I never feared Lobo cause I always thought his bark was worse than his bite. But this time I could see he had somethin in him. He looked over to Santo, who was now standing in a corner of the faintly lit room, couldn't even see his face, only his scruffy beard and the outline of his wavy brown hair. Lobo asked him—

"Aint that right, Santito? Aint all this shit been for the music?"

"I only hear murmurs, Lobo—no melody in madness," Santo stepped out of the corner and into the light; his face was straight—no emotion. He was also strapped.

"Then I'm special," Lobo said, "cause all I hear are Little Toons making up big tunes—a symphony of undercover homeboys and even homegirls, and we'll have this whole motherfucker sewed up, stitched up, and ready to wear. Sing me a song, Toon."

"Fuck you, nigga," I said. "You want me to sing and dance, bust me out some grits."

Lobo smiled. "That's music—the money mix. Listen to the boy, Bros! He got heart like none of us could ever have. He got the heart to live, live for the finer things. You aint gonna pull no fast ones on Toon cause he knows every song. Aint that right, homes?"

241

That fool was tryin to play me. Lookin back now, though, they were just playin each other and themselves, their whole fuckin lives, and I was just another sucka gettin played, bein used for another fool's agenda. All I wanted was to get the fuck out of there cause I knew wasn't no good gonna come from them three heads crashing.

"S'up?!" I demanded. A bit taller than me, Lobo could box, but I didn't give a fuck.

Lobo laughed. "I'm sayin you could take it all, boy, like you got the world in your fuckin hands, but don't flex on me; don't worry about that chicken shit."

Lobo was lookin at me stupid, like if he thought I was dumb or some shit, insulting me cause he had masterminded the lick, and all I did was drive. I didn't like it. "You wantta step outside with that shit," I invaded his special three inches of private air space.

"I'll put you down, Lil Toon. Don't waste your time with a homeboy like me. You're tops, Lil Bro. You gotta learn that shit now." Lobo put his hand on my shoulder. I pushed it off.

"Who you tryin to school?" I asked.

Lobo got serious real quick. "Don't tell me you need an ass whuppin. I'm over here givin you answers to all your problems, and you want to act like a *puta?*" Lobo was practically kissing my nose, he was so close to me.

I right-crossed him in the mouth. Lobo's head whipped back and came forward biting. I stepped back and put my hands up to protect my face. He locked onto my left arm with his canine teeth. I was up against the sheetrock wall and was hittin him in the head with my right. Lobo wouldn't let the lock go. Blood escaped from my arm.

"Lay off the boy, Lobo," Toro said, even though I was the one pounding on Lobo's skull. Lobo lifted up his hands and started digging into my eyes. I kept punching, but he just got more energy from each blow. That's when I sprained my hand. I stopped punching. Lobo stepped back. He shook his head a couple of times, stared me down, then threw his arm around me.

"Pull up a chair, homes," he puffed out of breath. "Stay awhile and peep how real game works." Lobo spit on his hands and spread it over his playboy looking face. He slicked back his shiny black hair with more saliva and then turned to Santo, who was now crouching down on the mattress on the floor. Toro was lying down next to him, breathing in slow and steady bursts, loud enough for us to hear them. I pulled up the steel folding chair that we also used as a card and eating table. Lobo massaged the growing knots on his forehead.

"Now, *carnales,* we've made that move, and we got more than tradition to uphold. We're makin up the rules now—new traditions and ways to measure this ever-changing world. All that old shit is out the windows. What we got is innovation—the opportunity to teach old dogs and young pups new tricks. This is the ticket right here." Lobo put his palm on the back of my head.

From outside, screaming cop sirens squealed. Even though it wasn't for us, I got paranoid. "Throw the tube on, man, let's see if this shit hit the world yet," I said.

"Yeah," Toro said with no color in his squat face. "I think that shit was too sick to ignore." He massaged his leg bone. Santo got up and turned on channel two.

Santo's mug was the image on the screen. No one said anything. The news lady reported from right in the middle of bloody Chinatown. White sheets and yellow tape filled the background of the picture. Like clowns in a circus, policemen ran around in circles. Mrs. News Lady held the mike like a dick, whispering wicked words to our ears.

"Looks like we're famous," I joked. Lobo dropped his head into cupped hands. Santo's head tilted up. Toro looked straight ahead at the TV. "Yeah! Movie stars and shit," I added.

"Shut the fuck up," Lobo demanded, raising the volume on the TV. The news-lady reporter said that an unexplainable mass murder had taken place. Witnesses reported that a lone gunman had been hanging around the park when he suddenly opened fire. Some tourist had been taking pictures and gave them to the cops. They showed Santo's face on the screen again. It was Santo standing straight, dressed all in black, lookin goony as fuck, wild wavy brown hair and a beard to boot; but Toro was up in it too, in the background, but there was no word of him being involved. I figure it was cause Toro was in the wheelchair with his shades on and camouflage uniform. Them fools must have just assumed he was a bum. The news lady said that the gunman got away on foot. She said nothing about any loot gone. Three dead and one critically wounded.

The lady tried to interview a few of the locals passing by, but they walked away covering up their faces. When she caught up to a tourist, he spilled his guts for the bright lights.

"I thought I heard some firecrackers going off," the white dude in the pleated khaki shorts and plaid baseball cap said, "and I sure wanted to see that famous lion dance, so I rushed to the festivities. I turned the corner into the park and saw this Hispanic man jog up to an old Chinese man and shoot. Pop! Some giant Chinese guy tried to stop him, but the hero tripped over some crippled homeless guy and became the gunman's second victim. Then everyone started dropping down. I stayed standing, perhaps in shock, until the crazy guy pointed his gun in my direction. I threw myself to the ground, and then I heard screaming and shouting, and the shooter started yelling, 'No sings!' That's when everyone started running out of the park in a panic. The Hispanic guy chased a thin Chinese gentleman with glasses and started shooting again. Once again, everyone threw themselves to the floor. I couldn't move." The tourist looked baffled.

With her eyebrow cocked, the news lady listened to him while he was telling the story. Once he finished, she faced the camera, said thank you, and brushed him off. They again showed Santo's stoic face. Lobo turned the TV off. Everyone was silent.

"We got to go," Lobo finally said.

"I'm not leaving," Santo answered. Lobo looked at him, and then at Toro lying down.

"I can't go anywhere," Toro muttered.

"I'm going out to the streets. See what I hear. This place is gonna be too fuckin hot. I know it, but let me see what's up," Lobo turned to me. "You're comin with me."

I nodded my head. "You strapped?" he asked. I shook my head. Lobo dug into his waistband and handed me a pistol. He went into his pants pocket, pulled out a smaller gun, and then stuffed it into his waistband. Lobo grabbed one of the M16s and wrapped it into a Mexican blanket. We took off, Lobo driving, in a new Tercel. He said he stole it after we took off on him. He understood that we had to get on once Santo went sick. It was good we left him, he said, cause he saw a few fools try to be stars and follow us, but he just shot at them from the tower, so they stopped chasing us and ducked for cover. He ended up hitting one of em. That was why no one had ended up following us.

Lobo cruised the quiet Sunday streets, fired up a cigarette, and asked me what I thought. I told him that this shit was sick with it, that Santo was probably gonna get popped. I didn't tell him, but I felt we were all gonna get busted, too. Lobo looked down the road.

"He fucked up. Again. I told motherfucker to be cool on the trigger, but nah, stupid ass had to start trippin. I saw everything from the tower. Shot the old shot caller first. Then took care of Sasquatch and Kwai—before I even had a chance to aim—like if he wanted to take all the heat for this. 'Kwai, just Kwai—real red' I had told him. I didn't even have to clip anyone, but now they got his portrait. Now they got us all." Lobo was talkin to himself.

We went up and down *Varrio Montaña* and the Swamp and then drove down a dead end alley and got blocked in by a Caddy that suddenly appeared behind us. Lobo had been hunting, and now we were the hunted. He switched the car in reverse and told me to hold on. He was peeling back quickly when Rey stepped out of the car that was blockin us. Lobo stomped the brakes. It was Rey, the main *chignon* from the hood. I knew it from the way Lobo got scared. Lobo never got scared. Wearing a burgundy *guayabera* and creased black slacks, Rey stood with a suited Chino right next to him. Two other Chinos and a big ass homeboy stepped out of the back seat of their whitewalled Fleetwood.

Lobo laughed, got out the car, and put his hands up. "Hey, what's up." He shined them his smile. Sideways in the seat, I watched Lobo walk up to Rey and give him a homeboy hand-shake. Rey looked into the car to see who was in it and then put his arm around Lobo and walked him back to his Caddy. While they stood out there, Rey whispered some things into Lobo's ear. Lobo shrugged his shoulders and said things I couldn't hear. Rey again went to Lobo's ear, and Lobo stepped back and shook his head.

Rey did some kind of hand sign, and Lobo nodded yes. Rubbing his Fu Manchu style moustache, Rey pointed at me in the car, then turned and looked Lobo straight in the face; he lightly hit his closed fist against his own heart. Rey turned away, the gangsters loaded up in the Caddy, and the car peeled out.

With a giant smile, Lobo walked to the driver's side of our Tercel. When he got into the car, he was as white as a *sábana*. His face dropped. He turned off the radio that automatically came on when he started the car. He drove halfway down the block, pulled over, and puked.

"What happened?" I asked him when he put his face back up in the window of the ride. He looked at me as if I was stupid, and I felt like cappin his ass right there. He looked away from me and told me to just drive. Jumping in the driver, I rolled. He squirmed in the passenger seat. "Where to?" I asked.

"Back to the shack," Lobo said. He stayed silent for awhile and then shot off. "This is the beginning, not the end, Bro. If you can stick through this shit, you can rule the world. Shit has to happen the way that it falls. Sometimes we can't do nothin about it. We just got to accept it: Evil can't be redeemed. *Entiendes?*"

"Yeah, I got you," I said. Lobo pulled out his gat, a dull black .380.

"No complaints, Lil Toon. You can't argue with the sun or fight with the moon. It's gonna rise, and it's gonna shine. You just suck that shit in. No looking back. No regrets. No pity. Don't ever be stupid and fight the losing fight." Lobo put one in the chamber.

"Yeah." I nodded my head.

I pulled up to the shack. We got out, and Lobo started picking rocks off the ground and handed some to me. We walked up to the streetlights and busted out all the block's light posts.

"Keep all the lights off," Lobo said entering the room, but the full moon that invaded through the crack of the window shades couldn't be turned off.

"So what's up?" Toro asked, waking up.

"Peaches and cream. We just got to lay low for awhile," Lobo answered.

"How about Santo?" Toro asked. Lobo looked across the room at Santo. He was sittin in a dark corner, but I could tell he was staring back. They just stood there like that for at least a minute, and I can't say they were mad dogging each other cause they didn't have any fear or anger in their eyes. They just looked as if they were trying to understand.

"Santo's sick," Santo said before Lobo could say anything. "He has a disease that only Lobo can cure. One antidote. Ain't that right, Lobo?"

Lobo's pistol dangled in his hand.

"That's the remedy, Lobo," Santo said. "You're an MD with the miracle drug. Call him doctor from this day forward cause he's that damn bright. Too bright and I can't even look at you cause you hurt my eyes." Turning his head away, Santo faced Toro. "I know you would never let anything happen, Bro, and I know you would die in the process." Santo looked back at Lobo. "Lobo, didn't you know that, or did you come to cure us both?"

"Nigga," Lobo responded. "I aint as bright as you make me out to be." Lobo looked at the pin-up calendar on the wall. "See, I know there aint enough medicine for all of us, cause I'm sick as fuck myself—throwing up all the damn time. Don't you think my stomach turns?" Lobo walked over to me. "No, it's not for me or us that this day came; it's not our party. Ever since that *familia,* we should know where we're headed and what we rate. Only a real

248

genius can make all this right." Lobo pushed me towards Santo. "You take Santo to where he needs to go," Lobo said this to me, and I was ready to go wherever the fuck I had to. I accepted both the mission and car keys from Lobo.

"Let's go now, cause I'm already tired as fuck," I said. It was already two in the mornin.

Santo got up from his chair. He walked for the door without saying anything to anyone or even looking at anyone's face.

"Bro," on the mattress, Toro was drenched in sweat, "you just gonna leave me here like this?" We all knew Toro was gonna be gone in a few hours if he didn't see no doctor. He had been bleeding way too much and the open wound had started to smell rotten.

With a blank stare, Santo turned back and looked at him soft. The lights off, all the lights from outside busted out, only the glare from the moonlight barely lit the room. Toro lay on the mattress shaking, bleeding to death, and Santo rubbed his hands swiftly together. Smoke rose, a tiny fire between his hands, a glow inside of his palms. Caressing the light, Santo lifted the spirit above his head and slowly opened his tight grip. Santo shone. I mean, his whole body blazed, and me and Lobo stepped back. I aimed my gat at him. Lobo fell on his knees.

Toro rose. He got up out of his shit, moaning and groaning, on a shattered toothpick, little steps forward, brave walking, faithful strides. Toro's leg was fucked, forever would be fucked, but he wouldn't die from poison; Santo had cleansed him. We knew that now. Toro sidestepped the hole in the floor and put out his shake to Santo. Santo pushed the hand aside and embraced him. They embraced each other.

I couldn't breathe, so I opened the door for air. The fire escaped and lit up the whole block like noontime. I stumbled outside to catch my senses. Toro fell to the floor, putting out his hands before he smashed his grill. Then Santo was beside me, ready to go. The lights out, we got into Lobo's stolen Toyota.

"Where we headed?" I asked Santo.

"To the hardware store," Santo said, "for the proper tools."

"Ace?" I asked.

"Yeah," he said. "I got to prepare the way for the homeboys, scope out the next scene, and make sure all's cool on that next level. Infiltrate behind enemy lines." Santo smiled.

When we got to the hardware store, I didn't think there was any way to bust in cause the entrance was a solid steel door. Santo floated over to it, and it seemed to just open for him without any alarms going off. We immediately went down to the Skilsaw aisle. He inspected a few saws and plugged one into the wall. The harsh motor hurt my ears. Santo grabbed a shelf with two hands and ripped it off the rack. Nails, bolts, and washers smashed to the floor. He took the shelf and roared the saw through it. Splinters of wood flew through the air, but the motor stuttered at the final cut. Hitting the wood against the wall, Santo broke it neatly into two.

"This won't work," Santo said. "We need something more powerful."

I walked over to the lumber section and called him. "Here," I said. There was a table with a saw sticking right through the center of it, a saw used for cutting down two by fours and big lumber of all shapes and sizes. I pressed the ON switch, and the saw vroomed like a 454 big block. I grabbed a two by four that was lying on the floor and raced it through the saw. Quick and clean. His calm, bearded face blushing, Santo nodded his head.

"It's time to go," Santo told me. "We need some heavy duty bags, the burlap kind, potato sacks. Go find some." Santo gently glided his light brown fingers across the top of the prickly table saw. I jogged down the aisles and realized we had hit a gold mine. I started grabbing shit from all over the place. First, I grabbed some light bulbs and stuck them in my pockets cause I always wanted a clear view. I stuffed hella batteries in my jacket cause I wanted to stay powered. I got to the garbage bags, and above them I took all kinds of insect repellents and rat poison cause I wanted to keep the bugs and vermin away. I busted open some Hefty bags and went back to the Skilsaw section and started packin saws, but the blades cut through the bag, and then I remembered Santo had told me to get the potato sacks, so I went back to the garbage section, and I looked for burlap sacks. At first I couldn't find them, but I looked to my right, right on the bottom next to the wooden and steel mice and rat traps, and there they were. The bags were thick and itchy, heavy duty, no fake shit like Hefty bags made for plastic garbage, papers, and softness. These potato bags were for the crooked saws and the heavy fruit. The potatoes and the grub. And so I opened up a sack, and it was full of possibilities, full of options. I went down them aisles, and I discovered hammers, and chisels, and notepads and rulers, radios and model airplanes and cars, puzzles of castles and green beautiful landscapes. Fishing poles and synthetic bait. A bag of cement for a solid foundation. Everything I stuck into the bags.

I was a kid up in Santa Claus's toy factory. Happy as a fat fuck and full as a pig. I was so excited I was shouting out "Santo, hey Santo, come on, Bro, they got hella shit around here. More than we can carry in our hands. I'm a stuff the car; shit make a few fuckin trips back. Hey, Santo, Bro, we got this motherfucker sewed up, you know." I laughed. I ran down the aisles and threw the shelves over. I splattered glue all over the walls and grabbed some spray paint and was about to hit up all the homeboys and the *varrio* when I heard it. I heard what I had heard waiting in Chinatown from the parked car, what Santo had been shoutin as gun fire and rockets exploded—"No sins! No sins!" And I discovered the power of words.

I sprinted back top, right to the back of the store where all them table saws were, and I heard the machine going strong making the music of madness, the magnificent melody of machismo, the maestro orchestrating machine guns' *trat trat trat trat.* I stepped slow, maybe a little scared, unsure of what that noise meant.

I looked low.

Santo was in the corner of the room pushing something into the big saw. He was bent over reaching for something; no, he was leaning forward looking for something, and I crawled even slower cause I didn't want to shock him, didn't want to make him lose his place and lose sight of what he seemed to be lookin for. I stepped small. Looking down, I saw his feet planted solid. His legs were locked up straight, the creases in his pants thick. His chest was on top of the table. His right hand was pushing the ON button. His left hand was stuck in the ever-propelling saw, blood spurted out of it, and the *varrio*'s bloody fame was splattered all over the walls. Santo's chopped head was on the floor.

I stepped back, and the sacks in my hands crashed to the floor. I did not know what to do. I looked at his right hand that could not stop pressing the on button and realized that his left hand was stuck in the machine because he had pushed his head as hard as he could through the saw. Fuck. I fell to my knees and bent my head. I stared at my chest then looked down on the floor. Santo's eyes were still open. The saw was still cutting. On my knees, I walked to his head, and I closed his eyes. I cradled his head in my arms as if it were a baby. I lullabied myself to sleep.

I was slobbering on Santo's head when after awhile I woke up, groggy, disoriented, but awake, nevertheless. I pulled out a burlap sack and put his square, wavy brown haired head in it. His right hand was still pressing the ON button. The grind, the racket, the saw cut into my heart.

I never went to get stitches cause how the fuck you gonna mend a broken heart? I grabbed all the shit, threw it into the ride, and went back to the shack. They waited in the cover of darkness, hid against all the evils of the world. When I walked in, there were blankets and towels covering every crack of window space. Lobo looked at me as if I had betrayed him. He saw the sacks in my hands. I had two sacks full of necessities from the hardware store in my left hand, and I had Santo's head in my right.

"This *vato* had no sins," I said holding up the sack with Santo's head in it. "Even though he was bloody, he died clean."

Toro nodded.

Lobo went and grabbed some paper plates from the bathroom, which we also used as a makeshift kitchen. He reached inside Santo's hole in the ground and took back the sack that he had brought back from after the craziness. Another grape was inside, I realized.

"Bury his cut. No money from our *sangre* should be spent," Lobo said. Santo's money remained exactly where he had left it, inside his hole.

"I've gotta go serve the main course," Lobo said, stretching out his ostrich neck. I gave him Santo's head and dropped the other bags in a corner of our one room shack. "People got to know how we really come up." Lobo left with two heads.

"I'm gonna turn on the tube, Bro," I said to Toro.

"Bro," Toro said. "You think I should let it go? I mean, I think

I'm gonna be all right now." Toro's color was back in his face, and he had stopped sweating. "But fuckin Santo's gone, homes. My only real *carnal*. You think I should let it all go? Fuck it? I'm ready." In his hand he held a pistol, caressing it against the light stubble of hair on his face.

I swallowed bitterness. "You got up just a little while ago, Bro, cause of Santo. Now that he's gone you wanna punk out. You gonna leave the show to Lobo? Cause he sure aint never gonna let shit go. You aint good to no one in the ground." The steady leak from the faucet could be heard throughout the room. "Toro, you aint gotta die like a man, homes, just fuckin live—live like a real man. Shit, prove you're a fucking Marine. Like you told me one time, Bro—You aint gotta love it; you just gotta hack it."

"I sure can hack it," Toro said. He was in shorts and the way he was lying down his chest looked like loaves of bread. He was a buffed little bull.

"Sins aint gotta be no fatal thing. Or else we'd all be dead the day we were born."

"Then you do it, homes. You make me live. I leave it in your hands," Toro said no more. I turned on the tube and sat down. I watched for a minute without recognizing what I was supposed to be doing, or maybe I did know, but I just wanted to ignore it with the stupid box. Whatever the reason, I got up and went to the corner of the room and searched inside one of the bags. I grabbed the little bag of cement mix and poured it into a bucket and added some water and stirred. I poured all the whiskey we had on Toro's wound and then tightly wrapped cut up blankets around his bone, what remained of his leg. I pasted the cement mix on top of it and told Toro not to move around for awhile, to remain completely still until the cement dried and hardened. It was all fucked up, a monster's job. Toro would be a limper forever. But the blood and infection were stopped; his leg wouldn't have to be chopped. I sparked the leftover roach of the *leño* and put it to his lips. He inhaled and closed his eyes. I took the joint out of his mouth, put that shit out, and never hit it again. I dropped to the floor and slumbered.

The morning sun assaulted my dreams. Lobo had come back, and all the sheets and dirty clothes were off the windows, inviting light to breakfast. Lobo had some *pupusas* and OJ out for us. I rubbed my eyes and thought that maybe the night before, the whole sixteen years past, had been some kind of dream, some kind of imaginary acid trip.

But the lights were even brighter than usual. People were outside, great big crowds of people walking by the shack, going up the block in formations. Cameras clicking. Red, white, and blue cop lights swirling around. After peeking out the window, I stepped out. There was a table set up, a long cafeteria table from the rec center was at the top of the block. I pushed my way to the front of the crowd, and there was a stack of paper plates and utensils on one end of the table. In the center of the table there were two paper plates. On those plates lay the heads of Santo and Sheila, Lobo's old lady. People gawked in disbelief and horror, yet they couldn't stop staring. Even the police didn't know what to do. They were calling up the investigators to hurry the fuck up to the scene of the crime. Kids were trying to push their way through, but they were held back by old folks with good intentions. No one covered my eyes.

The cops figured out that one of the heads belonged to the same dude who started all the shit in Chinatown. They never figured out who Sheila was—they had no prints and no one came to claim her. She was a down homegirl. Later, Lobo told me that he had gone over to her pad after the heist, to see if he could still save her. There on her bed, he found her brain. Howling, he had put her head in a pillowcase and then come to see what was up with us.

That was it, the beginning of the end. That craziness was the reason they started raiding the neighborhood. Toro had to go back to his mom's cause he needed proper care. Lobo knew he couldn't give it to him, but Toro still refused to go. He was talkin about "Can't leave the homeboys behind." So one day Lobo lit up a duster, and while Toro was spaced out, Lobo pushed him in his wheelchair and left him in front of Toro's mom's pad with a note around his neck— "Please take care of me." A few days after that, the cops rammed through the shack. Me and Lobo had still been stayin there. They took us in, but we had already buried the artillery. We kept our mouths shut. Once they realized we wouldn't crack, they assigned me to the custody of a group home. They kept Lobo cause he had warrants for other shit, but he too eventually got out after the prosecutor knew she couldn't prove shit. Toro never got sent up, and that was all good.

No note or plea could save the *varrio*. Everywhere I turned places were getting busted down. The streets were a greasy pan on full blast, too hot to even walk through. And homeboys were put on ice for a nickel or a dime or twenty blinks, and I'm sure they never thought that the streets, the actual tar and cement, would be rehabilitated before them. Other homeboys had to move onto other parts, outside the city of Inten—cause the Santo craziness had been the perfect opportunity for City Hall's kings and queens, the buffed big boys with corporate muscle who made real deals for people's souls. Property was gettin scarce in the richest city in the world, and then bam! Invasion of the body snatchers. The living dead—drunk ass President Grant and wise old owl Ben Franklin—

they knocked on doors and terrified homeboys and homegirls and working class folks with tired hearts into leaving their apartments and houses. The dead said, "Hey, you ever seen me before? You got any of my Bros in your house?" When the *gente* shook their heads no, they had to pack up their shit and get on. Luring loans were offered to old folks for their houses. A year later when they couldn't pay the interest, they were foreclosed. The shack was demolished and lofts were put up in its place, a great big five-story condominium mansion, and I knew that that shit wasn't for no *gente*. Aristocrats pranced into *Varrio Montaña*.

Economics knows no friends. I partied away all my fare from the heist, treated homies and homegirls to paradise for a flash, so I didn't even know where the fuck I was headed to until one day, out the blue, I see a shiny new black 1993 Mercedes rolling down the street, and I just figure it's one of the newbies, but it pulls up right next to me. And I want to jack the fucker, but I know it's a sure bust. The cops are super tight around there now cause of the new yuppies in the hood. So I just mad dogged it hard. The tinted passenger window automatically rolls down, and someone calls me by name from the driver's side. Lobo invites me inside.

"Looks like you're doin pretty damn good," I said, jumping into the plush leather. "Cool. Got even more dope and hope than ever before," Lobo said. He caught me up to where he was. He'd taken over Kwai's operation and spread out to running some shit for Rey.

"Here," Lobo handed me a C-note. I hadn't seen him in over a year.

"*Orale*, but what's this for?" I asked.

"This has all been for you, Toon. Remember?" He handed me a card. "You come by this address tomorrow, no bullshit, at three on the dot, clean cut and sober minded, and you get what's comin to you." He pulled over to the curb.

"Done," I told him. For the next twenty-four hours, my stomach turned thinking about the crazy mission I'd be goin on. I knew it would be the craziest, most insane mission of all.

I showed up dressed in black, gloves and beanie in my inside coat pocket. It was a great old Victorian house on the outskirts of the *varrio*. A tall suited homeboy answered the door, a youngster at that. He showed me into this beautiful ass living room with a burgundy velvet pool table, a shiny chandelier suspended above it. Lobo glided down some stairs, shiny goateed face, smiling white teeth, and told me to sit down in a tight ass golden throne.

"Homeboy," Lobo said as I sat down like the pope, and he sat next to me. "I'm gonna be direct. This has all been for you. Times are changing and we need real steel to deal with it. I'm in too deep, but you're still a runt just craving for the big time. Well, all right, I've chosen you cause you got qualities that I think can be transformed into other avenues of opportunity. Lil Toon."

"Yeah," I said.

"I'm going to ask you to be brave, and show me some strength."

"Anything," I responded. Lobo looked at the wall behind me.

"Forget me. Forget all my bullshit or ignore it or however the fuck you got to psyche yourself out of the game, and get the fuck on. Motherfucker, we're getting kicked out anyway—accept it now or later."

"What the fuck you talkin bout, nigga. This is *mi varrio,* my fuckin hood." I did not understand what he was talkin about. Lobo grinned at me for a brief second, then looked back at the wall behind me—

"Go and be selfish, homeboy. Go and fuckin have your own mind, cause you can't help me or any of us any other way. Don't feel sorry for nothin or no one and don't cling to shit that is gonna stop you from getting to where you need to go, even if it's the thing or person you love most." Lobo clasped his hands together. "Let it go, young Brother. You got to be ruthless, and that means you got to be alone."

"I know what you're trying to say, Lobo, like I can't help anyone else out unless I first help myself. But I'm already down, Low, and I aint your average bear," I said.

With the bottom of his fist, Lobo thumped the arm of the chair.

"We already got too many average bear motherfuckers out there ready to die now," Lobo said. "Think they're bad cause they can give up the ghost. They're sellouts to the man up above— traitors to this world, and this is the world we're living in. I aint asking you to die for shit. I'm asking you for something even harder. Toon—fuck everything you've ever known. I got faith that that shit will always stick to your ribs, so I aint worrying about you forgetting the life and the values, but I don't want you to just walk around here like a fuckin zombie. Sheila's life has to have been for something." Lobo's guilt leaked into his voice. "I want you to sacrifice everything you've ever known, yet I know in the end you'll come back to where you need to be." Putting his gold ringed fingers on my shoulder, Lobo scooted closer.

"Learn. Cause I've been making paper for the last few months, and I realize, even with gold and platinum, I aint got shit. We aint got shit. We're fuckin laughingstocks. These motherfuckers moving in see *gente* as jokes. We're maids and housekeepers, and aint nothing wrong with bustin your ass, but there is something wrong with gettin no respect. There's somethin wrong when *putos* treat you like a boy. Cause the establishment thinks they got us all figured out. They think we're a bunch of dummies who can't even put up a fight in their world, and their world is where the big *lechuga* is at. They want to pacify us with talk of peaceful, non-aggressive bullshit and have us happy with crumbs. But, check out, outright revolution won't work; *evolution* is what's needed. Toon, we need sacrifice like only a *vato* like you can give."

Lobo handed me a Cuban cigar, lit it up for me, and lit one up himself. He blew O's out into the air, and I held in my coughs. "Go get some education, young blood. I don't want to see you unless you got something positive to give me. If you hang around, I'll put you down. No fuckin pity, you will sleep with the fishes, cause I aint gonna let you waste *our* potential. If I see that you do, I'll take that shit as a personal insult, and I'll choke you out my damn self, even though it would kill me." Lobo serious, I rustled around in the throne. He gave me an envelope.

"This money's yours. I won't baby you. Do what you have to do. You got freedom from this day forward. You belong to no man, no gang; when you're done, you'll come back, and I'll be waiting with arms extended. We'll toast to the tests of life. Now," Lobo said rising to his feet, buttoning up his double-breasted cashmere coat, "take off." Two suits rushed behind me.

I got up trying to smile like if this was all some big ass joke. The two hefty *vatos* started scooting me out, and I turned around to protest. Motherfuckers clipped me in the back of the neck with blackjacks. I fell to the white and red Persian rug. Lobo walked to me, and I stared down at my reflection in his glossy black Stacy Adams.

"Remember," Lobo said, "we fly even when we fall."

His shoes were the last I saw of him.

I was a nomad. I went to check out homies, and motherfuckers walked away like I was a leper. I wanted to buy a *torta*, but stores wouldn't sell me shit. No one got crazy with me, but they just ignored me, and it was the most fucked up feeling I could imagine—not even being recognized. Bored as fuck, I went to see a movie, but them bitches wouldn't even sell me a seat. And it started drizzling outside, so I called up the homeboy who would never let me down.

Toro.

That fool will let me kick it over there, I thought. I mean, shit, he was crippled, couldn't fuckin walk no more except with a metal walker. All he did was stay up in that room of his and hustle fancy computer shit—he even had some young homies learning how to fix and hack computer systems like how in the old days motherfuckers used to strip cars and steal decks. He'd have crates full of computer shit from overseas shipped to his house and sell everything at a discount. I dug in my pocket for change and pulled out a little scrap of paper that had his phone number on it. I dialed the number and the phone started ringing.

"Hello," Toro said.

"What's up!?" I said jumping up and down.

Toro slammed the phone in my ear. I was about to call him back like if it was some kind of fucked up connection or something, but then I realized I was completely ostracized and homeless. I was desperate. I had nothing except my memories: dust dreams and high skies, so I walked to the cemetery and looked for Santo, like if Santo could help me out of this torture.

And it was the first time I had visited Santo's grave. It was the first time I saw his headstone, and the stone was black marble and the fresh roses and carnations surrounding it were different rainbow colors. Lobo must have paid for that shit cause I knew no one else would have put up the bread just on the strength of remembrance. The lettering on the marker was gold and shiny and when I seen it, I knew what I had to do.

Santo's name and birth date were centered in the middle of the marker, and above it the following golden words paved the way for me to begin my own journey, to start what I started ten years ago, the moment it hit me, and I aint landed yet; it was stated boldly and without regret:

This is takeoff.

Barrio Bushido Timeline

1982 Toro (age 12) and Santo (age 13) fight; Toro joins gang.

1987 Toro joins Marine Corps.

1989 Lobo (age 19) starts working with Kwai Chung.

1990 Toro sent to Persian Gulf.

1991 *March*
> Toro home on leave.
> Homeboys attack family.
> Lobo meets Sheila.

April
> Toro climbs Mount Fuji.

July–August
> Sasquatch's plot.

August
> Toro discharged.
> Santo and Maricela make plans.

September 11
> Kwai sends Lobo after Sasquatch.

September 13
> Lobo draws homeboys into his scheme.
> Toro in hospital.

September 14
> Trip to wilderness.

September 15
> Lobo launches scheme.

1992 Lobo recruits Lil Cartoon for master plan.

Glossary

BARRIO SPANISH

*Note: Spanish is adapted to its use in a
California barrio of the 1980's and 1990's.*

carnalismo: brotherhood
Chapin: slang for Guatemalan
chignon: literally fucker or tough guy
chiva: heroin
cholo: Latino *vato loco* or gangster
corazon: heart
cuete: gun
ferria: fare, slang for money
filero: crude knife
firme: ultimate firmness or strength, also cool
frajo: cigarette
guayabera: men's shirt popular in Latin America
huipil: Mayan ladies' blouse
hyna: homegirl
leño: cigarette containing angel dust
loco: crazy guy
mano a mano: hand to hand boxing
maton: angel dust joint
mojado: illegal immigrant; "wetback"
morillo: a complex of muscles over the shoulder
    and neck which gives the bull its distinctive profile
orale: "right on," "hell, yes," usually said
    enthusiastically
pendejo: fool, jerk, coward; literally pubic hair

pinta, la: the penitentiary

primo: cousin

puto: male prostitute

que no?: Isn't that correct?

sábana: white bedsheet

Salvatrucho: person of Salvadoran descent

sangre **in their veins:** blood in their veins

Varrio Montaña: varrio is an intentional corruption
    of *barrio*. In Latino neighborhoods in the time
    setting of the novel it was popular to corrupt the
    word as such. In the novel, the homeboys have
    named *Varrio Montaña* for the big mountain that
    is in the center of their neighborhood.

vato: dude, guy

veterano: Latino veteran gangster or *vato loco*

Vida Loca, La: The Crazy Life

LEXICON

angel dust: the drug phencyclidine (PCP)

C-note: one hundred dollar bill

dime: time in prison. Nickel=five years, dime=ten
    years, twenty blinks=twenty years

drop a dime: to call the cops

dust: angel dust

forty or forty ounce: forty ounce bottle of malt
    liquor or beer

G ("at least a G"): one thousand dollars

mad dog: to stare at with intentions of intimidating
    or fighting

Mad Dog 20/20: Mogen David fortified wine

OG: Original Gangster

Old E: Olde English Malt liquor

pleather: fake leather

red devil dust: angel dust

Red Man chew: chewing tobacco

shank: to stab

MILITARY TERMS

.38: .38 caliber small arms revolver

.45: .45 caliber small arms pistol

AAV (official designation AAV-7A1; formerly known as LVT-7): Armored Amphibious Vehicle, a fully tracked amphibious landing vehicle

AT-4 tank and bunker destroyers: an infantryman's 84-mm unguided, portable, single-shot recoilless smooth bore weapon built to destroy tanks

Boot: enlisted Marine

butter bar: slang term for a second lieutenant, the lowest officer rank in the Marines

C-4 line charge: a type of plastic explosive used to clear mine fields

deuce gear: standard issue web gear, combat gear, or field equipment

Devil Dog: US Marine. Derived from the German word *Teufelhund*. During World War One, the German soldiers nicknamed the Marines this for their fighting prowess

DI: Drill Instructor

frag: grenade

Jarhead: United States Marine, called such because of Marines' high and tight haircuts

Jughead: corruption of Jarhead

Lewisite: an organoarsenic compound, specifically an arsine. It was once manufactured in the US and Japan as a chemical weapon, acting as a vesicant (blister agent) and lung irritant

M16: lightweight, 5.56 mm, air-cooled, gas-operated, magazine-fed assault rifle

M249 machine gun: previously designated the M249 Squad Automatic Weapon (SAW), and formally written as Light Machine Gun, 5.56 mm

M60: formally the United States Machine Gun, caliber 7.62 mm

SMAW: The Shoulder-launched Multipurpose Assault Weapon is a rocket weapon based on the Israeli B-300. It is primarily a portable assault weapon ("bunker buster") and secondarily an anti-armor rocket launcher

track: slang term used by Marines for the AAV

Acknowledgments

Para todos los homeboys and homegirls of every color, creed, and creation. You have transformed me into who I am today. Like true homies, you always open your arms. Your warmth and strength comfort and inspire me to go beyond myself. My dear family, for allowing me the time and freedom to pursue my passion. For my transgressions: there can only be redemption in the future. For St. George, patron saint of soldiers, who protects, strengthens, and blesses me. Tom Farber, for loving literature and for always leading the way. Shawna Yang Ryan, your grace has been my blessing. Peter Yedidia, my generous benefactor. El León Literary Arts, for injecting your faith and excitement into this project. UC Berkeley's and San Francisco State University's writing groups. The United States Marine Corps: Bravo One Five and Weapons Three One. Nami Mun. Maxine Hong Kingston. Amy Williams. Kit Duane. Andrea Young. The "Ashby" Writing Group. My student-teachers, you teach and I learn; my pleasure is to serve you.

About the Author

The son of Guatemalan immigrants, Benjamin Bac Sierra was born and raised in San Francisco's Mission district, then the heart of Latino culture in Northern California. Living the brutal "homeboy" lifestyle, at seventeen he joined the United States Marine Corps and participated in front line combat during the first Gulf War. After his honorable discharge, he completed his Bachelor's degree at UC Berkeley, a Masters in Creative Writing from San Francisco State University, and a Juris Doctor degree from the University of California Hastings College of the Law. Currently, he is a professor at City College of San Francisco.